THE LADY OF LARKSPUR VALE

ALSO BY KASEY STOCKTON

Ladies of Devon Series

The Jewels of Halstead Manor

The Widow of Falbrooke Court

Women of Worth Series

Love in the Bargain

Love for the Spinster

Love at the House Party

Love in the Wager

Love in the Ballroom

Stand-alone Historical Romance

His Amiable Bride

A Duke for Lady Eve

A Forgiving Heart

All is Mary and Bright

Contemporary Romance

Snowflake Wishes

His Stand-In Holiday Girlfriend

Snowed In on Main Street

The
LADY
of
LARKSPUR
VALE

LADIES *of* DEVON 2

KASEY STOCKTON

For Emma, my own little Pippa

CHAPTER 1

*Y*uck.

Mabel scraped stiff fingers over her eyes and removed as much of the thick, gooey mud as she could from her eyelids. She cleared her vision enough to see the culprit hiding behind the tree at the edge of the pond, snickering behind an adorable little hand.

"Pippa, you get out here right now!" Mabel yelled, continuing to rub at the mud covering her eyebrows and dripping down her cheek. She bent over and scooped a handful of the murky pond water before splashing it on her face in an attempt to further clear the mud away. Dirty liquid slipped between her lips, and she immediately spit it out most unbecomingly.

"Pippa isn't here!" a tiny voice squeaked through peals of giggles.

"Philippa Jane Sheffield, get your hide over here this instant before I lose my patience and withhold your pudding this evening!"

A tiny gasp pierced the warm air as little hands slapped against tiny hips. "You wouldn't dare!" the sassy seven-year-old exclaimed indignantly.

"Oh, wouldn't I?" Mabel countered with an identical pose, eyebrow hitched as she glared down at her formidable opponent. It was irrelevant that she did not intend to stay true to the threat; Pippa just needed to believe she meant it, and she would get her way. "Or shall I add it to my next letter to Papa?" Mabel tapped a finger to her chin, ignoring the crust of drying mud as she angled her face toward the warm sun. "Let us see. I could write, 'Dearest Papa, among making strides in both French and Italian, our *sweet* Pippa has taken to launching gooey mud pies in her spare time at unsuspecting—'"

"Oh, *fine!*" Pippa stomped her tiny foot.

Mabel crossed her arms over her chest in victory as she raised an eyebrow at the little girl, staring into a copy of her own navy-violet eyes on her sister's face. Mabel and Philippa were nearly perfect likenesses of their deceased mother—or so they were told—except for their stubborn streak, which was wholly Sheffield.

"Now, come," Mabel said with barely-felt authority. "Giulia is waiting to resume your lessons, and I will have no more mud slinging today. Is that understood?"

Mabel realized her mistake. A miniature jaw jutted forward as Pippa crossed her arms over her chest, once again mirroring a larger version of herself. Despite growing up the daughter of a captain for His Majesty's Royal Navy, Pippa didn't take kindly to being told she could not do something. "Write the letter, then. Papa thinks it is fine to play in the mud. He likes my throw-jeck-shun anlee-suss."

"Your *what?*" Mabel asked, completely at a loss for what Pippa could possibly be referencing. The little mite was always doing this in the days and weeks immediately following a visit or letter from their father—and they'd had a letter just a fortnight before. He was a good man of moral character and took his role as Captain in the Royal Navy quite as seriously as he took the responsibility of being a parent. But for all of the love

2

and affection he bestowed upon his two daughters when on leave, he still had yet to master conversational etiquette with a seven-year-old, always using too-large words and concepts that were not quite within Pippa's reach.

"You know," Pippa drawled, obviously frustrated by Mabel's inferior understanding. "With his cannons. His throw-jeck-shun anlee-suss."

"Oh, right." Mabel nodded as she inched closer to Pippa, who now stood in front of the tree with her hip cocked, and her arms still crossed. "The cannons. Papa's throw-fleck-ton army-sass."

"No." Pippa shook her head, a tiny hand rising to her forehead in condescension.

Mabel took the opportunity to lunge, forcing a squeal from her younger sister as she swooped her into the air and threw her over her shoulder. She spun toward the house and strode in long, fluid steps, ignoring the small ache in her leg, the hollering for release, and small fists pounding her back. She reached the back door to the Sheffield house and stopped as enlightenment dawned, effectively halting all opposition as Pippa was stunned silent by the immediate pause.

"You mean *projection analysis*," Mabel said. She could nearly feel the weight of Pippa's chest shift as the little girl sighed, a tiny hand swatting her backside.

"I *know*, Mae. That's what I said!"

Chuckling, Mabel set down the infuriatingly mudless girl and patted her behind. "Get those hands rinsed and then run upstairs and locate Giulia. Now."

"I'm going, I'm going," Pippa called over her shoulder as she scurried away.

It was Mabel's turn to shake her head as she watched her little darling dodge through the kitchen and up the back stairs. They were for the sole use of the servants, but no one minded that Pippa preferred the inner workings of the large house to get

3

around instead of the luxuriously carpeted staircases specifically designated for the family. Mabel preferred her younger sister using the servants' stairs, actually, as Pippa was, more often than not, covered in dirt or wet from the pond or dirty from some other malady; it was a wonder she had remained so spotless today. For the most part.

Mabel could hardly blame her sister; she had been much the same way when she was younger. But that was to be expected when a child grew up with mainly boys for companions. Her cousin, Charles, had been orphaned young and grew up right alongside Mabel as the brother she never had. They had resided together with Gram, the owner of their estate, which Charles was set to inherit.

Mabel had two close friends in Hattie Green and Amelia Mason—or now Amelia Fawn, she supposed. The woman's name had changed often with her shifts in husbands, so it was sometimes hard to recall. Every second of her time that had not been spent in their company had been spent following Charles and his band of miscreants and trying to get into whatever trouble they found themselves getting into.

"Goodness!" Mrs. Henderson jumped back with a hand to her chest as she stepped into the kitchen to find a muddied and disheveled Mabel. An elderly housekeeper who was often more pretentious than the gentility she worked for, Mrs. Henderson was known for her theatrics and was skilled at elevating the most minor oddity or flaw.

"I was attacked by the little terror, Mrs. Henderson, but the situation is under control." The mud on her face was beginning to dry, crusting and pulling her skin taut.

"I think not," Mrs. Henderson announced with widened eyes and pinched lips. "That child needs a firm hand, Miss Mabel. She needs to understand that soiling one's superior is thoroughly unacceptable."

"Certainly, Mrs. Henderson. I assure you that I will make

sure she understands how improper it is to *soil* one's superior."
Mabel sniffed to fight the levity that sparkled in her shoulders,
for Mrs. Henderson did not take kindly to being laughed at.
"Now if you'll excuse me, I must wash up."

"*Hmmph*," Mrs. Henderson grunted with a nod before
turning back to whatever task she had been diverted from, her
keys jangling as her ample hips swung to and fro. Mabel snick-
ered as she turned for the servants' hall and scanned the busy
staff, looking for the jet-black hair and pale green eyes that
belonged to her lady's maid.

Spotting Payne in the corner with a needle and thread to the
tear in Mabel's forest green riding habit—the one she had
chosen because it intensified her eyes—she crossed the thresh-
old, effectively ceasing all work as every seated employee rose
and every moving employee halted and turned to attention. She
briefly wondered if this was how Papa felt aboard his ships,
having complete authority over the men that made up his crew.
Although unlike her, Papa loved the control of being in charge—
something that Mabel was talented at, but not entirely content
with, yet.

"Payne, if I could see you upstairs?" Mabel said in her most
kind and authoritative tone, clasping her hands before her. If she
was going to stand in front of the large majority of her staff
while covered in dried, crusty mud, she would do so with as
much dignity as she could.

Payne seemed to collect herself and stammered, "Yes, miss.
Of course."

"Very good. Thank you." Mabel directed a nod to the occupants of the room, indicating they could resume their duties.
She was tempted to say "at ease" as her father often did but
refrained, chuckling to herself at the odd looks that would most
likely follow her.

"Am I correct to assume," Payne asked as she sidled up to
her mistress, "that you would like me to draw a bath?"

"Yes, Payne. A bath sounds simply wonderful."

"Right away, miss," Payne said as she moved for the kitchen.

Mabel shook her head as she turned toward the servants' staircase. There was no sense in trailing mud along the carpeted stairs within the house. It would be much easier to clean if she remained on the bare, wooden set.

As she reached the upper level that contained the schoolroom, nursery, and family rooms, she heard giggles layered with rich, feminine laughter and smiled to herself. Asking her friend Giulia Pepper to come and help her with Pippa had been the best decision she had ever made. The two had taken to each other like flies to honey; no other tutor or governess had ever been able to reach Pippa quite like Giulia had. Mabel was able to get through to the little spitfire, but they tended to butt heads more often than not, and she found that their relationship thrived better when they practiced intervals of healthy breaks between their time together. Something that Giulia gladly helped to implement.

Giulia had come to the nearby estate, Halstead Manor, the previous year in an effort to kindle a relationship with her uncle, Lord Hart, the earl that resided in that castle, misnamed in an effort by the previous Peppers to avoid taxes hundreds of years ago. While there, Giulia had made the acquaintance of Mabel and her friends, Amelia and Hattie. The four had become friends quickly and easily. Mabel had a difficult time remembering life before Giulia entered it.

She had now been a guest in the Sheffield home for six months while helping with Pippa's schooling and courting the heir to the earldom, Nick Pepper, a distant relative of hers.

The two had come together while she stayed at the castle, but to give herself a little freedom and a pinch of propriety, Giulia had come to the Sheffield home to live for the time being. But that would soon be at an end. Giulia would marry her uncle's heir, leaving Mabel alone with her sister and elderly grandmother. Not that Mabel complained. Giulia and Nick were obviously made for one another.

Mabel slipped into her bedroom and began peeling off her mud-soaked dress. Payne came in a moment later with the first of the hot water and set up a screen quickly.

"I've got Peter helping with the water, Miss Mabel, if you would like to step behind there."

Mabel nodded and jumped behind the screen just as the door opened and Peter came in, a bucket of steaming water in each arm. The footman's gaze leveled on her face over the top of the screen and she felt her cheeks warm. Blast her ridiculous height! She hunched her shoulders slightly, but it did little to lower her and she settled on looking away as Peter and Payne made multiple trips to fill the tub with hot, steaming water.

Payne closed the door and turned the lock before Mabel stepped over and lowered herself in the water. She sighed in contentment as she sunk in the warm liquid and let Payne wash the mud from her hair.

"Miss Pippa practicing her aim again?" Payne asked with levity.

"Naturally," Mabel replied soothingly, her eyes closed as she enjoyed the fingers massaging her scalp.

"That little spitfire is a handful." Payne chuckled. "She sure keeps things interesting."

"Interesting is one word for it." Mabel laughed. Payne had it right, though. Pippa was a ray of sunshine in the Sheffield house —the young, vibrant foil to Gram's spirited, aging soul.

The thought brought a wave of melancholy over Mabel and she sucked in a breath of air when Payne's hands moved away before plunging her head under the water. If only she could erase Gram's irritable mood as easily as she could the mud from her skin.

"Go on now. Have your dinner, and then Hope will bring you down to the parlor for games," Mabel said, indicating the table set in the corner of the room.

Pippa's nose scrunched up. "But I don't want to eat my dinner in the nursery. The nursery is for babies."

"Who told you that?"

A defiant little nose shot into the air, and Mabel struggled to keep her calm as she waited for the answer. Everyone else was most likely already assembled for dinner, and Mabel was having a beast of a time getting Pippa to let her leave the upper level of the house. The small, navy-violet eyes stared back into Mabel's, and she considered giving in before the voice in her head reminded her not to. The child was not going to learn to be obedient if she was spoiled and given everything she asked for, no matter how much easier that would feel in the moment.

Mabel let out a breath and dropped to her knees, trying for a gentler approach. "Pippa, did someone tell you that the nursery was for babies?"

"Yes." Pippa let out a long breath.

Mabel fought a smile. The girl mimicked adults so well, she seemed like a tiny grown-up herself at times.

"Was it a friend of yours or someone in the house?"

Pippa's face immediately reeled back as disgust marred her precious little features. "Jacob Tucker is no friend of mine!"

Aha! Mabel thought inwardly, puffing up at her success. "Well," she said softly, "what Jacob Tucker may not realize, Pip, is that *our* nursery is not simply a nursery."

"It's not?" Pippa said with a scrunched nose, tilting her head to the side and infusing Mabel's heart with a rush of love for her younger sister.

"Of course it is not." Mabel placed a hand to her heart to drive her point home. "Is it not where Giulia teaches your lessons?"

"It is."

"And is it not where we have our very grown-up tea?"

"I suppose."

"Then, you see, it is not just a nursery, Pippa Jane. It is a *schoolroom* and a very dignified parlor on occasion."

"I suppose that is true," Pippa said, standing a little taller, no doubt from Mabel's use of their cousin Charles's pet name for the little girl.

"Then run along and don't keep Hope waiting. A lady is never late, Pip."

"Right, and I am a lady."

"You most certainly are," Mabel replied through her grin as she watched the little lady turn and run toward the nursery and her maid who waited there. Well, she was only seven. There was plenty of time to teach her that ladies don't run in the corridors. Or sling mud at their sisters. Or throw rocks at the neighborhood boys.

Mabel's smile faltered at that last one. She had to remember to call on Mrs. Tucker the following day with her apologies. And perhaps a basket of muffins. Yes, Mrs. Tucker had seemed to like the blueberry muffins last time—that would be just the thing to smooth over the uncomfortable conversation.

"Where is Mabel?" a gravelly voice hollered from the parlor, followed shortly by a couple of thumps from the heavy cane Gram used to move from room to room.

"I am sure she will be here shortly," Giulia's voice soothed. "She was saying goodbye to Pippa when I came down."

"Grinding pepper?" Gram yelled. "Why was she grinding pepper? That's what the kitchen maids are for."

"I am here!" Mabel said as she flew into the room, trading a knowing smile with Giulia before approaching her elderly grandmother and placing a kiss on her wrinkled cheek. The old woman sat in her customary chair near the fire that she insisted must always be lit to warm her chilled bones, no matter how warm it was outside. The tall, wingback chair was a deep chocolate, infused with gold embroidery, and was well worn from years of daily use. When Gram was not holed up in her room for one malady or another, she was camped out in that chair.

"Has Carson announced dinner yet?" Mabel asked, her volume slightly louder as she addressed her near deaf grandmother.

Gram stared, unblinking, and Mabel found herself noting the wrinkles that folded skin over her eyes. Did that make it more difficult for Gram to see? She took note of the pinched lips and offered a smile as dignified as her posture before holding out a hand.

Gram batted Mabel's hand away and used her cane and the armrest to propel herself to a standing position. Gram's once tall frame was now condensed by the unseemly hunch in her back, but she remained as regal and dignified as ever as she led the mismatched group into dinner.

Mabel hung back to follow alongside Giulia and accepted the smaller woman's arm as she strung it through her own. Where Mabel was extremely tall for a woman, rivaling many men as well as towering over every female she knew, Giulia was the exact opposite, a petite woman whose compassionate heart made up for what she lacked in height.

"I heard you had a bit of a battle against Pippa today. Something involving cannons and lots of mud?" The mirth dancing in Giulia's chocolate-colored eyes was infectious, and Mabel found a smile turning up her lips in response.

"I would prefer to describe it as an ambush," she responded flatly.

"Oh, dear," Giulia said, giggling. Her hand came up to rest on her heart as she laughed, and Mabel found it hard not to laugh as well. It may have been irritating at the time, but now that she was warm and dry and quite a bit cleaner, she found the humor in Pippa's antics as well.

"That little one sure keeps us on our toes," Giulia said.

"That she does," Mabel agreed.

They took their seats on either side of Gram as Carson began serving dinner, along with Peter and Jeffrey, the two footmen that rivaled Mabel in height. She shook out her napkin and laid it across her lap as her mind trailed to the many men in her life and how she scaled them based on how tall they were in comparison to her. Most were about the same as she, if not an inch or two taller, but not nearly enough to make her feel dainty or feminine, as one young man blatantly pointed out long ago. A mocking laugh swirled in her stomach, for 'dainty' was not a word used to describe her. It fit Giulia perfectly, and Pippa on occasion, but no, Mabel would never be able to claim that description. No matter how much she longed to.

"Mabel, your brother has written," Gram yelled, though she only sat an arm's length away.

"And what did Charles have to say?" Mabel asked. Charles Fremont was her cousin, but as they were raised as siblings, she never corrected Gram.

"He inquired after my health, the dear boy."

"Oh, how kind of him."

"What?" Gram yelled.

Mabel set down her fork and knife and gave her grandmother a patient smile. "That is very kind of him."

"I don't know the time, Mabel. I am telling you about Charles's letter."

"And what did he have to say?" Mabel yelled.

"Well, he inquired after my health."

Mabel refrained from flicking her eyes toward Giulia, though she could feel her friend struggling to remain composed on the opposite side of the table. "How very kind of him," Mabel yelled.

Gram seemed pacified and returned to her meal.

"How is Charles?" Giulia asked.

"Good, as far as I know." Charles was studying abroad,

finishing his grand tour now that the war was over, and Napoleon finally defeated for good. Mabel took a sip of her soup and then continued, "Last I heard he was in Italy, though he spent a good deal of time in France before that."

A look of sorrow passed over Giulia's face, but it was gone as quickly as it came. Mabel wondered momentarily if she should have refrained from mentioning the country where Giulia's mother's family was from.

She thought a change of direction was the best course of action. "I can't believe it's been so long; the last time I saw Charles was the day after Nick's ball when he said his farewells to Pippa, Gram, and me."

"That was the very ball when I had the opportunity to meet your cousin," Giulia said with a swallow. "Though, I believe he really only had eyes for one," she finished with a wide grin.

"Yes," Mabel said, her eyes tracing the rim of her soup bowl. She looked to Giulia, hoping to quell the pain that scenario brought to her heart. "He has been smitten with Amelia for years. Probably our whole lives, to be honest."

"Poor man."

"Who's poor?" Gram asked, darting her gaze between Mabel and Giulia. She snapped her fingers. "The reverend mentioned on Sunday that a new family is moving into the house behind the school."

"Oh, splendid," Mabel called. "I will prepare a basket and take it over."

Gram nodded and went back to her plate.

"Are you going to see Nick tomorrow?"

"No," Giulia answered. "He is leaving to visit his mother and sister for a fortnight. But I am going to Halstead Friday for dinner. Would you like to join me?"

"Perhaps," Mabel answered. "Though I'm loath to leave Gram alone."

"It is up to you. Uncle Robert likes the company, so you would not be a burden."

Mabel raised an eyebrow and gave her friend a pointed look.

"He does." Giulia laughed. "He's too crotchety and grumpy to admit it, but he enjoys company. Particularly that of lovely young ladies." She took a bite and then pointed her fork at Mabel. "You cannot repeat this, but Nick told me once that Uncle Robert has called us the daughters he never had."

"That is too sweet," Mabel said, thinking of the grouchy old earl with long scraggly hair and a permanent frown.

"I agree," Gram said, causing both Giulia and Mabel to jump in surprise. "These yams are far too sweet." The old woman smacked her lips with a look of disgust before pushing the yams to one side of her plate and eyeing Carson as if the over-sweetened vegetable was his fault. Carson, ever the stalwart butler, remained composed and took the fiery darts as if they were his due.

Mabel glanced over her goblet and caught Giulia's mirthfilled eyes before choking on her water and coughing to cover the laugh. A moment of silence endured before both women let out their laughter, causing Gram to look between them in surprise and the ever-stoic butler's mouth to curve in a very slight, and completely uncharacteristic, smile. Until, of course, he caught the footman's grin and snapped back to attention.

CHAPTER 2

*T*he windows were dark, reflecting the flickering candlelight against their panes. Mac crossed his ankle over his knee, lowering the missive in his hand and pinching the bridge of his nose. He had not been back to Graton since the day he had left to join the navy, six years prior. He couldn't help but feel concern about returning.

According to Charles, everything was much the same in the small town they had grown up in. People had come and gone, relationships had formed, but the houses, the land, the Sheffield family—all of that remained unchanged. And *that* was what plagued Mac. He'd been a thoughtless youth, even a flirt, that he would readily admit. But what young man truly knew his own heart, or even thought about love? Surely his misdeeds could be blamed on his inexperience and youth.

Mac had grown up in the shadow of the Sheffield estate. He'd had a close friend in Charles, and he'd never *wanted* to leave Graton—the navy had not been his goal as a young man—but his father's choices had made it impossible for Mac to do anything else. His foolish actions had ruined everything, and his shame bled down to Mac, ruining his chance at a peaceful life in the town he loved.

Smoothing out the letter in his hands, he ran his eyes over the words once more. The war had ruined many lives, but it had also lined Mac's pockets—or, it would as soon as the prize courts finished reviewing his ship's prize money and determining whether or not they would receive it. The chance remained that the prize courts would deny them—their claim had been tied up for months now—and that worried him excessively.

He could not help his father without that money.

The library door opened, and Charles stepped inside, crossing the floor and lowering himself in the plush wingback chair. He rubbed his temples, expelling a noisy breath.

"Something troubling you?" Mac asked.

"Not exactly." Charles glanced up, holding his friend's gaze. "I'm looking forward to a respite in the country, though."

"A respite, huh? I didn't realize building cottages was such languid work."

Charles grinned. "I plan to leave most of the work to you and Desmond."

Mac let out a booming laugh. "You're bound to be disappointed, then."

"What I fail to understand is why my uncle won't hire laborers."

Mac would have wondered the same thing just a few years before, but his time in the navy had changed his perspective. He'd worked hard and learned the value of using his own hands to build or create, to accomplish a goal. Charles's uncle had been Mac's captain for much of his navy career, so he'd grown to know the man very well. Captain Sheffield was nothing if not industrious. Why would he hire men to do a job he could—with some help—accomplish himself? But that was key: the captain would not do this alone.

"Last I heard, Captain Sheffield planned to acquire *some* help from Graton to supplement our labor." Mac stretched his long legs and crossed them at the ankles. "But yes, I must agree. I am tired of Town life, and the wide, open skies of Devon are calling my name."

"Careful, you're sounding poetic."

Mac chuckled. "We wouldn't want that."

"The ladies might."

"All the more reason to curb my tongue."

Charles sighed. "Perhaps I'll borrow your turn of phrase. I don't hesitate to admit that I would be more than happy to find myself leg-shackled soon."

"It is different when you have a particular lady in mind." Mac did not, and despite one woman's particular attention, he was not in the market for a wife. "Where is Desmond?"

"Asleep." Charles rose, stretching his arms high above his head. "Which is where I should be. We will make an early departure, yes?"

Mac nodded. "I'll be along shortly."

He listened to Charles's footsteps retreat down the corridor and thump up the stairs. They hadn't been in London long, but it was long enough to determine that Mac was ready to leave the metropolis—and the fawning women to be found here. He didn't know how the rumor had spread that he was set to receive a sizable sum from the prizes his ship had attained during the war. But the word *had* spread, and the *ton* mistakenly believed him to be a wealthy man.

One woman had gone as far as attempting to force Mac into a compromising situation, regardless of his insistence that he was unsure if the money would ever reach his hands. For all Mac knew, he could remain poor and become forced to join back up with the navy.

But for now, an escape to the countryside with his friends,

where no fawning women might find him, was precisely what he needed.

Mac shifted on the narrow seat, trying to make himself as small as possible. It was difficult to fit himself into an average-sized chair; the small interior of the carriage made him feel like an absolute giant.

His knees knocked against Charles's across the way, and he caught his friend's gaze as a snore ripped through the carriage.

Desmond shifted in his sleep beside Mac, leaning further against the side of the vehicle.

Charles lifted the window covering to peek outside. "Another hour or so and we should arrive."

"Are you nervous?"

Charles shook his head. "I've only been gone for a year and yet I am eager to return. The estate might belong to my grandmother, and be run by my cousin, but it is still my inheritance." He shrugged. "I will probably always be drawn to it."

But Mac stopped listening, his mind caught up on two words that had slipped from Charles's lips. *His cousin.* Mac swallowed, a slow ripple of apprehension moving through him. He could not hear about Charles's cousin, Mabel Sheffield, without remembering his own misdeeds from years ago. When she'd put her heart on the line and he'd dashed it away as easily as flicking lint from his sleeve.

Passing the summer under Mabel's roof was an intimidating prospect. Perhaps Mac would get lucky and she wouldn't remember the way he'd treated her during their final interaction before he'd left for the navy. He cringed. No, she was unlikely to forget such a scene. But he *had* changed significantly in the last six years. He'd grown very tan, his hair lightening quite a bit from the sun. He'd grown from a lanky boy into a strong man.

What would Mabel think of him? He shook his head. He was likely overthinking this.

Charles's voice broke through his thoughts. "You have not met Pippa yet, I assume."

"Not formally. She was just a babe when I left," Mac said.

A contented smile lit Charles's lips. "I am eager to see her again. I hope she has not forgotten me."

Mac laughed, and Desmond stirred beside him. "It has only been a year, Charles. Of course she hasn't forgotten you."

He gave a self-deprecating smile. "I suppose we will find out within the hour."

Charles's steady announcement of how close they were drawing to Graton and Sheffield House did nothing but heighten Mac's trepidation. He lifted the window covering and turned his attention to watching the countryside roll by.

He didn't yet know how he was going to manage it, but he most certainly owed Mabel an apology for his past indiscretions. He only hoped she allowed him the chance.

CHAPTER 3

"*N*ow, listen to me very, *very* well," Mabel said, "for there are rules you must agree to before we can set off."

Pippa sat on the edge of the worktable in the kitchen, her hands folded delicately in her lap and her eyes wide, soaking up every word in a rare moment of acquiescence. The two baskets beside Pippa on the counter were full of still-warm muffins that Cook had just pulled from the oven and a tin of ginger biscuits she had baked earlier. Heavenly smells wafted to Mabel's nose and she considered sneaking a muffin of her own. She turned her attention to her sister and looked her square in the eye.

"Delivering baskets of goods is a…" Mabel trailed off her words in a question, a common method of hers to test Pippa's understanding.

"Act of charity!"

"Right." Mabel nodded. "And a duty of ours in being…"

"Women!"

"Good neighbors," Mabel corrected.

"Right, good neighbors," Pippa repeated quietly to herself.

"And as good neighbors, we will deliver these baked goods to the Tucker family—"

"No! You never said we were going *there!*"

"—and the family that has just moved into the vacant home behind the school, with good Christian charity and *kindness* in our hearts and our thoughts."

"Ugh!" Pippa said, folding her arms and glaring. "I changed my mind. I don't want to learn how to deliver baskets like a lady."

"No, no, no," Mabel said with a wag of her finger. "Lesson number two: once a lady commits to something, she does not back out. Pippa, you have given your word; you must see this through. Besides, which Sheffield lady was it that threw rocks at a certain Tucker lad?"

"Me," Pippa grumbled.

"So which Sheffield lady is going to deliver the apology basket of muffins and biscuits to the wronged gentleman?"

"They weren't *rocks*, they were *pebbles*—"

"A-hem," Mabel cleared her throat in a loud double syllable.

Pippa pouted. "Fine. *Me.*"

"Exactly. Now, take your basket," Mabel said as she lowered her sister onto the floor and handed her a basket, immediately stilling the arm that began to swing it rapidly back and forth. "And hold it still so as not to lose any of the muffins along the way."

Mabel selected two muffins from the cooling rack on the counter and led the way outside before handing one to Pippa and taking a bite into her own, a moan slipping from her mouth as the pastry melted on her tongue with an explosion of blueberry when she chewed.

"Cook makes the best muffins. I wish we didn't have to give any of them away," Pippa said through a mouthful.

Mabel swallowed her own bite and then turned to Pippa, closing her mouth again when the little sprite put up a hand to stop her. "I know," Pippa said, swallowing. "A lady does not speak with her mouth full."

"Right you are," Mabel said with a smile, taking another bite of her muffin to cover the laugh that wanted to break free. Her heart swelled with love for her sister, and she stepped closer to sling an arm over Pippa's shoulder.

"I love you, Pip."

"I love you too, Mabel."

They walked the rest of the way in companionable silence, Pippa asking the occasional question, and Mabel only needing to remind her one time that a lady does not run down the lane or splash in puddles.

They reached the farm that the Tucker family ran as tenants of Hattie Green's family, and Mabel nudged Pippa forward. The girl moved slower than a snail, but eventually, they made it to the front stoop where Mabel picked up Pippa's hand and knocked it on the door for her.

Pippa let out an irritated sigh before the door swung open, forcing her to stand at attention. Mrs. Tucker stood in the doorway, wiping her hands on her apron; gray peppered her dark hair pulled back into a tight chignon, and kindness crinkled the edges of her eyes. How such a sweet, kind woman had begotten such monsters for sons was beyond Mabel. One of the mysteries of the universe.

"Good afternoon, Miss Sheffield," Mrs. Tucker said to Mabel.

"Good afternoon." Mabel smiled as she nudged Pippa.

"Good afternoon, Mrs. Tucker," Pippa said quietly. She coughed a little dainty sound and then squared her shoulders before shooting her arms forward. "We've brought you muffins as an act of char—"

Mabel kicked Pippa's shoe, and she delivered a strained smile. "As an apology," Pippa continued. "For throwing the tiniest pebbles—"

Another kick. Pippa turned to glare at Mabel, who moved her attention to Mrs. Tucker, her smile innocent.

"For throwing rocks at Jacob," Pippa finished in one breath, holding the basket out farther and turning her face toward the yard.

"Thank you, Pippa," Mrs. Tucker said, taking the basket.

"There's ginger biscuits in there too. They are the best ginger biscuits in England," Pippa said begrudgingly.

"Then I look forward to tasting them."

Pippa turned back to Mrs. Tucker, who was now lifting up the cloth on the basket and sniffing the contents.

"You know, you should eat *all* of the biscuits and the muffins, for they are best when they are fresh, and they only just came out of the oven."

"Very good to know," Mrs. Tucker said with a straight face before flicking a look over to Mabel.

"Ewww. What's a baby doing at my house?" a little voice called from above them.

Pippa's face turned red before she pivoted to the right, clenching both of her hands at her sides in a rage.

"Pippa's a baby 'cause she sleeps in a baby room. Pippa's a *baby!*" the boy taunted from high up in a tree to the right of the house.

"Am not!" Pippa yelled back.

Mabel could feel the anger emanating from the small child and couldn't entirely blame her. Jacob Tucker really was something of a brat.

"Jacob, get down from that tree this instant," Mrs. Tucker called, her cheeks becoming rosy. "That is not how we speak to our neighbors. Especially a lady."

"But she's not a lady, Mama," Jacob yelled back. "Didn't you hear? Pippa's a *baby*."

"Am *not!*" Pippa yelled again. "It's not a nursery, anyway,

Jacob. It's a schoolroom. Because I'm a lady and I'm *learning*. I'm not some poor kid—"

"*Enough*," Mabel said through clenched teeth, grabbing Pippa's arm and pulling her back. The young girl immediately stopped, and when Mabel turned her to face Mrs. Tucker, Pippa's face was beet red. "Apologize," Mabel said in her steeliest voice. It hit its mark because she did not have to repeat it.

"I am sorry, Mrs. Tucker."

"And to Jacob," Mabel said.

Pippa turned and gave her sister a death glare. They stared off for a moment before Pippa shouted, "Never!" and pulled her arm from Mabel's grip, turning and running out of the yard and down the lane.

Mabel shot Mrs. Tucker an apologetic look, received a sympathetic one in return, and turned to chase after Pippa, yelling the little mite's name as she ambled down the road. Horse hooves sounded on the lane to the side that ran through their own, and Mabel turned, the blood leaving her body in one fell swoop. She screamed Pippa's name like she never had before.

Pippa halted and looked back to Mabel, her face blank. The girl lacked fear. She could not see the team of horses heading straight toward her from the highway that intersected with their small country lane. Mabel dropped the basket at her feet and reached a hand toward her sister as if that would magically pull Pip out of harm's way and screamed. Pippa turned toward the highway, the thundering of horse hooves, and her mouth dropped open before the man driving the ornate traveling carriage yelled at his animals, swerving off of the road and maneuvering onto the country lane, missing the ditch by an inch.

Mabel collapsed to the ground, shooting up a prayer of gratitude and savoring the sweet relief that filled her body. She lumbered to her feet and sprinted to where Pippa lay on the ground, having fallen back from the wind and the fear of the carriage, undoubtedly. Scooping her sister into her arms, Mabel fell to her knees once again, squeezing Pippa and rubbing her back as tears fell down both of their faces and sobs wracked the tiny girl's body.

"Amabel? Pip?" A deep voice called hesitantly ahead of them, and Mabel lifted her head, shocked by the image of the chestnut-haired man with deeply tanned skin who slightly resembled Charles—and certainly sounded like Charles. No one besides her closest family would call her by her given name. Everyone else knew her as Mabel.

"It is you!" he yelled as he closed the distance and dropped to his knees, throwing his arms around Pippa and pulling her from Mabel's embrace, leaving her bereft. "That was too close," he said as he squeezed Pippa tighter, his eyes screwed shut and obviously unaware that the child in his arms was not returning his affection. After a moment he looked down at her and noticed the confusion before glancing up at Mabel and laughing. "What?" he said. "You don't recognize me?"

"Charles?" she questioned.

"Of course I'm Charles!" he responded. "I know I have tanned, but I cannot look that different."

Mabel lifted her brows and shut her mouth. She could do nothing but stare at this man that had been much like a brother to her for the last two decades, and Pippa, too, for the duration of her life. He rocked back on his heels and released Pippa, who stood and screwed her eyes, tilting her head to the side.

"But why are you so dark?" she asked innocently.

"It's from the sun, Pip. I've spent quite a bit of time on a boat, you see, and that dratted sun got the best of me."

"If you're Charles, then you have to prove it. When did Mabel break her leg?" Pippa asked, crossing her arms over her chest. Mabel flinched, but Charles didn't look her way.

He smiled at Pip and answered, "A few years back from

26

falling through the loft in that wretched barn she and her friends insist on meeting in."

"It *is* you!" Pippa squealed and jumped back into his arms, causing Charles to fall back and laugh as he squeezed Pippa to his chest.

"I thought you were in Italy," Mabel said, rising to her feet and ignoring the pulsing in her calf, a result from the sprint. She had broken her leg three and a half years earlier from falling through a rotten plank and onto the ground fifteen feet below. She'd been told that she was lucky and could have broken her neck, or worse. She wondered what there was to be lucky about when she had gained an unseemly, albeit slight, limp and had lost the ability to ever dance with grace and finesse again.

"I *was* in Italy. I decided to come home." Charles grinned at Mabel, and she smiled back, confused at the easy manner and radiance that exuded from this once reserved man. Apparently, Europe had been good for him. Perhaps he had been able to move on and forget the childhood infatuation that had trampled his spirit and broken his heart not once, but three times, as Amelia had married and remarried twice more without ever giving Charles a chance. It always secretly bothered Mabel, though she would be loath to say so to one of her dearest friends—particularly when that woman had been forced to bury three husbands.

"Well, I am glad you did." Mabel grinned. "Gram missed you," she said with a saucy smirk.

"How very fortunate for me," he said drolly before setting Pippa down and lifting his arms to Mabel.

She stepped into his familiar embrace and reveled in the strong arms that came around her, in their familiarity and warmth. She tilted her head back and smiled. "How long are you home?"

His grin was contagious, and she felt her soul lighten. "As long as I'm wanted, of course."

"Yes!" Pippa shouted, jumping up and down. "Now you can make that abominable Jacob leave me alone once and for all!"

Charles stepped back and lifted a brow at Pippa. "Jacob Tucker giving you trouble again?"

Pippa nodded in her adorably exasperated way.

"And since when," Charles continued, folding his arms over his chest and cocking a hip, "has Pippa Jane needed help from anyone to keep that bully in line?"

Pippa stood up a little taller, her chin poking dangerously high into the air as she huffed. "Never. I can handle that rat."

"Names," Mabel reminded gently.

"Fine!" Pippa yelled at her sister before turning back to Charles. "I can handle that bully."

"Very good. Now shall I give you a ride back to the house in my fancy carriage, or would you like to walk?"

"Oh! A ride, definitely a ride!" Pippa said as she jumped up and down. "Can I sit up by the driver?" Her wide-eyed plea looked as though it dissolved Charles into a puddle instantly.

"Of course."

"Yippee!" Pippa ran toward the carriage, and Mabel watched her go.

"That was close," Mabel said quietly.

"I know," Charles agreed, standing beside his cousin and watching Pippa run along carefree. "I saw her fall back when the carriage swung to the side. I didn't even know what was happening when I heard the scream. That was you, wasn't it?" He turned toward her.

"Yes."

He shook his head, releasing a breath through his teeth. "Have you heard from your father?"

"My father?" Mabel stilled. Her father was aboard a ship somewhere in the East Indies. "We aren't due a letter quite yet."

"I think you will see him yourself before any missive reaches your door," Charles said softly, his words lifting on the wind and soothing her battered heart.

"What do you mean?"

"He's coming home, Mae. He should be here very soon." Charles squeezed his cousin on the shoulder before releasing her and moving toward the carriage. He took a few steps before turning back. "Coming?" he asked.

"No." She waved him off and then gestured behind her, her heart still racing. Papa, coming home? She would believe it when she saw it. "I've got a basket of muffins somewhere back there that I have to deliver in Graton, if they did not turn to crumbs when I tossed them. You just get settled. I'll see you at home."

He nodded, shooting her another smile. "It's good to be back."

"It's good to have you."

Mabel turned back to find the basket that she had thought-lessly dropped somewhere along her heart-stopping run. With her luck, it was somewhere in one of the ditches on the side of the lane.

"Oh, Mae?" Charles hollered.

She stopped and turned back to look at him.

He rubbed his chin, a sheepish look on his face. "I've brought a few friends. Any special rooms you have in mind?"

Her jaw dropped and her gaze shifted to the carriage, but it was shadowed, and she could not make out who was sitting inside it. This was so like Charles to foist visitors upon her without any warning. Would that she actually had the chance to prepare linens and beds, air out rooms, or plan for meals. She was tempted to point out that the only prepared rooms she knew of were at the inn in Graton but bit her tongue when she caught Charles's candid grin. She shook her head but couldn't help the smile which formed on her lips.

"I will manage it when I return," she responded, before

lifting a finger and pointing it accusingly at him. "But you make certain they know they are only waiting for their rooms to be prepared because I wasn't given a hint of warning."

Charles lifted his hands in surrender. "Sure, Mae. Whatever you wish."

A chuckle rolled over Mabel's shoulders as she turned back to search for the basket. She spotted it just down the road, on its side about halfway down the embankment. She reached it as the carriage pulled up behind her and lifted a hand in farewell when it ambled past. Checking her basket, she was pleased to note that while the biscuits in the tin were a little disheveled, the muffins were in perfect condition.

Releasing a sigh of relief, Mabel straightened her skirt, wiped the dirt from her knees as best she could, and began walking toward the town of Graton again. The scare with Pippa and the carriage had sapped her energy, and she found that the peaceful stroll was exactly what she needed. Particularly if she was going to return to a house full of guests. At least Giulia was planning on dining with her uncle this evening. Then Mabel could ease into entertaining Charles's friends.

Hopefully, they were only planning on staying for a day or two, and then she could have her pseudo brother all to herself.

CHAPTER 4

The Traynor family seemed grateful for the muffins, and Mabel always found herself glad to meet new people in the area. She knew that what she spouted to Pippa was true, and in acting neighborly and welcoming she was giving the family a sense of peace and belonging. Moving to a new place could not be easy, or so Mabel assumed, and if she could lighten their load in any way, she would. And in this case, she was going to lighten their load considerably when they sent their two girls over tomorrow to play with Pippa. Both girls were around the same age as Pippa, so Mabel immediately invited them, forgetting, at the time, of her house full of Charles's friends; she only recalled that bit of information after the time was set and the directions given, and it was too late to back out.

Mrs. Traynor had seemed a nice sort of woman, maybe three or four years older than Mabel was herself. She wondered if they could have been friends in another world. A world in which Mabel Sheffield was not a giant but instead had gotten married and had children of her own, instead of growing into a spinster as she raised her sister and cared for her grandmother. With the help of a small army, of course.

By the time Mabel reached home, her limp was more pronounced, and her leg was aching—a sure sign that either rain was on the way, or, and much more probable in this case, she was enduring the aftermath of overworking it—and she was ready to put her feet up and steal an hour's respite before meeting with Mrs. Henderson to discuss the arrangements for the guests.

That dream was not to come to fruition, however, for upon entering the house, Mrs. Henderson swooped on Mabel immediately, dragging her into the housekeeper's parlor downstairs with a most stricken look on her face.

"Mrs. Henderson, this is not the first time we have entertained guests on such short notice. Tell me what has you so vexed, and I am sure we can work together and come up with a solution," Mabel said diplomatically.

Mrs. Henderson set down the tea her shaking fingers held and folded her hands in her lap. "Master Charles has not only arrived home with two guests in tow, but he informs me that three more are on their way."

Mabel's mouth dropped. "Five? Charles has invited *five* people here? Where on earth did he even meet five people?"

"Precisely," Mrs. Henderson said as she lifted her teacup and took another sip, satisfaction on her face, seemingly content now that Mabel shared in her distress. "And we've got considerable work ahead of us readying the master's suite with no notice. But to bring five guests home on top of it is beyond anything."

Mabel lifted her tea and took a sip of the steadying liquid. Drawing in a fortifying breath, she set it back on the table between her and the housekeeper. "Well it will be improper for them to be on our side of the house, so we must—"

"That is just it, Miss Mabel." Mrs. Henderson leaned in.

32

"Two of them are *female* and bring with them a hired companion."

Mabel stilled, speechless.

But Mrs. Henderson was not. The older woman droned on about the inconvenience, her complaints extending far past her worry over where to put the guests. After listening for nearly a quarter of an hour to the housekeeper over changing menus, altered plans, and increased workloads, Mabel rose, halting Mrs. Henderson's speech with a slightly lifted hand.

"We'll put the ladies in the rooms on either side of me. The companion can take the Rose Room, and move Giulia to the Blue Room. She won't mind the broken wardrobe for a few days but take the drapes from my window to replace the missing ones in that room, because she *will* mind being woken by the sun, I am sure. Then Charles can take his room and his male guests can take the Princess Room and the Green Room. Deliver the menus to my chamber, and I will glance over them and make notations. We can still serve whatever Cook planned for this evening. Just ask her to find some sort of filler to stretch the meal."

Mrs. Henderson nodded.

"But do not, on any account, take from what she has prepared for the servants' dinner. Cook is resourceful, and I know she will find something." Mabel lifted her hands, clasping them lightly before her. "The truth is, Charles gave us no notice, and I am sure our guests will understand for this one evening if we have to be a tad unconventional. Giulia is not dining at home anyway, and I can eat with Pippa if Cook is concerned over quantity."

"Very good, Miss Mabel."

Mabel turned to go and stopped when Mrs. Henderson spoke.

"Oh, but the Green Room is out! The chimney smokes in there, and it hasn't yet been repaired."

"Drat," Mabel said under her breath, ignoring the glee in Mrs. Henderson's eyes at finding a flaw in the plan.

"The Romeo Suite, then?" She frowned. "No, that is too close to the nursery."

"There are no babies in the nursery. It would not be an inconvenience in that regard."

"True." Mabel nodded. There would be no babies to bother the guest. Only a feisty little seven-year-old. At least she no longer woke in the night to eat or cried all hours of the day. And the truth was that all of the other available rooms would put the guest next door to a lady, a blight that would not pass under Gram's nose at all. Not even if it was her room that a young gentleman was placed beside.

"Princess and Romeo it is, then."

"Very good. I will get started immediately."

"Thank you, Mrs. Henderson," Mabel said as she left the room.

She made it to the door and heard the raucous sound of men's laughter combing through the corridor and invading her eardrums in all of its unwelcome entirety. She turned toward the stairs and hurried to the top, nearly colliding with Giulia as she came in the opposite direction, holding her valise with her bonnet slung over her arm.

"I apologize," Mabel said after she righted her friend and took a step back. "I was not paying attention. *Please* do not tell me you are leaving on Charles's account." Mabel gave a very pointed look at Giulia's valise.

"Uncle Robert is always begging me to stay. And with the ball just a few weeks away, I ought to be at Halstead helping with the preparations," Giulia said sheepishly.

"So this has nothing to do with the hordes of people Charles has unsuspectingly cast upon us?"

Giulia smiled. "You need my room." She pointed a finger right at Mabel as she continued, "Do not say you don't need it, for I heard there are two ladies on their way with a companion, and you know it would not be proper to place them next to the men's rooms."

Mabel groaned and dropped her head into her hands. "Have I ever told you how much I dislike entertaining? Particularly those who I do not know?" She heard a thump on the planked floor as Giulia dropped her valise and two arms snaked around her waist.

"I can come back every day if you would like. I will bring reinforcements with me as well. Just write, and we will be here straight away. You do not have to ever do any of this alone."

Tears gathered in Mabel's eyes as she nodded her silent acceptance. Giulia was right. If she needed them, Giulia, Hattie, and Amelia would be at her door without hesitation. And she always had Pippa and Charles. She would not be alone. There would be people around her that loved her and cared for her and did not judge or mock her enormous height or odd limp. She took a sustaining breath and released a hesitant-looking Giulia.

"I really can stay," Giulia offered.

"No, go and be with your uncle. I know you are still building a relationship, and this time will be good for you both. Besides," she added with a halfhearted laugh, "you have done quite enough for me this last year. You deserve a break."

"Don't be silly. Pippa is not getting off so easily. I have left her a list of tasks to complete every day until I return."

Her heart swelled with gratitude as she pulled Giulia in for a final hug. The woman was a blessing in more ways than one, and Mabel was grateful for the addition to her life Giulia had become.

"Now be off with you." Mabel laughed as she watched her friend walk away.

She took in a deep breath and let out another, repeating the process to calm her pulse and remind herself that she was going to be fine. This was simply...a house party. The thought gave her pause. Charles had sprung *a house party* on her. Still, if there was one thing that Mabel was good at, it was playing the hostess and running her house like a fine-tuned ship. Besides, they couldn't possibly be staying that long, right? House parties lasted one, maybe two weeks at the most.

And this particular house party was going to fly by.

"Charles, you *didn't*," Desmond Pemberton said in his high-brow manner, swirling his brandy in the glass before throwing it back in one gulp. The amusement on his face was opposite the chagrin on Charles's, and Mac glanced back and forth between the two before rising and crossing to the open window.

Mac cast his eyes to the ceiling before glancing across the open expanse of land.

Land. Sand filled his throat at the thought, and he returned to his goblet before gulping down the refreshing liquid in an attempt to quench his insatiable thirst for water.

It did not work. It was saltwater he craved, and he had no particular wish to drink that.

"You could have written to her. Warned her." Mac interrupted their banter, his deep voice echoing in the small library.

"Come on, Mac. I've got enough guilt," Charles said, tilting his head like a small puppy and beseeching his friends to cease berating him. "I hadn't expected to bring anyone home with me, and *you* aren't even my guest, Mac. Not when you've come at the request of my uncle. Besides, if anyone can receive guests with little warning, it's my cousin. She's...dynamic."

Desmond laughed as he poured a refill, spilling some of the amber liquid on the sidebar and leaving it there when he sauntered back to his chair. "Is that a compliment?"

Charles let out a low whistle. "With her it is. She's...productive. Practical. She was made to be a hostess. Literally made for it."

Mac shook his head. He was half-tempted to pick up his still-packed bag and hit the road. No one deserved to have three men shoved on them unannounced. Especially since these men were planning on remaining for the whole summer.

"Productive? Practical?" Desmond chuckled. "You make her sound terrifying, Charles. Is she also prudish?"

"It is possible for a woman to be possessed of both a sound mind and a degree of beauty." Mac did his best not to remember the last time he saw Mabel, all those years ago, tear-streaked cheeks and eyes burning with hurt. But if she was the same now as she was then, she embodied dignity, grace, and beauty.

"The ladies should be arriving soon and that should help smooth things over," Desmond said, shooting Mac an odd look before taking another gulp. Mac walked over and took the glass from his friend, ignoring his protests, and returned the glass to the sideboard.

"You'll thank me when you can still sit up straight in an hour," Mac said, irritation feathering his words. He halted by the sideboard and spun around. "Wait, Des, did you say the ladies were coming?"

Charles sat up and shot a look of surprise to Mac. "Don't tell me you didn't know?"

"How would I? I came here at the behest of Captain Sheffield, not in anticipation of a blasted house party," Mac said, his voice as cold as the empty hearth. Fury bloomed in his center and began seeping into his limbs. He stood, shaking his arms, hoping to dispel the itch to hit something. Someone. Anyone.

Pacing before the window, he stopped when a tiny person walked across the gravel driveway, skirted the fountain in the center, and continued on as if it—no, she—was heading for the stables. He watched her walk and found himself cooling considerably, his attention distracted. He pressed his forehead to the glass and got a good look at the girl. She had to be a young girl, for she was just a mere slip of a thing, with dark hair circled on her head in a crown-like style.

He found it interesting that the anger dissipated so easily at times. But at others, he felt like he was going to explode until he had released himself of every ounce of anger or passion built up in his body. He took a calming breath and turned to face his friends, not surprised by the slight looks of caution they each held. He leaned against the window sill, crossing his ankles and casually folding his arms. "Who?"

"My sister, Lydia," Desmond offered enthusiastically. Too much enthusiasm, to be frank. Enough that the next name was not going to be one that Mac wanted to hear.

"And?" he drawled. He wanted to hear her name. A small part of him wanted Charles to say it out loud. Or Desmond. It didn't really matter which. But he needed the name spoken aloud for them to all reach the same understanding: Mac was feeling murderous, and he had good reason to.

"Miss Sophy," Charles said, defeated. "Mac, listen—"

Mac held up a hand to halt his friend's defense. He didn't want to hear it. He wanted the silence to bubble and fester as Charles and Desmond realized their mistake. He would count to a hundred before he spoke, and he knew that they would let him. *He* was driving the carriage now, so to speak.

He didn't actually count to one hundred, but he waited an uncomfortably long period of time. And then he waited a little longer. "You will understand, my *friends*," Mac said, emphasizing the false title, "why I have chosen to leave your house party a little early. You can tell the captain that I'm putting up at the inn in Graton."

"Come on, Mac," Desmond said. "Sophy may have been a little misguided in her intentions, but I know my sister well, and she has—"

"No!" Mac thundered. "Why would you do this to me? Do you think it will be different? Do you think she has suddenly had a change of heart?"

They both averted their gazes, and he steeled his jaw. "I remember where my trunk went. I will see you around. Perhaps." *Or maybe I won't.*

Mac stormed out of the library and up the stairs to the room that his things had been placed in earlier. He was nearly blind with anger, but there was something else there, too. Something that he could not quite put his finger on. Betrayal, or hurt maybe. It was something.

"Oof!"

Mabel's arms went up to her face instinctively as she bounced off the wall she had just run smack into. A bizarrely soft yet firm wall, and in a place that had previously been an open corridor. So, perhaps not a wall at all, but a...person?

Strong hands gripped her shoulders, righting her, and she rubbed her nose to dispel the pricking feeling that was bleeding up into her eyes and causing them to blur with tears. She took a fortifying breath and stepped away from the wall before stilling. She had run right into it—or him—and hadn't collided with a face. Or a chin. This had to be a very, *very* tall wall. And this wall was most likely one of Charles's guests.

"Forgive me," Mabel said as she took another step away. She lowered her hands and found her vision cleared as she took in the monstrous man before her. It occurred to Mabel that *this* was what most women likely experienced, to gaze straight ahead and see a man's chest, instead of directly into his eyes—or worse, over his head. She tilted her head back—another novelty —and her mouth dropped open at the handsome, yet vaguely familiar stranger. His face was cast in shadows from the dim corridor, the sun having reached the other side of the house by now.

It was too dark to see the man clearly—whoever was supposed to light the wall sconces likely had been delayed due to the extra bedchambers they suddenly needed to prepare. But something about the man tugged at her mind, something about his expression told her she knew him from somewhere.

He had a perfectly chiseled jaw, a straight nose, and eyes that were...dark? Perhaps. There was so much fire behind them that it was hard for Mabel to tell. She would have been embarrassed by her frank perusal if the giant opposite her wasn't doing the very same thing to her.

She cleared her throat, giving the stranger a smile and hoping, with a small part of her, that he was neither dumb nor a servant. "You are one of my guests, I assume?" she said. That was a safe bet. Even the servants she considered guests. They were not coming to live forever, after all.

"I, um..." he stammered, before clearing his throat and hesitantly holding her gaze. "Yes, I suppose. I am a guest of Charles." He spoke the words slowly, with calculation, and Mabel cocked an eyebrow.

"Are you well, sir? I apologize. I was checking the bedchambers and must have had my head in the clouds."

"No. Yes. Well, er, I don't know if I..." He trailed off, staring at her mutely. His direct gaze was unnerving, his mouth hanging open.

Well, great. This friend of Charles appeared to be in possession of a half-empty brain box.

She waited for him to continue, but he remained silent, staring. She clasped her hands. "Shall I escort you downstairs? I believe they are gathering in the library. Or perhaps you'd like to be directed to your room? It has been prepared by now." She was doing her best impression of a put-together hostess and hoped the man wasn't offended by her eagerness to deposit him somewhere. But the truth was she had piles of things to get done and standing around the corridor was not accomplishing any of them.

"No, I...I mean, I don't think..." He cleared his throat. "I know my way," he said quickly.

"Very well," Mabel said, wondering if perhaps this *was* a servant and she had understood him wrong. "I shall see you for dinner then, I suppose."

"Yes. Dinner."

"Good day, sir." Mabel backed away slowly, receiving his nod and then turning toward the stairs. Perhaps she'd been mistaken earlier. This visit felt more and more as though it was going to drag.

CHAPTER 5

"We've received word that the other two guests and their companion are not arriving until tomorrow," Charles said, leaning against the balcony and breathing in the country air. "And I imagine your father will be shortly behind them. He has some business to wrap up in London, but when I left him there, he assured me he would come along soon."

Mabel nodded in response but felt utterly drained. It was welcome news, but she could not summon the energy to feel glad.

Charles seemed to notice. "Are you well, Mae?"

"Yes." She let out a long, slow breath and relaxed another fraction. "It has merely been a long day. Pippa nearly getting struck by the carriage…then all of the preparations for this surprise visit…" She shot him a look, and he had the decency to look sheepish. "I'm contemplating skipping dinner and just falling into bed."

"Then do that," Charles offered. He folded his arms, leaning against the railing, and looked as far over to the right as he could. It was a habit of his, and she knew what he was doing.

He was looking toward Amelia's house—Falbrooke Court. Not that he could see it from here.

She shifted, leaning against the railing beside her cousin. Lifting her feet one at a time, relief flowed into her heels from removing some of the pressure. Access to the terrace came from her father's room, which was right where Charles knew she would be. Papa had the balcony added on when she was a small girl. He'd said he needed a vantage point for when he was home. She had made a joke about him adding a ship's wheel to one side so he could remain at the helm when at home and had been elated when he took her advice and brought home an old wheel on his next leave. When Mabel found herself in need of guidance, or simply missing her Papa, she gravitated to the steering wheel on the balcony and wondered if he was at the helm as well.

"Maybe I will," she said tentatively. Charles shot her a look of surprise. He never expected her to take his advice, and she knew it. "But that wouldn't make me a very good hostess now, would it?"

"The choice is yours. But with the ladies not present yet, I say you've earned the night off. Gram can play hostess. Technically that's *her* role anyway, right?"

Mabel smiled. "You know, you're right."

Charles nodded once, succinctly. "Then it's settled. I will sacrifice myself by finding Mrs. Henderson and telling her that you would like a tray sent to your room, and you can go put your feet up."

Mabel laughed at the jest and knew as well as Charles that he would simply find the nearest footman and ask him to relay the message. She watched him a moment longer, searching for evidence of his alteration. *Something* had altered within him— she'd noticed it since first seeing him on the road earlier in the day. But what?

"You seem different," Mabel hedged.

"I feel different," Charles answered, looking toward Amelia's home once again before dragging his gaze away and sitting against the railing beside her.

She wanted to be delicate, to tiptoe around the question which had plagued her all day. There was something about his bearing which had very much altered since she'd seen him last, and there was only one thing she imagined could be the cause of such an alteration. But how did one come right out and say, 'are you finally over your imagined love of fifteen years yet?'

Well, maybe just like that.

"Have you overcome your affection for her, then?" Mabel whispered.

"You may not believe me," Charles said with a hint of pride, "but I am past that childish passion I held on to for so long. I fancied myself in love with her for what…fifteen years? It feels good to be over her now. Liberating. Free."

Mabel placed a hand on his arm. "I am really glad for you, Charles. I can see it; you seem happier now. Lighter."

"Yes, well, enough sentimentality now." He shooed Mabel back into the house, his cheeks glowing pink.

Mabel grinned, happy for Charles. "Yes, yes, I am going."

Mac sat at the large dining table and pushed the food around his plate with his fork. He reached for his goblet and tipped it to his lips before realizing, again, that it was empty. Returning it to the table with a thud that was harder than he intended, he glanced up to the footman who scurried around the table to refill his drink. Where was the butler? Wasn't that his job?

He mentally shook himself to release his anger. He wasn't truly mad, not really. Irritation was more the vein his feelings were taking at the moment. At least Miss Sophy and her sister would not be arriving until the following day. That gave him a bit of a reprieve. Or, more apt, time to plan his strategy.

Miss Sophy. The name alone brought fresh humiliation to the surface, boiling his blood and searing his skin. Seeing the actual woman again was not going to be good for him. Charles better be up for acting as his sparring partner, because Mac was surely going to need to vent his feelings somehow if he was forced to remain under the same roof as that woman.

Why was he subjecting himself to this again? Oh, right. *Her.*

Mac felt a combination of excitement and unease when he thought about Mabel. She was the one reason he had hesitated to return to the Sheffields' home in Graton—and now the one reason he was willing to remain. He was certain he was the last person she wanted to see, but when he had run straight into her —or had she run right into him?—he'd felt like he'd been struck in the side of the head by a fist. He had stood on the tips of his toes waiting for her to recognize him. Metaphorically, of course, for he did not need to add to his already massive height.

But that was just it—she didn't either. She was tall, lean and graceful, much as he'd remembered. And when she fell into him, he immediately noted how perfectly she had fit into his arms. Mabel Sheffield was not too tall. No, she was perfect. Standing beside her, Mac didn't feel like the monster that most women, and some men, made him feel. He felt almost *normal.*

A guttural laugh escaped his lips at the thought, and he dropped his fork.

"What's so funny, Mac?" Charles asked from the head of the table. The man had spent the better part of dinner yelling updates at his grandmother, who was comically misunderstanding and forcing him to repeat himself. Mac was impressed; the man had patience. A little thin at times, perhaps, but Charles was gentle and kind with his grandmother, nonetheless. That was to be expected, however, when the woman was the closest thing to a mother Charles had had in his life. With his own parents dying tragically young, and then Mabel's mother, his aunt, giving her life through Pippa's birth, Charles and Mabel were both left with their grandmother as their sole female relative.

"Just imagining how I'm going to throttle you both," Mac replied, popping a potato into his mouth and grinning at the colorless faces peering his way.

"You want another bottle?" Gram asked. She snapped her fingers and turned her head from side to side. "Carson! Where's Carson?" Pointing to a young footman on her left, she said, "Where's Carson? These young men would like another bottle."

The puny footman—well, puny to Mac at least—glanced up to Charles, no doubt having heard the correct interpretation and understanding that no one had requested another bottle. Desmond was nearly asleep where he sat, and Mac believed the table had had enough to drink, but he wasn't in charge. Charles gave a nod, and the footman left the room immediately.

"What made you decide to stay?" Charles asked, curiosity furrowing his brows.

Mac picked up his glass once again before setting it back down. He pushed his chair back a fraction and stretched his legs under the table. How much should he say? *Your cousin, Charles, has grown more beautiful than I could have imagined and sets my pulse to rapid. The prospect of spending time with her is nearly worth staying in a house with Miss Sophy again.* Nearly? No, it was worth it. Or so he thought.

Mac sighed, trying for nonchalance. "I promised Captain Sheffield I would help him, and that is precisely what I intend to do."

"And Miss Sophy?" Charles asked, his eyes flicking to Desmond.

Mac scrubbed a hand over his face. Charles may be conscious of ill-talking a woman around her brother, but Mac did not hold the same scruples. Desmond was perfectly aware of what his sister had done. "Perhaps I was being too rash earlier. Miss Sophy may have had a change of—"

"Circumstances?" Desmond supplied sleepily.

"I was going to say heart. But yes, perhaps she has had a change of circumstances. Though if that were the case, you would know, wouldn't you, Des?"

"Well," Charles said, mirroring Mac and stretching out his own legs. "Whatever the reason, I am glad you changed your mind. And to make it up to you, I will take you fishing in the pond first thing tomorrow morning."

Mac grinned. "Deal."

"What is happening with the servants tonight?" Gram shouted with an exasperated breath. "That's it." She brought her frail frame to a stand and threw her napkin onto the table. "Without Mabel, nothing runs smoothly. And where is Carson? I'm off to bed." Gram lifted her cane and stalked off without so much as a farewell; each man shot to their feet to bow their mistress away from the table, their murmured 'goodnights' undoubtedly bouncing off her ears unheard.

"Where is Miss Sheffield, anyway?" Desmond asked, and Mac secretly thanked him. He had wanted to ask the question all night but was afraid Charles would see right through him if he did. He'd made it to the second course before he quit watching the door and realized she was not joining them for dinner.

"Tired," Charles said. "We gave her quite a scare with Pippa earlier, and then she had all the work involved with preparing our rooms."

"Your perfect hostess shirked her duties in lieu of sleep?" Desmond smirked, his pompous attitude seeping into his words.

"I told her to," Charles defended. "Besides, Gram is the hostess in this house." Charles brought a hand up to his tanned face and pinched the bridge of his nose. "To think what almost happened today..."

"But it didn't," Mac reminded him gently. He had been looking out the window when the carriage had veered away, too, and had seen how close they had come to trampling the small child. He had been away too long to know Pippa, except through Charles's letters and stories, but he had been affected by the ordeal as well. That, compounded with the way Mabel had held Pippa after the near-collision, had pierced his heart. He hadn't been able to see from the distance that it was Mabel and thought the woman to be the child's mother. But the shock was unmistakable in the bend of her shoulders, and his heart had ached for her and the child.

When Pippa had skipped over to the carriage and climbed up to ride with the driver, Mac had the unmistakable pang that this little girl reminded him of another little girl he used to play with, and the thread of guilt that accompanied that thought was emphasized when he remembered, once again, that he had been headed to her house.

"Just wait until you see Mabel," Charles said unexpectedly.

Mac looked up and was surprised to find the comment was directed to him. "Oh?" he said noncommittally. "Is she so very changed?"

"No, she is the same old Mabel. But with the shell of a diplomatic hostess now." Charles laughed to himself. "Trust me though, she's the same girl that used to follow us around, drop mud bombs from trees, and terrorize poor Akkerman's precious tulips."

Mac laughed at the image and was instantly transported to the blissfully carefree existence of his youth. A youth that was cut short by the start of his navy career. He sobered instantly, remembering the callous young man he had once been—the boy who had laughed in Mabel's face.

"Mr. Fremont, you have visitors." The stately butler spoke

from the doorway, causing both Charles and Mac to startle, and Desmond to snort awake.

"At this hour?"

"Yes, sir. Miss Lydia Pemberton and Miss Sophy Pemberton have arrived with Mrs. Boucher. I have placed them in the drawing room awaiting further directions."

Charles looked at his butler like he was a foreign object, his mouth hanging open in a dumb manner that belied the man's years at university.

"And have you inquired of the mistress of the house?" Mac asked helpfully. Or, so he hoped. In truth, his body was battling the desire to hear that Mabel was on her way downstairs with the irritation of knowing that Miss Sophy was in the house.

"Mrs. Henderson has awoken her," Carson said with barely veiled irritation. So this was what the man had been doing for the last half-hour during his mysterious absence. "Their rooms are prepared, and she has offered to dress and come greet them if you wish, sir."

"No, no, of course not." Charles swatted a hand through the air. "I will greet them. Mrs. Henderson can show them to their rooms. If you will call for a tea service, I will go and attend to our latecomers."

"Very good, sir." Carson bowed and turned to leave, surprisingly spry for such an old man.

"Why so late?" Charles asked, rubbing a hand over his face.

Mac shrugged his shoulders and stood. "I'm off to bed. Give them my greetings." He stopped at the door. "Or don't. It doesn't matter much to me."

"Right. Goodnight, Mac," Charles said, his exhaustion showing in the drooping of his shoulders.

He heard Charles rousing Desmond as he mounted the stairs, and hastened his stride, eager to escape before the women discovered his presence.

CHAPTER 6

*I*t was a dream, wasn't it? Mabel sat up in bed as the faint beginnings of day crept between her drapes and pooled on the floor. Stretching her arms high above her head, she yawned, glad she had chosen early retirement the evening before, for she felt rejuvenated and rested now.

She glanced around her room, noting the additional meal plans Mrs. Henderson had left on her table the night before when she had come to inform Mabel of the late arrivals.

No, it was not a dream. Three additional guests who were scheduled to arrive today had, indeed, arrived late last night.

Groaning, Mabel pressed her fingertips to her eyelids before rising and tying her wrapper around her waist. She opened the drapes—grateful she had gotten to keep them since Giulia didn't need them now—and stood at the window for a moment, soaking in the fresh morning light. She noticed two figures climbing into the boat on the pond. Squinting her eyes, she leaned forward until the tip of her nose rested on the cool glass, and she recognized the men. One of the men was most certainly Charles, made known by the old, ratty fishing garb he deemed good luck and refused to replace.

The other was that monstrously tall man she'd met in the corridor the day before. There was something about him that again struck her as familiar, but she could not place what it was. She was certain she had not met him before, for she would have remembered someone of that magnitude. In fact, she only knew one man who had ever towered over her in that way, and his memory did nothing but stir her stomach in an unpleasant manner and raise bile to her throat.

No, this man was different. Aside from his breadth and lack of a brain, Liam had darker hair. No, he was nothing like Liam MacKenzie.

Heat flooded her cheeks as the giant man down in the boat lifted a hand in greeting, shortly followed by Charles. She raised her hand back and left the window immediately, depositing herself at her writing desk with the menus Mrs. Henderson had delivered and the food orders which would need to be subsequently altered. She pulled a sheet of paper from her desk and began a list, scrawling at the top a reminder to speak with Mr. Akkerman about cutting tulips for the guests' rooms.

Mabel worked on the menu until she felt satisfied that it would please both Gram and Charles's guests, which took quite a bit longer than she would have liked. Ringing the bell, Mabel waited for Payne to come help her dress, anxiety mounting as her list of things to accomplish steadily grew. Moving to the desk, she added to the list, *Convince Charles to buy new fishing equipment.* If he had a pole that was not so outdated, surely he would catch a few fish and they could add trout to their menu. Perhaps she could just gift him with new supplies? No, that would never work. It would only offend the man.

Payne entered the room with a breakfast tray, pleasing Mabel's growling stomach. She took her time eating and dressing, reveling in the few quiet moments she would get before welcoming her guests and playing hostess. She was dawdling and found herself wishing she could escape to Halstead with

Giulia as well and wait out the duration of this blasted house party.

Why she disliked being around people when she was rather talented at hosting was a mystery in itself, and one that she did not care to delve into solving. If only she had been blessed with other gifts, more practical gifts, like patience with Pippa, or a strong talent at hunting, riding, or even fishing, then she could at least be useful in a pleasant way. She could supply the house with an endless stream of trout from the pond.

But no, she had to be blessed with the ability to easily manage the house and its odd occupants, and the ability to take on a decent-sized house party with absolutely no notice. Mabel laughed to herself. Very well, so her skills *were* rather practical. But that was beside the point.

The thing was, Mabel detested people. She could not stand the way they made her feel monstrous and large and awkward and...*ugly*. There, she admitted it. Maybe she could get through this next week or two. Even though her insecurities were real and valid and based on true experiences, they did not stop her from being the mistress of this house—at least in theory—and in complete charge of herself and all of the Sheffield home, if nothing else. At least Charles valued her opinion above all else. She could always count on him to see her and value her contribution.

Mabel descended the stairs after checking Pippa's room, which she had found empty, and her teeth grated together as musical laughter floated from the drawing room. Steeling her nerves, she put on her most regal air and stepped into the room, stopping abruptly at the scene that lay before her.

Two women were seated at the card table playing a game with Charles and another man. The man had the same dark blonde hair as the woman he was seated beside and bore such a strong resemblance to her in the pointy chin and arched eyebrows that Mabel was positive they must be related in some way. Opposite from the dark blonde was another young lady who's rich, brown hair in no way resembled that of her table-mates. Both of the ladies' gowns were fit for London's elite drawing rooms, and the stark contrast made the Sheffield home shabby in comparison.

The men at the table stood upon her entrance, along with the one who was seated on the sofa facing the card table: the half-witted giant.

"Mabel, welcome!" Charles crossed to her and pulled her further into the room.

Her heart beat rapidly at the four sets of strange eyes peering at her, and she tried to smile and walk with grace and poise.

"Please let me introduce you to my dear friends," Charles began, placing a reassuring hand on her back before gesturing to the golden-blonde lady. "This is Miss Pemberton, her sister, Miss Sophy Pemberton, and their brother, Desmond Pemberton. You remember my mentioning Des from school? We met up in Italy and have been traveling together ever since."

Mabel nodded, smiling to the siblings who gave her concilia-tory nods. Desmond Pemberton was a dandy, to be sure, if his bright purple waistcoat and dashingly tied cravat were any indi-cation. A chain hung from his vest, replete with fobs of all sorts, and no sooner had Mabel noticed it than the man pulled the eyeglass from his pocket and secured it to his eye to get a full look at her. Pink tinged her cheeks, and she was grateful when Charles turned her away from that table.

He clutched her shoulders, directing her gaze to the man on the couch. The man she had met in the shadows of the corridor, whom she had not recognized until this moment. No, it couldn't be, could it? Her chest swelled with indignation that she did her best to conceal.

Charles swept a hand to indicate his friend. "And of course you know—"

"Mac!" the giant shouted, a slight panic coloring his words. Did he think he was fooling her? His gaze shifted between Mabel and her cousin. "Everyone calls me Mac."

"But surely in company you'd prefer Mr. Mac—"

"No," Mac said, his mouth turning down as he gave a small shake to his head. "Mr. Mac would be fine, but I'm so used to being called Mac, anything else feels quite uncomfortable."

Charles nodded slowly, a crimp to his brow. "Mac," he repeated, as if it was unknown and the taste confusing on his tongue. "Everyone"—Charles beamed, gesturing to his cousin as if she was someone to be proud to announce—"this is my cousin, the closest thing I have to a sister, Miss Mabel Sheffield."

"Pleased."

"Charmed."

"Pleasure."

The soft-spoken greetings rolled in with slight nods, dips, and bows as Mabel did her best to spread her smile to the occupants of the room, dusting them each with her greetings while her heart hammered wildly against her breastbone.

Mac. Charles had said Mac, but he'd meant *Liam*. Liam MacKenzie.

She'd had a flicker of doubt the moment they had collided in the corridor. He'd certainly seemed familiar then, but it had been so dark, and he really was very changed.

And the name. Mac *surely* had to be shortened for MacKenzie.

She drew in a fortifying breath. Liam MacKenzie was sitting in her drawing room, requesting to be called an absurd name, clearly under the impression that he was actually fooling Mabel into believing his farce.

The shadowed corridor was one thing, but did the giant truly believe Mabel to be so dull that she would not recognize him in the fully lit drawing room? They had grown up as neighbors, and at one time she had actually fancied herself in...well, that was irrelevant. She snuck a look at him and caught his hazel gaze before it flicked away.

"Care to join us for a game?" Charles asked, drawing her attention. He was beaming, and Mabel was determined to discover why he was so pleased with himself. He could not be that glad just to see her. "We are nearly ready to begin a new one."

But it could wait. "No, thank you. I must go and find Pippa. I've yet to see her today."

"She is out with her maid. Hope, I think her name was?" Charles supplied. "They should return shortly, though. They must have left nigh on an hour ago."

"Right," Mabel said, her excuse thwarted and leaving her in a lurch. She crossed to the chair normally occupied by Gram—where *was* Gram, anyway?—and lowered herself slowly, positioning herself near where Mac sat on the sofa. She watched Charles return to his game and grin at the ladies, a slight wave of jealousy washing over her for how easily she had been dismissed.

If she was forced to endure Mac's presence, then she ought to give herself the upper hand. Turning toward the sofa, she offered him a smile that did not quite reach her eyes. "You found Charles on the continent, then? Did you all travel here together?"

Mac opened his mouth to respond but was cut off.

"Yes, pure luck," Mr. Pemberton said from his seat at the card table. "Pure luck it was to run into such an old friend." The man swung his eyeglass from his finger before artfully flipping it up and perusing Mabel from head to toe once more. She felt a blush creep up her neck and turned her attention away from the dandy and toward Liam. Or should she call him Mac? She was undecided about whether or not she wanted to reveal that his ruse was all for naught.

But, no. She would not give in too easily. If he believed her to be unaware of his true identity, she would take advantage of the opportunity.

It would take some training in her mind, but she could do it. She could remove *Liam* altogether and think of the man who'd once broken her heart as Mac.

"Sir, are you well?"

It took a moment for Mac to realize that Mabel had addressed him. He swallowed the lump in his throat and nodded. She gave him a look somewhere between condescension and uneasiness, and he felt a blush fill his face. She must think him as dimwitted as a common mule.

But at least she hadn't recognized him.

Mabel tilted her head and offered him an easy smile, no doubt finding the prospect of his conversation less demanding than the rake that had ogled her moments ago. Mac could wring Desmond's neck, the ridiculous dandy, pulling out his eyeglass and sweeping his gaze over her like that. The action had made Mac's temper rise faster than Miss Sophy's suggestive glances had all morning. And if anyone could raise his ire, it was certainly Miss Sophy—the fortune-hunting chit.

"I noticed you were fishing this morning," Mabel said. "Did you have any luck?"

Mac cleared his throat before shaking his head awkwardly. If he spoke too much, would she recognize his voice? Probably better to keep quiet as long as possible.

"Do you know what I think?" Mabel quieted her voice and leaned in to impart her secret. Mac leaned in as well, his pulse quickening at her proximity, a faint floral smell tickling his nose.

Gardenias, wasn't it? He recalled the moment Charles had bought the fragrance for his cousin while they were in London. His gaze fell into hers. He could reach out and graze her smooth jaw with his thumb if he wanted to. And man alive, did he have a sudden desire to do just that.

"I think," she said, raising her voice slightly, "that if Charles would replace his lucky fishing gear, he might actually have some luck on that miserable pond."

Mac had to smile at this. He had said the very same thing earlier that morning, but Charles had steadfastly refused.

"Did I hear you were fishing this morning?" The sickeningly sweet lilt of Miss Sophy's voice floated to them from the card table, and Mac tensed.

"We did. Not that we caught anything. Right, Mac?" Charles said, his lovesick face directing everything he said to the blonde beside him. Mac wanted to scoff at how smitten his friend had become with Lydia Pemberton. She was nice enough, he supposed, and certainly pretty. But there was something about her that didn't settle right with Mac. But to be fair, her fortune-hunting sister could be the source of his doubt.

"That is correct," Mac said dutifully. "But we have time."

"Perhaps if you acquired new gear..." Mabel playfully directed to her cousin.

Charles shot her a playful scowl. "You know I could never."

"But that pole is nearly as old as we are, Charles." She laughed and the musical sound filled Mac with unaccountable joy. He took a breath and shook off that strange feeling. He had known Mabel for the majority of his life and never had she, or anyone really, elicited such a warm reaction within him. He would have been ashamed if it was not downright enjoyable.

"Oh, Charles, you are not speaking of that ratty old thing you showed me this morning, are you?" Miss Pemberton said with a pretty little pout. "It is positively ancient."

"And full of luck, my dear," Charles said as he lifted her

small hand to his lips and kissed her knuckles. Her cheeks blushed becomingly, and she turned away from him, with just the right amount of coyness that society matrons taught their daughters to portray.

Mac shot a glance at Mabel, and his heart wrenched when he saw the shock written on her features. She clamped her jaw shut and looked away, but not before he noticed her surprise melt into sorrow.

"Surely it cannot be that lucky if you failed to catch a single fish?" Miss Pemberton pressed. "I'm certain we could get you something much better than that wretched excuse for a pole."

Charles smiled endearingly down at the little minx and sighed. "You are probably right. I don't know why I hold on to that old thing. Especially when its luck faded out long ago. Didn't it, Mae?" He shot a look over to Mabel.

Her face flushed, and she tried to smile, but Mac could see the slight tremble of her lip as she answered, "I suppose that is true."

She stood before another tick of the clock could sound and crossed to the door. "I must see to the altered menus. If you'll excuse me."

A chorus of halfhearted answers fueled her escape, and Mabel fled, passing Mrs. Boucher, the older companion traveling with the Misses Pemberton, as she came into the room. Mac stood to follow Mabel and caught up with her just outside the door that led down to the kitchens.

"Wait!" he called.

She paused but did not turn around. He had acted before considering his situation and remembered that, while she would not welcome any consolation from the man he truly was—the man who had known her and Charles and the significance of that pole—she would most certainly find it bizarre to be consoled by an utter stranger.

"You ran out of there so quickly," he said, searching for the right words. "I merely wanted to make sure you were—"

"I am fine, Mr. Mac. Thank you," she answered tightly. Judging by the firm set to her shoulders, she was trying to hold herself together.

Mac reached for her arm, squeezing it in encouragement. "If it's any consolation, the blockhead wouldn't take my advice either. I am under the impression that he has eyes for Miss Pemberton alone at the moment. The rest of us pale in comparison."

Mabel let out a breath, and her shoulders relaxed beneath his hand. She turned, and he cringed at the sheen in her eyes but warmed at her attempt to smile. "If only he felt me important enough to inform me that his heart even *had* a desire."

"Has he had the chance?" Mac asked. They had not yet been in Graton for a full day.

"Actually, yes, he has. Not only could he have written, but we spoke last evening for a length of time." She seemed to lose herself in a memory when her eyes glazed over. "I asked him about his previous love, and we discussed how he has finally moved past his feelings for her. He could have told me that he had gotten over Amelia *because* he had moved on to someone else." Her features hardened as she focused on Mac's face again. "Someone who was coming to stay in my home."

Mac shrugged his shoulders. "Not that it is any excuse, but that is just the way Charles is."

"I know." She released an exasperated breath before her eyes darted to his hand where it was still resting on her shoulder. He jumped back, and a blush crept up his neck.

Mabel collected herself and gave him a sly grin. "Apparently you *are* a man of many words."

He chuckled. "You thought otherwise?"

"You gave me little reason to think much else. Thank you,

though. I do feel better." The smile of gratitude she bestowed on him melted his heart and raced his pulse simultaneously.

He watched her walk away while his body filled with lead, and a heaviness settled on his bones. If Mac knew one thing, it was this: he had to do everything in his power to get that smile back on her face again.

Or maybe two things. For under no condition was Mabel to make the connection that he was not plain and simple-minded Mac. If anything was going to put the sorrow back in her eyes— or worse, anger—it would be if she found out that he was, in fact, Liam MacKenzie. The man who had once broken her heart.

CHAPTER 7

"*P*ippa, we must go now. Please come down," Mabel said, drawing in a sustaining breath. Her gaze sought the clouds above, tracing them with her eyes as she waited for Pippa to climb down from the tree, forcing herself to feign patience where it was far from natural.

"But I don't *want* to come down. I would rather stay in this tree all day than play with those silly girls."

Mabel clenched her teeth. "The Traynor girls are perfectly lovely, and just about your age. They will arrive any moment, and I would like for you to meet them in the house like a proper lady and *not* from the branches of that wretched apple tree."

Pippa's tiny head poked out from between two full branches, wrinkles above her small nose as she scrunched it in distaste. "But what if they don't like me?"

Her delicate voice pierced Mabel's heart. "Oh, Pippa, of course they will like you." Her voice dropped, a wry note lilting her tone. "You do realize it is impossible not to love you, right?"

"You *have* to say that," Pippa said. "You are my sister."

Mabel resisted the urge to stomp her foot like her younger sister did so often, clenching her hands instead. "Phillipa Jane

Sheffield, you vex me to no end. Please come down from that tree and prepare to greet your guests."

Pippa's scoff ripped through the air. "I will not!"

Mabel held her breath, watching the branches for any sign of movement. But the girl refused to climb down. If anyone understood the fear of not belonging, of fearing a lack of acceptance, it was Mabel. That she had suffered in her youth with the same insecurity was little balm at present, however, and she stepped closer to the trunk of the tree, lifting her gaze to find her sister; the girl's head was squarely turned away.

As a child, Mabel had often trailed behind Charles and his friends, begging for inclusion before finding her place among other local girls, Hattie Green and Amelia Fawn. Those friendships had changed Mabel's life, giving her a sense of belonging and love.

"You will never know, Pippa, unless you meet them," Mabel said softly. "What if these girls are about to become your dearest friends?"

Pippa's head came around, her eyes holding Mabel's. The air seemed to freeze until Pippa let out a tiny, long-suffering sigh, her shoulders dropping. Without a word, Pippa began to climb down the tree, and Mabel stepped back, relief filling her chest. She had enough to worry over with her papa's return and her cousin's guests without the added anxiety of sending away the Traynor girls because Pippa refused to play.

"You will remain with me, will you not?" Pippa asked.

Mabel considered her younger sister. The girl had such confidence in every other regard—at home with visitors, with the servants, and even when facing her nemesis, Jacob Tucker—this insecurity was coming as something of a shock. "Of course I will. Though you only have the three dolls."

"You needn't *play* with us, Mae. Just be there."

Mabel smiled, taking Pippa's hand in her own to lead her back to the house. She was unsure how much longer Pippa would rely on her so heavily. The child was already independent to a fault. Mabel would enjoy being wanted while it lasted.

"That sounds perfectly reasonable to me."

They stepped in front of the house as a gig came through the trees lining the gravel drive, Mrs. Traynor at the reins, and her two young daughters nestled snugly on either side of her.

"Good day," Mabel called as the horse came to a stop. If they couldn't meet in the drawing room, at least Pippa was out of the tree. "We are so pleased you could make it. Do come and meet my sister."

Mrs. Traynor stepped down from the gig, clutching the skirt of her rose-printed cotton gown as one of Mabel's stable hands ran to hold the horse's head. Turning to help her daughters hop to the ground, Mrs. Traynor whispered something to them, and they both nodded, their curly blonde hair bobbing in rhythm.

"You must be Miss Sheffield," Mrs. Traynor said, bending her head as she spoke to Pippa.

"I'm the *younger* sister, ma'am. You can call me Miss Pippa."

"Well," Mrs. Traynor said, sharing an indulgent smile with Mabel, "will you allow me to present my daughters to you, Miss Pippa?"

Pippa inclined her head softly, and Mabel had to swallow her amusement. It appeared Pippa was learning from her comportment lessons, after all. And perhaps taking a few tips from elsewhere. The girl was mimicking a fine lady beyond anything Mabel had taught her.

Mrs. Traynor continued, "This is Katie, my oldest. And her younger sister here is June."

"Pleased to meet you," Pippa said, spreading her pinafore as she bobbed a curtsy. "Would you care to see my dolls?"

"I'd much rather climb trees than play with dolls," June, the younger of the sisters, said abruptly.

Mrs. Traynor gasped in time with Pippa. Though the mother's cheeks colored, Pippa's eyes lit at once.

"June," Mrs. Traynor admonished, "that is not—"

"I *love* climbing trees," Pippa said, "and I have just the perfect one in the back garden. Come,"—she gestured for the girls to follow, her voice as regal as a queen—"I will show you."

"I would not mind seeing your dolls," Katie said meekly.

Pippa's gaze ran over the older of the sisters before nodding. "Very well, but come look at my tree first. It's *far* better than Jacob Tucker's tree, whatever he says."

"Pippa, shall I come?" Mabel asked when the girls were already halfway across the lawn.

Pippa turned back, her narrow eyebrows lifted. "Really, Mabel. I am old enough to climb a tree without help, am I not?"

"As long as you are cautious."

Pippa smiled saucily before turning back, flanked by the Traynor girls. Chatter could be heard as she led them toward the back garden.

"I would invite you inside for tea, but I understand you have much to do," Mabel said, turning toward Mrs. Traynor.

The woman smiled appreciatively, her gaze trailing her daughters as they rounded the corner of the house and out of sight. Nodding, she faced Mabel. "You are so kind to invite them, Miss Sheffield. I hope I might return the favor sometime in the future."

"Though next time perhaps we ought to arrange to share tea," Mabel said, doing her best to be welcoming.

Mrs. Traynor hooked a blonde curl behind her ear. "I would enjoy that."

Mabel smiled. "They seem like very sweet girls. I'm happy to have them here. It is not often my Pippa is distracted in a manner that does not lead her to mischief."

Mrs. Traynor's eyes sparkled. "I think our girls shall get along rather nicely, Miss Sheffield."

The woman climbed back onto the driving seat of her gig and accepted the reins from Mabel's stable hand before clicking her tongue and leading them away. Mabel stood on the drive, her hands clasped lightly before her as she watched the woman leave, aware of the giggling drifting from behind the house.

A smile touched her lips, and her shoulders relaxed. If Pippa could make friends such as Mabel had found in Hattie and Amelia, it would do the girl a world of good. To constantly be at odds with a neighborhood boy was not doing Pippa any favors.

Footsteps crunched on the road behind her, and Mabel turned toward the sound, her heart nearly jumping into her throat when Mac approached. The midday light touched his hazel eyes, reminding her of honey drizzling over the edge of a spoon.

Mac cleared his throat. "Have you seen Charles, Miss Sheffield? I rather thought he told me to meet him out here. But perhaps I misheard him."

Mabel's stomach constricted. Had the sound of Mac's voice caused the sensation or the sudden desire she developed for honey spread over a muffin? "I have not seen him. Are you planning to venture to the lake again?"

His lips tipped into a smile, and he shook his head. "Not at present, no. Your father has plans pertaining to the south field, and Charles thought it prudent to ask my advice."

"You have experience in agriculture?"

"Agriculture? No," he said, shaking his head. A moment of heavy silence passed before he cocked his head to the side. "Are you waiting for someone?"

She shook her head, unwilling to continue the deception. Did he *truly* believe she still did not recognize him? How daft could he be?

Well, if Liam MacKenzie wanted to pretend that he was not the same man who had shredded her heart six years before, then Mabel was going to do everything in her power to force him to confess his identity.

She ran through her childhood memories, certain there was

something she could say to show him that she knew who he was, before settling on one in particular. She turned to study Mac.

"You know, it would do Charles a world of good if he was able to catch a fish. Perhaps you can help him."

"How might I do that?" he asked.

"I think I know what his trouble is. I learned this from a friend." She ran her gaze along the roof of the house. If she was going to successfully play this idea out, then Liam could not look into her eyes. He would understand her intent at once.

"A friend?"

"To be quite frank," she shifted to hold his gaze in a moment of bravery, "he was not a friend of *mine* per se, but he was a friend of my cousin's."

"A friend of Charles?"

Mabel nodded, looking to the chimneys stacked like squat birds on the roof. "He was quite a good friend to Charles, and he would be utterly mortified if he was to hear me now, so if I take you in my confidence, will you promise not to reveal your source?"

"I will do my best."

Mabel looked to him, her eyebrows pulling together. She could not help it; she was drawn to him without her consent. She very much wished she could keep her gaze from searching out his honey-colored eyes, but it was moot. She swallowed a sigh. She would just have to be utterly convincing.

"If that is the best you can promise, then I suppose it will have to do. Now—" She leaned in, her voice lowering in preparation to impart her secret. A scent tickled her nose, husky in a comfortable sort of way, nearly thwarting her scheme by its distraction.

"Yes?" he asked, leaning closer, his scent growing stronger and further clouding Mabel's mind.

She cleared her throat. "Please remember that I only tell you this so you might help Charles catch a fish. I am certain he would like to impress Miss Pemberton."

"Of course," Mac said, shifting on his feet, his boots crunching the gravel.

"This friend often fished with Charles and nearly always caught fish when my cousin was ever so hopeless. So one day I asked Charles's friend if he might tell me how he was able to catch fish when my own cousin returned empty-handed nearly every time—despite his lucky equipment."

Liam's face became a work of stone, the only movement a quick flash of recognition in his eyes. He must have thought he knew where she was heading, but he couldn't. Mabel's stomach fluttered, but she could not back out now. She had already gone this far. Liam surely knew she was telling him a story of his own childhood, that he was the boy from that day. The only difference now…well, she could only press on.

"This friend told me that Charles would never catch a fish because he was wholly ignorant. He'd never been taught the proper way to do so. According to this friend, Charles was incapable of catching anything because he never let the pole rest. He was constantly pulling his pole from the water and re-casting it somewhere else, hardly giving the fish time to nibble and completely disrupting the water in the process."

"That seems like sound advice," Mac said, gazing at her.

It was sound advice. But she was not finished.

"What he proposed Charles do, however, was not bother with recasting his pole at all, but to leave it in one place and hum fish songs ever so softly." She leaned in, holding her mirth close to her chest, doing her utmost to keep her expression neutral. "Charles's friend actually told him that humming softly drew the fish toward him, that it was something he did so very quietly, that he was always successful in making a catch. I am afraid Charles has never ceased this practice."

Mac's eyebrows drew together, doubt clouding his eyes. "Are you absolutely certain you are remembering it correctly?"

Mabel drew in a gasp, her chest puffing in umbrage. "Sir, do you call my memory faulty?"

"Never," he said, though she could tell he did not stand behind his claim. For him to believe that she would not know him by now, he would certainly have to think her memory increasingly faulty.

"Then you doubt my story?" she asked, tilting her head to the side. He was close to disputing her claim, she could tell. She merely needed to add something, to make the story even more ridiculous, and *surely* Mac's pride would force him to contradict her.

Mac opened his mouth as though to speak but promptly closed it again. Glancing just over the top of Mabel's head— something she wholly loved—Mac's gaze settled firmly on something behind her.

"Are you ready?" Charles asked, gathering their attention. "I've been waiting in the stables this last quarter-hour."

"You told me to meet you here," Mac said, though his gaze flicked back to Mabel. There was a measure of uncertainty lurking within the pools of honey, and Mabel wondered if she had gone too far. Mac would either think her a liar now, or he would begin to doubt that she didn't remember him.

"Mabel, the women are in the drawing room, and I took the liberty of inviting them to use the music room and the library as often or as much as they please."

"But Charles, the pianoforte has not been maintained. Surely it is out of tune."

Distress passed over his face. "Will you see that it is put in working order?" Stepping closer, he took hold of Mabel's hand. "I would appreciate it ever so much, Cousin."

"Of course," she said, nodding. "I will see to it right away." Offering the men a tight smile, Mabel turned for the house.

Heat seared the back of her neck as she felt the gentlemen's gazes follow her across the gravel drive, and she quickened her pace, reaching the door in swift, long steps. She refused to glance over her shoulder, to find if the owner of the fiery gaze was her cousin or his friend, but her heart told her that Charles could never incite such a feeling within her.

But why would Mac? The man had all but told her on that fateful day in the vale that she was undesirable. Just to remain in the same room with him now caused nothing short of distress.

The tinkling of high-pitched female conversation lilted down the corridor and ran disagreeable shivers up Mabel's arms. She was not comfortable in the presence of other women—those who were petite and lovely and everything a gentleman desired in a wife.

It was not the ladies' fault Mabel felt so at odds against them, and she understood that. But it did not make the drastic differences any easier to bear. She would forever be the last lady chosen, the one left standing against the wall as all others were asked to dance.

Leaning against the closed door, Mabel drew herself up to her full height, her pride rearing its head and commanding that she not cower.

Rubbing at her temples as she ran the list of things she needed to do through her mind, Mabel closed her eyes and imagined the reward she would give herself for completing the duties of the day: she would remove to the nursery following dinner, and she would read to Pippa. Surely the guests would not find fault in her absence if she was with her sister.

With that delightful prospect, Mabel willingly went to check the pianoforte.

CHAPTER 8

"*Y*ou want to build in the vale?" Mac swallowed, scanning the vast field. It was empty now, save for the waves of long, green stalks, but soon it would be resplendent in a violet carpet of flowers. And the idea made Mac's stomach clench.

Charles nodded, his smile widening. "The plan is to build four cottages. Six if we can manage it, but I am not sure we need that many men."

"What does the captain think of this?"

Charles shot him a confused glance. "He has approved the venture."

"In the vale, though?" Mac asked, gripping his hands tightly behind his back.

Charles turned, eyeing his friend closely. "Does that trouble you?"

Mac clenched his jaw. He could never admit so, but yes, it did bother him. He could not look over the field without imagining the heartrending scene of his final day in Graton before he left for the navy.

It had haunted his dreams during his time in His Majesty's

Royal Navy; seeing Mabel again had not helped, even if she had failed to recognize him. Though, that conversation they'd held earlier on the drive had been confusing. Mabel was either lying, or her memory was indeed faulty.

"My uncle has approved the vale," Charles said, a slight edge to his voice. "Is there a reason we should consider another location?"

"No." Mac shook his head. "I was merely surprised. If you are planning to farm the south field, this is quite a distance for the men to travel."

"The men will certainly not mind. We are not asking them to travel to the south side of Graton, for heaven's sake. Just to the south field."

"When does the captain return?"

"He should have been here yesterday."

Yesterday? "Is that cause for concern?" Mac had been under the captain's tutelage for the last five years and had never known the man to be anything less than perfectly punctual.

"No," Charles said, turning back to run a hand along his horse's neck. "He had business to take care of in London. My uncle assumed he would be a day or two behind us, but that could have easily changed."

The field spread out before him, and Mac allowed his eyelids to drift shut, to imagine the barren stalks ripe with deep violet petals, vibrantly washing over the curves of the ground like peaceful waves along the lakeshore. A soft breeze tickled his chin and he opened his eyes, subtly shaking his head to remove the image from his mind.

"Shall we look at the south field?" he asked, turning toward his horse. He climbed onto the saddle in a smooth motion, desperate to ride hard and rid his limbs of the anxious prickles unsettling his body.

Charles agreed, and Mac didn't wait for his friend to mount before he spurred his horse forward, skirting the edge of the vale and heading toward the south field. Mabel's story earlier had unnerved him, and he knew it had little to do with the falsity she had shared.

He could not put his finger on precisely what it was that bothered him, though. She couldn't possibly know, could she? Surely if she had recognized Mac, she would have been angry or sad, or worse, cold and disinterested, all of which she had every right to be. But this woman? This strong, stable woman who looked at him kindly and shared ridiculous untruths from her youth? He did not know her.

But he wanted to. And that realization startled him.

"I didn't know you wanted to race," Charles called from behind, spurring his horse even faster.

Mac glanced down, feeling the tightness in his grip, the reins cutting into his palms as he rode hard across Charles's land. Mabel's family land. He needed to remove her from his mind. But this ride wasn't doing much to help.

He reached the proper field, kicking his horse for added speed. It was once farmed but had become overgrown in recent years. There was a lot of potential for land such as this, and with all of the men returning from war with nothing to return home to, it would be a blessed thing for the captain to put his plan into motion.

But to build the tenant cottages in the vale felt like sacrilege. He was clearly alone in this thought, but Mac could not like disrupting the vale. He turned back, coming upon Charles and reining in his horse. "It's quite a distance," Mac said, unable to hold back a final disagreement.

"Where else would you propose the cottages go? The vale is large and of little use—"

"Not to the women. Do you not think your cousin ought to be consulted?" The words, once escaped from Mac's mouth, could never be recalled. Did he want Mabel to be consulted?

Could he manage his feelings if she admitted that she did not care for the place?

"Mabel will not mind. I am fairly certain she has not come out here herself since we were children."

Mac knew that to be untrue, but he was not about to share the information. Charles would only want to know why Mac was aware of Mabel's frequent trips to lay among the violet flowers and read or nap, as he had once found her doing.

The image brought a smile to his lips.

"You know," Charles said, his mouth pursing in consideration. "What a splendid idea. We ought to bring the ladies to the vale to enjoy a picnic or some such thing before it is dug up. It is only too bad the flowers aren't in bloom."

"No," Mac said, his curt reply startling his friend. "What use will it be to show them the vale if we are to ruin it with cottages shortly thereafter?"

Charles studied his friend. "Why do I feel as though you are withholding information?"

Because I am, Mac thought. He merely shrugged, directing his horse back toward the house.

"You may not wish to share with me yet, but I will get it out of you. You've acted strangely since arriving in Graton."

"It *is* odd being back," Mac said. "The last time I was in Graton, I still had a home."

"Your mother is not unwell?" Charles asked.

Mac shook his head. "No, she is content in Bath. She writes that her sister is a tolerable companion."

"Is it the memories from your childhood that bother you?"

Mac was becoming dangerously close to lying to his closest friend. "Yes, of course," he finally said, opting for honesty. "This will never feel like home as long as my father is in the Marshalsea and my mother is living out her days in only tolerable contentment with her sister, no house of her own to manage."

"You could pay your father's debts," Charles said softly.

Mac clenched his teeth, his hands flexing over the thin, leather reins. He planned to, of course. It was left to him to get his father from the clutches of the debtor's prison. But he needed to wait until he had the funds to support his parents once again. If only he could convince his mother...but no. She would never return to the town where she had felt such acute embarrassment.

Shaking his head, Mac turned his horse from the field. "Shall we return?" His voice sounded strained even to his own ears.

"I wish I could help." Charles pulled his horse alongside Mac's as they cantered toward the house. "If I had the money at my disposal—"

"This is my burden and mine alone," Mac said crisply. He had intended to bring enough prize money home from the war to both help his father and purchase an estate of his own, but so far, things had not gone the way he had planned.

What ever did?

Mabel stood in the dim corridor, her ear pressed against the door as she listened to the girls playing in the schoolroom. Once they'd had their fill of climbing trees and the subsequent tea Cook had prepared for them, they had disappeared into the schoolroom and spent the better part of an hour quietly ensconced in the room, the charming sound of young voices intermixed with giggles floating into the corridor.

It was rather a shame the Traynor family did not live closer, but that was not going to deter Mabel from furthering their acquaintance with the family. Her papa had never been one with snobbish airs, and even if he had, nothing would stop Mabel from pursuing a friendship with a family of two perfectly lovely girls for Pippa to play with. The poor thing needed friends that would be kind—anyone to replace the dreadful animosity between Pippa and Jacob Tucker.

It had felt like watching history repeat itself to hear Pippa complain of Jacob, to watch the boy tease her from up in his tree when they had gone to deliver the apology basket of muffins. Mabel had acted very much the same way when she was younger, when Mac and Charles had been younger, as well. She had longed to play with them, to be included in their adventures, but the boys had been so bent on refusing to allow her to join their games.

She needed to interrupt the girls now—it was time to return the Traynor girls to their house—but couldn't bring herself to do so yet. Mabel pressed her ear to the door, laying her palm flat against the solid oak as she strained to hear what the girls were saying.

"Does Pippa realize you are spying?" a deep voice said just behind her.

Startling, Mabel straightened, her cheeks growing warm as she caught Mac's gaze. He took up the majority of the narrow corridor, his head nearly reaching the top of the doorway behind him.

"I am not spying," Mabel defended, her voice barely a whisper. "I am merely listening."

"Perhaps traitors to the Crown might give that same defense. Do you think it would work in their favor?" he returned, his low voice quietly matching hers.

Duly chastised, Mabel shot him a wry smile. "It is different when I am the sole person in charge of both Pippa's happiness and wellbeing, do you not agree? I am merely doing my duty to ensure my charge is being treated well, and that she is treating her guests with the same courtesy."

"*Touché*, Miss Sheffield."

The name sounded strange on his lips—too formal—from this man who had been used to calling her Mabel.

"Was your outing with Charles a success?"

Mac looked at her sharply, his eyes flashing before his gaze flicked away. What else was he trying to hide?

"You did not run into any trouble, did you?" she asked.

"No, no trouble," he agreed, offering a tight smile.

Her stomach clenched. "What is it, Mac?" she asked softly.

Mabel detected a nearly imperceptible widening of his eyes before he focused, studying her. "Actually," Mac said, "I spent a lot of time today considering your request."

"Oh?"

"Yes."

Mabel waited, holding her breath. Had he considered it so long because she had gone too far? Because she had given herself away? That had indeed been her objective, but the prospect of being discovered, of Mac knowing she had not been fooled, was now somewhat frightening. It meant she could no longer pretend to be indifferent to him. She would be vulnerable to anger, and no facade would sit in the way to stem the flow.

"You see, I cannot think Charles would believe such a wretched tale, that humming to fish would ease them toward the hook." He took a step closer, and Mabel's heart pounded harder in her chest. "In fact, I have a hard time believing *anyone* to be foolish enough to tell such a story."

"Uh—"

"Present company excluded, naturally," he said swiftly. "For you were merely relaying a tale."

Mabel swallowed, her pulse racing. Had Mac grown since just that morning in the front drive? He seemed so much taller now, towering over her with an intelligent glint in his honey-hazel eyes.

"What are you proposing, then?" she asked.

His gaze flicked between her eyes, and she watched them shift back and forth, her breath coming in rapid spurts from how close the man stood to her, afraid too deep a breath would meet her buttons to his.

"I think, Miss Sheffield, there is something you are not telling me."

She'd been caught. But she could not breathe in such proximity.

Stepping back, she bumped softly into the doorway to the nursery. "Oh?"

"Yes," he said. Did he come closer, still? It felt as though he was growing nearer, regardless of her efforts to put space between them. "But what I cannot tell is *why*."

She stilled. Whether or not Mac realized it, he was playing her game. Giggling floated through the door from three very young girls, and Mabel's heart reached out to her former self, to the girl who wished to play with the boys but was told she could not. To the girl with the bundled lock of hair which was destined to remain lonely in its cherrywood box on her table. She was not going to stand idly by any longer.

She was not going to pretend.

"Do you mean," she said, straightening her shoulders and clutching the folds of her gown at her sides, "that you *didn't* tell Charles to hum to the fish in order to bring them closer?"

Shock registered momentarily in Mac's eyes before he shuttered them again. Silence sat heavily upon them while Mac seemed to regain his bearings.

"Have you known from the first?" he asked, his voice dipping to the low timbre only a man could achieve.

The stripped bare tone squeezed Mabel's heart, and she couldn't help but smile. "As mortifying as it is to admit, I did not know that day in the corridor. You are very changed."

"And you are very much the same."

CHAPTER 9

*M*ac resisted the urge to close his eyes and sink into the floor. Why had he spoken such foolishness? Mabel was anything but the same. She had altered considerably since Mac had left Graton. Her face had lost the roundness of youth, defining her cheekbones and the gentle curve of her jaw. She appeared to be a woman with confidence, very much in control.

And she was beautiful. Had he been wrong to push her away all those years before?

No. Mac shook his head. He was not worthy of Mabel Sheffield.

"I would like to think six years has allowed me to age somewhat," she finally said, her voice dry.

Surely the woman did not think he was referencing their last meeting before he left for the navy. "Of course," he said hurriedly. "You are much changed."

"But you only just said that—"

"Don't listen to me." Mac rubbed a hand down his face.

The door opened behind Mabel and Pippa appeared in the open space, a tiny scowl marring her lovely face. "We are right in the middle of a *very* important part, and you have distracted us to no end."

"Forgive us," Mac said at once, dipping at the waist. "I hadn't realized we were speaking loud enough to disrupt—er, what is it we are so rudely interrupting?"

Pippa studied him before her gaze flicked to Mabel. Drawing her tiny shoulders back, Pippa tilted her head and spoke in a regal tone. "We have decided to become actresses. We are in the midst of a *very* important scene where the pirate has come to demand his treasure, and I cannot faint for the life of me with all of this distraction."

"Perhaps you ought not to faint," Mabel said kindly, though the authority in her tone was unmistakable.

Pippa shook her head. "But I *must*. It is not in earnest, you see. I am merely feigning so I might distract the pirate long enough for Katie to hide the treasure."

"Unfortunately, you shall have to perfect your faint another day. It is time to take the Traynors home."

"Already?" Pippa asked, anguished.

Nodding, Mabel stepped past her sister into the schoolroom. She looked to the young guests. "You are both welcome here any time, but we must get you home now."

Mac stood in the corridor, watching Mabel gather the girls and motion them toward the stairs. She directed a brief glance his way before ushering her young charges out of sight. He leaned back against the wall and listened to footsteps retreating down the stairs. He liked Pippa. She had spunk—much like her sister.

Turning toward his bedchamber located on the other side of the schoolroom, Mac went to dress for dinner. There was no way he was going to be able to let that conversation be the final word on the matter. Somehow, he needed to find a way to get Mabel alone so he might explain himself. She had not asked why he had failed to reveal himself right away, though she had also failed to explain why she had pretended not to know who he was.

It was all quite silly, and Mac very much wished to make a clean breast of it. But more than that, he wanted to discuss the things he had said to her before he left for the navy. He needed to explain away his insolence, beg forgiveness for his rudeness.

The trouble was, he could not tell her *why* he had been so mean to her. There was no excuse for his foolish behavior.

<hr />

The drawing room was set up with a card table following dinner, and the Misses Pemberton, their brother, and Charles sat in the midst of a game of speculation. Mac stood beside the cold fireplace, his hands clasped behind him, as he pretended to survey the watercolor painting of the Sheffield estate on the mantel. Mabel sat behind him on the sofa beside the Pembertons' hired companion, Mrs. Boucher, deep in a tiresome conversation about the best age to begin teaching the languages, and how early dancing ought to be introduced to young ladies.

He'd overheard Mabel telling Charles that she thought she should spend dinner with Pippa that evening, but Charles must have convinced her otherwise. Not that Mac was complaining about Mabel's presence—he enjoyed simply being in the same room as her.

And he watched her far more often than he ought, hoping to see her gaze flick his way. She knew who he was, yet she appeared entirely in control of her faculties. He'd expected anger, hatred. He *deserved* it. But instead, the woman remained seated comfortably, her pleasant gaze fixed steadfastly on the Pemberton ladies' aging companion.

"Your cousin is awfully good at cards, Miss Sheffield," Miss Sophy called from the card table.

Mabel lifted her head, glancing toward the group at the table. "He has been known to win more games than not, I'll admit."

What had happened to Mabel in the last six years to change her from the spirited, witty girl he knew into this refined, careful mistress of the house? Mac missed her impish smile and sparkling eyes, the ones that had clearly told him she was up to no good. Was that playful thread sitting idly somewhere deep inside Mabel, or had she put it off completely in pursuit of this older, more mature woman?

Introspection drew his gaze over her now, noting the elegant sweep of her neck as she turned to glance at the card table and its occupants. Had he seen that very hint of mischief he so desired in her expression when she had spoken to her younger sister? Or had Mac merely *wished* he'd seen it?

"If I cannot claim skill as a fisherman," Charles said, holding his cards but grinning at Miss Pemberton, "then I ought to be able to claim skill in some other department. Cards will do, I suppose."

Miss Pemberton dipped her head coyly, a soft smile touching her lips. She was every bit as smitten with Charles as he was with her. But that was good. Better this brainless miss than Charles holding out for a widow who would never have him.

"Would you like to join us, Mac?" Charles called, and Mac glanced up to find his friend watching him.

He shook his head. "Not this evening. I'm afraid I need to catch up on my correspondence." He delivered what he hoped was a sardonic smile. "I've put it off long enough."

"Can you not put it off one day more?" Miss Sophy simpered, her lower lip jutting forward. "I would very much like to see if you can best Mr. Fremont."

"I cannot," Mac said plainly. "In the lake, perhaps. But never at cards. The man is far too cunning for me."

"But speculation is a matter of mere luck, is it not?" Miss Sophy asked.

Mac could not help but look at Mabel, his mind drawn to that day in the woods when Mabel had earned herself the title of cheater by rigging a game of straws. "Even in games of luck, *some* degree of skill is required if one would like to tip the hand in their favor."

Mabel sat up, straightening her shoulders and folding her hands in her lap. Mac held her gaze, unable to move his sight from the faint blush spreading up her cheeks or the way she watched him as if against her better judgment.

Did she understand his intent? His reference to her tampering with the straws that day long ago? Her cheeks grew pink in a most becoming manner, indicating that she did. There was something about inducing a blush in a young lady that sent a flood of achievement coursing through Mac's veins.

"Mac," Charles called, stealing his attention. "What say you?"

Mabel dropped her gaze to her lap and the restless fingers lying there. What had happened to change her so? The Mabel he knew would have challenged him, not acquiesced.

"Forgive me, Charles. I was not attending."

Charles glanced between Mac and Mabel, his eyebrows drawing together as his eyes flicked back and forth, his hand of cards going limp against the table. Warmth spread up Mac's neck, and he crossed the floor, bowing toward the table of card players. "I must clear my head," he said before quitting the room.

He was in trouble.

Had Mac meant to reference the game Mabel had orchestrated as a young girl? When she had convinced Charles and his friends to draw sticks in order to determine who would have to escort Mabel home after she'd twisted her ankle following them through the forest?

It had mortified her, after Mac had chosen the shortest straw, that he immediately accused her of having done it on purpose. She had, of course, but she would never admit so aloud. Not after the way Mac had grumbled the whole way back to Sheffield House or what he had said when they had stopped in the vale.

Mabel stifled a sigh. She had learned her lesson then. She would never meddle with a game of chance again.

"You have begun French, I presume?"

Mrs. Boucher's beady eyes blinked at Mabel, and she recalled herself to the present. Mac was gone, having left the room. The card players had returned their attention to their game, mildly raucous, on the other side of the room, and Gram sat undisturbed, slumbering in her regular chair near the fireplace. But Mrs. Boucher remained, and she persisted in her conversation. It seemed to Mabel the woman was itching to take over Pippa's lessons entirely.

With Giulia so wretchedly absent at present, that was a wildly appealing thought.

"We began French two years ago, ma'am," Mabel said, nodding. "Pippa is doing rather well. But my father has asked that we give Pippa a thorough understanding of science and mathematics, so there is not as much time to devote to language as I'd like. Still, we do our best."

"How very strange," Mrs. Boucher said, her mouth pinching in disapproval.

"Perhaps it *is* unusual to teach a young girl mathematics and science, but I will not go against my father's wishes." And though he was not present, Papa had strong feelings about the education of his daughters. If only he would arrive soon. His latest missive had explained that his business was taking far longer than he'd anticipated. Mabel had no notion of when he would be arriving.

A snort rent the air, and Gram adjusted her position in her chair, sitting up straight while her head lolled to the other side, her lace-gloved hand never releasing its grip on the ebony walking stick.

"Are you proficient in all of these subjects?" Mrs. Boucher asked.

"No. I rely heavily on my dear friend, Miss Pepper. Though she is to be married soon and we will not have her assistance much longer, I'm afraid."

"You will send the girl to school?"

"Not if I can help it," Mabel said. "I would much rather bring a governess here if it can be managed."

Mrs. Boucher nodded, narrowing her gaze until Mabel could no longer stand it. She rose, offering the companion a smile before escaping to the other side of the carpet.

"Gram?" she asked, interrupting the older woman's soft snores.

Gram sat up, blinking up at Mabel with no recognition.

"Shall I escort you upstairs?"

"I would *not* like the core of a pear, Mabel. That is utterly nonsensical."

Mabel nodded. "Of course." She raised her voice, leaning in slightly. "Shall I help you to your room instead?"

"I am tired," Gram snapped. "Come, help me up."

Mabel took her grandmother's delicate arm and hoisted the woman softly to her feet. Wrapping Gram's arm around her own, she crossed the floor, bidding the others farewell as she made her escape the best way she knew how. They made their way quietly up the stairs, arm in arm, as Gram leaned on her walking stick more than she leaned on Mabel. The older woman was stubborn—a likely source for Mabel's inherited trait. The thought brought a rueful smile to her lips.

"You will not let that woman come in here and take over Pippa's learning."

Mabel halted at the top of the stairs, turning toward Gram, whose chest heaved from the climb. "What do you mean?"

"The companion," Gram said, her white eyebrows rising on her forehead. "She wants to come in here and take your position, Mabel. She wants to marry off those wanton ladies to the two available men and insert herself into the role of Pippa's governess."

Mabel was stunned. First, her *position*? Did Gram view her as a servant? She shook the thought away, for surely Gram had only meant it regarding Mabel's authority over Pippa. Those thoughts aside, Mabel had not considered Charles's guests to be anything near wanton...let alone cunning and calculating, as Gram implied. And besides, there were two Pemberton sisters, were there not? Charles could not marry both women. And neither could they marry their brother. That only left...

"You think Miss Sophy has her eye on Mac?"

Gram managed to create another crease in her brow. Was Mabel blind?

"I need sleep," Mabel said.

"Indeed." Gram nodded as they set off toward her bedchamber. "You have those wretched dark circles under your eyes, Mabel. You must correct that if you plan to snatch a man for yourself."

Mabel could not help but laugh. "We are in no danger of that, I assure you."

"You will not play my nursemaid forever," Gram said with surprising bitterness. "You will wed."

Then *who* would play Gram's nursemaid? And what of Pippa? Mabel refused to send her sister to school. It was not as though she believed institutions to be inherently bad, but she could not send Pippa away, not when the girl already suffered for lacking a mother. Mabel was determined to fill that role as best she could and support her sister.

Gram reached forward, pulling Mabel's hand into her own. "It is not selfish to think about oneself on occasion, Mabel."

"I know that," she defended, though Gram's expression spoke to her disbelief. "Goodnight, Gram," Mabel said when they reached the door.

Gram's eyebrows drew together. "Will you not send for my maid and prepare my tea?"

Mabel could not help but chuckle. No, her Gram did not want her to play nursemaid, indeed. "I will send for tea right away."

CHAPTER 10

$\mathcal{H}$iding from one's guests was the very lowest of ladylike decorum, but Mabel flattened herself against the wall and prayed silently that the women walking down the corridor would turn for the stairs instead of continuing her direction. They had been in Mabel's home for nearly a fortnight now and their company had grown increasingly wearisome.

If Mabel was forced to endure their company for another fortnight, she was liable to burst. But her governess had taught her to conduct herself better than that. So instead of making herself known to the Pemberton sisters, she hid from them.

"But what of his cousin?" a soft, high voice said.

Mabel's ears perked up and she straightened, further pressing her back into the wall. Were they speaking of her?

"What of her?" the other voice said, sounding very much like Miss Pemberton.

"If you marry him, you'll have her to contend with. You know he will *never* force Miss Sheffield out of the house."

"You speak as though you believe the woman to be a permanent fixture. Do you think she is past marrying age?" Miss

Pemberton asked, a slight panic lacing her tone. "I am not sure I could become mistress of this house if Miss Sheffield remained. There's already the grandmother and the little girl to manage." Her voice lowered, growing gravelly. "It is positively overrun with women."

A beat of silence passed, raising the tide of anxiety in Mabel's heart. Now she *really* could not be found listening to the Pemberton sisters' conversation. She glanced over her shoulder, calculating the length of time it would take for her to sneak down to the end and around another corner. She could take the servants' stairs down—

"I have an idea," Miss Sophy said. "But do not speak until you have properly heard me out."

The end of the corridor, the freedom from eavesdropping, beckoned Mabel. But she could not move. Frozen in place, she pressed her shoulders further against the wall, silently pushing her head back as she strained to listen.

"Desmond."

"What of him?" the sister asked.

Mabel could very well imagine the sly smile taking over Miss Sophy's face as she explained. "He needs to settle down, and he could do far worse than a woman predisposed to care for others."

"You are suggesting we devise a scheme so that our brother might *marry* Miss Sheffield? Sophy, *really*, that is too much."

Affront reached up and clenched Mabel's chest. Did Miss Pemberton believe her to not be good enough for their brother? A tad tall, she might agree, for she could very nearly look into the man's eyes when they stood toe to toe.

"I don't see the harm in trying to make a match of Desmond and Miss Sheffield. We are not forcing them to post the banns, darling, merely helping them to see the benefit of this pairing."

"And why can we not do the same thing with Mr. MacKenzie?"

Mabel's heart constricted.

"You know very well why not," Miss Sophy snapped. Had her sister been goading her? "He nearly proposed marriage to me just last month. And after the way he spoke to me this morning, I am certain he intends to ask for my hand within a fortnight."

Mabel drew in a quick breath, her heart pulsing.

"Now," Miss Sophy continued, her voice drawing quieter as though she was walking away, "cut the foolishness and help me contrive a way to force Desmond and Miss Sheffield into prolonged, private exposure."

By the time Miss Pemberton responded, if she indeed did so, the women had fallen out of earshot. Shoulders slumping forward, Mabel blew a breath through her teeth. The very nerve! To attempt to contrive a match between herself and Mr. Pemberton, indeed. She was neither a young lady in the blush of youth nor a dainty, attractive female ripe for courting. Mr. Pemberton would not entertain illusions of the benefits of such a match, she was certain, and the idea of his sisters presenting the idea to him brought a blush swiftly to Mabel's cheeks.

Footsteps sounded on the staircase around the corner, and Mabel pressed herself against the wall once more, her eyelids drifting closed. Given her luck, it would be Mr. Pemberton coming next and he was sure to run directly into her. His face was bound to flood her cheeks scarlet. But all was not lost. *He* did not know the ridiculousness his sisters were planning.

"Miss Sheffield." Mac's voice came through the darkness, and Mabel felt it in her soul. Why was she so unlucky? Seeing Mr. Pemberton after overhearing his sisters' troubling plans would have been uncomfortable—seeing Mac was infinitely worse. They needed to discuss their situation at some point, but she was not ready for it to be now. If she kept her eyes closed, would Mac simply walk away?

A faint pattering of little feet could be heard overhead— Pippa playing in her schoolroom, no doubt—as silence sat between Mabel and Mac in the corridor, her eyes shut against the large man. Had he slipped away? Tempted to check, Mabel slowly lifted one eyelid, and immediately caught Mac's steady gaze.

Flushing, a wry smile found its way onto her lips.

"Were you trying to hide?" he asked, amusement clear in his voice, playing on his lips.

"Not exactly. I was hoping you would read the situation and slip away quietly."

"Do forgive me, madam. I was unaware of your thoughts."

"That is increasingly clear to me, sir."

Mac studied Mabel. The air felt charged, heavy. He stepped closer. "Do you think we could talk—"

"No, thank you." Mabel turned away, walking down the hall toward the stairs. She would find solace in the schoolroom with Pippa.

"Mabel—"

She glanced over her shoulder, her eyebrow lifting.

"Miss Sheffield," he corrected. "I called you Mabel for years and I *have* been trying to be more formal, but the habit will be difficult to break."

"I called you Liam for my entire childhood, and yet I haven't slipped once." She exhaled. "You haven't called me *anything* for years. I should think it wouldn't be a very difficult habit to break at all." Sliding her fingers along the bannister, Mabel lifted the hem of her gown and took the narrow stairs toward the top floor.

"Perhaps that is something we ought to rectify," he said, following, but pausing at the bottom of the stairs.

There was the flirt she remembered from before. Mabel paused mid-step, turning back. She was taller than him when standing this way, a few steps above him, though not by much. Looking down at him—however slight—she narrowed her eyes. "What is the use? You will be gone again rather soon, I should think, and I do not scruple to tell you that I have no pleasant memories of our time spent together before you left Graton."

Mac held her gaze, his mouth pinched into a firm line. Expelling a long, slow breath, he shook his head ever so slightly. "Has Charles not informed you of his plans, then?"

She stilled. "What plans?"

The bend of Mac's shoulders and his shifty gaze revealed just how uncomfortable he was with this situation. "This really ought to come from him."

"He isn't here now," Mabel said, unrelenting. She lifted an arm to sweep the staircase, pointing out just how alone they were. "What is it I should know?"

"Your father has invited me to remain here for the duration of the summer, and perhaps longer. We've developed a plan and he's asked for my help to see it through."

The *entire* summer? Her chin dropped. "You mean to tell me your presence here isn't due to a house party?"

"The Pembertons may certainly be, but I will not be returning to London when they choose to leave. I have committed to helping the captain with this project."

Mabel's breathing grew short, stilted. She had prepared herself to manage her discomfort in Mac's presence for the duration of a fortnight, but the entire summer was too long to bear. It was unfair of Charles to foist this upon her with no warning. Her papa may have orchestrated the scheme, but Charles could have informed her of it, at the very least.

"And your own house is not good enough shelter?"

Mac stared up into Mabel's beautiful, stone face, and his stomach clenched. "My house is not an option."

Was Mabel unaware of the debts? The Marshalsea?

She clenched her teeth—he could see it in her jaw.

Reaching forward, Mac laid his hand atop hers on the bannister and heard her breath catch. "I didn't realize you were unaware of the situation. I can promise you that from the very beginning, I vowed I would not make you uncomfortable. Whatever you ask, I will obey. This is your home and the last thing I wish to do is drive you from it."

"You could not," she said. Of course, he could trust Mabel to take a gesture of goodwill and trample on it with that dratted Sheffield pride.

"I am happy to hear it."

"Oh, hush," she said, removing her hand from underneath his. Mac felt the lack immediately and gripped the bannister instead. Lowering her voice, Mabel spoke in a harsh whisper. "You cannot return here six years later and force me to believe you are so very changed. I remember what happened that day in the—" she glanced away, blinking far too quickly for Mac's comfort. When she returned her gaze to meet his, he read resolve in their depths. And something far more vulnerable. Hurt, perhaps? It nearly killed him.

"Allow me to make amends," he pleaded.

"How do you propose you might make amends for something which happened all those years ago? It is childish of me to hold on to my anger, but I have never pretended to be a perfect person."

"It is not childish. I've never apologized for saying those things to you, for rejecting your offer. Please, allow me—"

"Can you not see how this might be difficult for me? Please, forget I ever said anything about it."

He watched her in disbelief. "Can *you* not see that failing to allow me to apologize might be difficult for *me*?"

She stared at him, dumbstruck.

He decided to press his luck. "I am sorry, Mabel. I can see the folly of my youth, and I wish I would have had the age and wisdom then to see how hurtful my words would have been.

Believe it or not, I was not in a good place that day, and I've often regretted—"

"Telling me I was tall and ugly?"

"Ugly?" Mac said, rearing back. "Never did I say—"

"Telling a young woman she was far too tall, and a lock of her hair would not be a favorable charm for any man is just as good as calling her ugly, Mac," Mabel spat. "You might as well have said I would never find a husband and would end up a spinster, caring for my sister and grandmother without a single prospect in sight."

Mabel's chest heaved, and Mac had a sudden, overwhelming desire to pull her down two steps and crush his lips on hers. But he valued his life, so he refrained.

"Surely you realize how very wrong that is," he said softly.

"Surely *you* realize how very true it is. I *am* a spinster, and I *am* caring for Pippa and Gram. And please, sir, show me one eligible gentleman who so much as wishes to take me riding."

Mac straightened. "That, I can do."

Mabel scoffed, crossing her arms over her chest. "Please, do. And if you say the grouchy duke who lives in Wolfeton House, I will pour vinegar in your soup tonight."

"No, not the duke. I was unaware we even had one of those nearby."

"Who, then?"

Mac swallowed. "Me."

CHAPTER 11

*W*as the man in earnest? Mabel could hardly credit it. He could not possibly believe Mabel would fall for his charms so easily, not when he had been a known flirt before, and she had been foolish enough to fall for it. She had believed herself in love with Mac at one point. His quiet, calm strength and the amusing glint in his eye had drawn her toward him when they were younger. But now? Now, she hardly knew him.

Mabel shook her head. "I hardly have time for these games."

"It is not a game," he said, reaching forward to stop her on the stairs, taking her hand in his. His large fingers wrapped around her own, making her feel delicate, protected, in a way no other man had before. "I would love to take you riding. Why not give me a chance to prove myself? I should like the opportunity to become your friend."

She paused, shock coursing through her body. His eyes were so beseeching, his face pleading, and she wanted to grant him whatever his heart desired. But what would that do to Mabel if she gave of herself so easily? Sometimes it felt that was all she did—give of herself.

Time. She needed more time to sort through this. And if this man was going to remain in her house for the summer, then evidently, they had plenty of it.

"Miss Sheffield?" Mrs. Henderson's voice drifted to them from the bottom of the staircase, breaking through the haze. "Forgive my interruption."

Mac was still, but his eyes never left her face, and Mabel could feel the weight of his gaze. "Yes, Mrs. Henderson?"

"Your father has just arrived, miss, and I wished to consult you on the sleeping arrangements."

Her heart jumped. Papa was here. Soon, all would be right. "He will have the master suite, of course."

"Yes," Mrs. Henderson agreed. "And his friend?"

A niggling unease slipped into Mabel's chest. "He has brought a friend?"

Mac turned on the stairs. "Who did he bring, ma'am?"

Mrs. Henderson's gaze shifted between them. "A man called Mr. Wright."

Mac's hand tightened on Mabel's and she pulled hers free, rubbing the tension from it.

"Forgive me," Mac said, his voice low. "I will let you attend to this. But please, consider my request. I would like to give you reason to call me your friend again, Mabel. I wish it, dearly."

His low voice washed over her, prickling her skin. Brushing past her, Mac mounted the stairs, and Mabel allowed herself a moment to regain her equilibrium, clutching the bannister for strength.

"Miss Sheffield?"

"Yes," she said, giving her housekeeper a tight smile. She started down the stairs. "Come, let us see what we can contrive. Did Papa say how long Mr. Wright would remain here?"

"No, miss."

"Then we shall see what we can do. And quickly. I should very much like to greet my father."

It took all of a quarter-hour to arrange a proper room for Papa's guest. He would be placed in the room next to Mac's and would have to be content to remain there until the Pembertons could be persuaded to leave. She trusted however old he was, he would be able to manage the stairs. Any friend of her father likely knew him from his ship, and that meant the man would be spry enough to handle both staircases. If he was too old or perhaps injured, then she would have to reassess, but she chose not to concern herself with that possibility quite yet.

Mabel's heart sped the closer she drew to the drawing room. It had been just under two years since she had set eyes on her papa, and their reunions were always sweet.

Soft, familiar giggling filtered into the corridor, lifting Mabel's spirits even further. Pippa spoke of their papa often, but in truth, the girl hardly knew him. This visit would be good for all of their souls.

"Mabel?" Papa's voice broke into her stupor, and she realized she'd halted in the doorway, watching him sit on the settee with Pippa on his knee. His weather-beaten face and long, white beard were the same as always, though the wrinkles around his eyes had grown in number.

"Papa," she said, crossing the floor.

He stood, setting Pippa aside and pulling Mabel into an embrace. It felt comforting and secure, his arms constant and strong. "You are as beautiful as ever," he said, dropping a kiss on her head.

Cheeks warming, Mabel stepped back, aware of the man standing just beside the settee, gloves in hand.

"Mabel, allow me to introduce Lieutenant Wright."

"Please, just Mr. Wright. Now that I've left the navy, you'll have to cease calling me lieutenant, sir."

Mr. Wright was anything but aged. He fell somewhere in age between Mabel and her father, but she wagered it was on the lower end. While he was tanned and his dark hair longer than fashionable, tied in a queue low on his neck, he had a degree of intelligence about his smile. And when he dipped into a bow, it was evident he was trained in the art of propriety. This man, her father's lieutenant, was clearly a gentleman.

"Mr. Wright," she said, dipping into a curtsy. "Welcome to our home."

A commotion in the foyer drew their attention, and Charles entered the room, shortly followed by Mr. Pemberton, the man's two sisters, each of them wearing broad smiles, and Mrs. Boucher lagging behind.

Mabel's gaze flitted between the numerous guests, her throat tightening. It was one thing to invite a few people for a short house party, another thing entirely to invite someone to stay for months. Where did Mr. Wright fall on this spectrum?

"Charles," Papa said, crossing the room and slapping her cousin on the back. He absolutely beamed and Mabel scolded herself. This was just as much Papa's home as it was hers—Gram had seen to that—regardless of how little time he spent there. He had every right to invite any man to stay for the summer, even her sworn enemy.

But *should* Mac remain her enemy? He'd as much as said he wanted to strive to create a friendship between them, and she was eager to allow him to. Fear aside, if he was going to remain in her house for the next few months, they would all be more comfortable if they were friends.

Hazarding a look, Mabel caught Mac's eye and stilled, surprised to find him regarding her closely. She shifted away, the warmth of a blush tingeing her cheeks. He was bound to think her as lovesick as she was the day he had left her in that wretched field if she continued to seek his gaze in a crowded room like this. Though, avoiding him felt all the more pointed.

"Uncle," Charles said, a wide smile on his lips, "I should love to introduce you to my friends. I hope you will be pleased to meet Desmond Pemberton and his sisters, Miss Pemberton and Miss Sophy Pemberton."

Papa bowed. "Pleased, of course. I am eager to speak to you, Charles, but I must take care of some business first."

"Of course, of course," Charles agreed.

"Mabel?" Papa gestured to the foyer. "Might we meet in the study? I assume my desk is still there."

"Of course," she replied, leading the way. She'd expected him to ask for a customary update of the household and its occupants, but not so soon. She'd known he was to return for a few days now and had prepared her report already.

His footsteps followed her down the corridor, and she opened the study door, stepping into the room that forever smelled of leather polish and old books. Papa followed her and she lowered herself into the seat across from the desk, making herself comfortable. When Papa took the seat on the other side, her home would feel complete again.

Papa cleared his throat at the doorway, and she turned to find him hovering there, Mr. Wright standing beside him.

"Perhaps," Mr. Wright said, holding her gaze steadily, "this might be better done in my absence."

"Nonsense." Her father swept his hand into the room, and Mr. Wright sent her an apologetic smile before coming to claim the chair beside her.

But she failed to understand why Mr. Wright was even here at all.

Papa followed, closing the door with a soft thud and crossing the room, his certain, even steps unrelenting. He always called his heavy footsteps his sea-legs, but Mabel had always thought it a tad overdone when on dry land.

"Shall I begin my report?" she asked, training her gaze on her father as he settled into the high-backed leather chair at the desk. She could feel Mr. Wright's gaze fixed on her person and anxiety began to quicken her heartbeat.

Waving his hand, he stroked his long, white beard. "We can do that later. For now, there is business I'd like to discuss. I've been in contact with Charles and he's assured me you do not have a beau."

A beau? Mabel wanted the floor to open up and swallow her entire chair whole, herself included. Her face went hot. What was Papa doing asking about such a thing in the presence of a complete stranger?

"That would be correct," she finally said.

Papa's smile grew wider beneath the beard. "Capital. Then you will be happy to hear that I've brought Mr. Wright home with the intention of creating an alliance between you."

The room began to spin. Had she heard him correctly? She opened her mouth to argue when it occurred to her that Mr. Wright was sitting beside her—close enough to hear her increased heart rate, no doubt.

She needed to tread lightly. "But Papa, Mr. Wright and I are not acquainted. We only met a few minutes ago."

"And you will have plenty of time to grow acquainted. I haven't any intention of having the banns read before the end of July. But that being said, we haven't much time to waste, and I would like the both of you to make an effort to spend time together."

"But, I just...to what end?" Mabel asked, her voice one degree shy of snapping at her father. He had been absent for years, save the odd letter here or there, and now he arrives with a man—a stranger, no less—whom he intends for Mabel to *marry*? He must have caught on to her distress, for his eyes settled firmly on her.

"To what end? Engagement and then marriage, of course." One could brook no argument with that tone, and it took all of Mabel's will to remain silent.

Mr. Wright cleared his throat beside her. "If I may?"

Papa nodded, though his eyes never left her.

"Miss Sheffield, I am beyond honored that your father finds me worthy of becoming your husband, and I should like nothing more than to join this family, but I want to make it very clear—and I have done so from the first," he added, shooting her father a look—"that I will not force you into a union which you find distasteful."

The silence stretched long enough for Mabel to shift in her seat, turning against her reluctance and giving Mr. Wright her attention, however awkward it was.

The small smile on his lips was little balm, but she recognized the effort Mr. Wright was making and owned that this situation was likely as uncomfortable for him as it was for her.

"I've come to help build the tenant cottages," he continued, "and I propose we take the time to get to know one another and decide between us if we should suit. Will that be agreeable to you?"

It was far from agreeable. Mabel was not in the market for a husband. She had enough on her plate with Pippa, Gram, and running the estate; taking on a husband was the last thing on her mind. Let alone a man she had never before met.

This was all too much for her.

Standing, Mabel clasped her hands before her. "I assume you will want to wash off the travel dirt prior to dinner, Papa? I will order a bath straight away, and"—turning to Mr. Wright, Mabel struggled to hold a steady smile—"Mrs. Henderson is waiting in the foyer to direct you to your chamber. We are entertaining far more guests than our household is used to, and you will forgive me for placing you on the third floor. Your bedchamber is situated beside Mr. MacKenzie's if you find yourself lost or in need of direction."

Mabel dipped a curtsy and escaped before either man could waylay her. She needed space, time to consider what had just occurred. Pausing in the foyer, Mabel saw Mrs. Henderson waiting to direct their most recent guest to his bedchamber and requested a bath brought to her father before she turned for the front door and let herself out.

She needed time to breathe.

CHAPTER 12

The breakfast table was full of steaming food and pregnant looks. Miss Pemberton and Miss Sophy shared meaningful smiles before glancing Mabel's way, which she ignored, hoping their schemes would die rapid deaths before coming to fruition.

Mr. Pemberton, however, sat beside his sisters with a pleasant smile and appeared to care for little more than the coddled eggs on his plate. Mrs. Boucher, his opposite, appeared to despise the bowl of gruel she rapidly consumed, if the expression on her face was any indication.

Mabel could do no more than push the rasher of bacon about her plate, afraid of glancing up and catching either Mac's or Mr. Wright's eye. Her brisk walk about the house the day before had not sufficiently cleared her head, and she was in need of more time away from the men to adequately get her bearings about her.

Gram walked into the room, leaning heavily on her cane, her face fixed in an eternal frown. "Mabel? Mabel?" she called, her gaze darting around the table. "Where are you?"

Pushing her chair back, she rose. "I am here, Gram."

Crossing the room, Mabel took Gram's bony hand and rested it on her arm before leading her down to the foot of the table. "Are you hungry? Or would you like some tea?"

"Of course I want to eat. That is why I came here, is it not? Who are all of these people? And what are they doing at my table?"

"Some are guests of Charles, and others are guests of Papa," Mabel said, guiding Gram to her seat and gesturing for a footman to fill her a plate at the sideboard.

Gram scoffed. "You must remind Charles that he doesn't own the house *yet*. When did you all cease to ask my permission?"

The room grew silent, awkward. Charles and Mabel were the only ones who knew that Gram's words were not to be taken seriously when she was in a cantankerous mood. They all likely thought her mad for forgetting the guests; she'd spent the evening before playing piquet with Mrs. Boucher in the drawing room. For finding the Pembertons' hired companion vexatious, Gram certainly enjoyed partnering the woman in games.

Mac started chuckling halfway down the table, dispelling the thick silence. "Mrs. Sheffield, we are all quite aware that we have you to thank for letting us stay in your home. You have been a very gracious hostess."

Gram narrowed her eyes. "You will not fool me, young MacKenzie. I know a tricky man when I see one."

Mac's smile broadened. "I will not pretend to find issue with that, Mrs. Sheffield. I appreciate a woman who takes my measure."

Miss Sophy straightened. "Then perhaps you'll like what I have to say, Mr. MacKenzie, for I believe I know *exactly* the sort of man you are."

He shifted, giving her a searching look. "I believe you and I both know the truth to that statement. Let's refrain from traveling that path further. Miss Sheffield?" he asked, surprising

Mabel by the sudden turn of conversation. "Will you do me the pleasure of walking out with me following breakfast? I would like to gather your opinion on a matter."

Miss Sophy had mentioned that she and Mac were on their way to an understanding. Had she been a victim of his over-flirtatious nature as well?

The entirety of the room seemed to shift their attention to Mabel, and she was grateful when the footman delivered Gram's plate. She busied herself with situating her grandmother.

"You've beat me to it," Mr. Wright said, while Mabel continued to arrange Gram's napkin over her lap. "I had a mind to request that very thing."

"As did we," Miss Sophy said. "It is too fine a day to remain indoors. My sister and I had hoped to convince Miss Sheffield to come walking with us. With so many like-minded friends, perhaps we ought to make an outing of it?"

"A group walk?" Mr. Wright said, smoothing back his dark hair. "What a splendid notion, Miss Sophy. Perhaps a jaunt around that quaint little pond."

The younger sister preened under the attention and the party broke into smaller conversations. While the others were distracted, Mabel took the chance to slip from the room.

Only, she didn't quite make it out of the room before hearing her name once more.

"Miss Sheffield?" a voice called, his tone pure and deep. Mac, again? He would not let things go easily, evidently. Rebuilding their friendship as adults was a good deal different from when they were children. Back then, she followed the boys around, wishing they would include her. *Now*, Mac was doing all of the chasing. It was entirely foreign.

Pausing at the door, she said, "I should like to join you all for a walk. Shall we meet in front of the house in a half-hour?"

General nods met her, and Mabel offered the room a smile

before escaping. She had thirty minutes, and she planned to use them wisely.

Wright was up to no good; Mac could feel it in his bones. He'd never much liked the man, and he was hard-pressed to understand what drove Captain Sheffield to invite him to Graton. Wright was lazy, power-hungry, and greedy. On the ship, if he knew the captain was watching, he was on point, displaying himself to best advantage. Otherwise, Wright would do whatever was in his power to avoid lifting a finger. A man with that poor of a work ethic could only have traveled to Devon with the captain with nefarious goals.

Mac bit down on his bacon and chewed. He'd searched his brain but was at a loss. Discovering Wright's purpose in being here had thus far proved difficult. They'd only spoken once after dinner the night before, and Wright was affecting his most amicable persona, the one which forced Mac to curtail his irritation and swallow his retorts. Arguing with someone who appeared good-natured did not do anyone favors. No matter how false the good nature was.

"Where shall we walk?" Miss Sophy asked.

"There is a lovely field just past the—"

"No," Mac said, cutting Charles off. "I think that too far a walk today with very little inducement. Were the blossoms in full bloom, I would agree with you, but as they are not..."

Charles nodded. "Right you are. Perhaps we ought to walk around the pond, then."

"A fine prospect," Mac agreed, relieved. The last thing he wanted was to take their entire party to a place he knew Mabel found sacred—a place she had once told him was her haven.

"I should like to have a tour of the entire expanse of property," Miss Pemberton said shyly, turning to Charles to offer him a smile. "Maybe not today, but sometime soon."

"Yes," her brother agreed. "Capital idea."

Wright's gaze searched the doorway, giving Mac the distinctive urge to hit something. Could the imbecile have set his sights on Mabel so soon? Mac had wanted to discover why the captain had requested a meeting with Mabel and had included Wright, but no one involved in that meeting seemed the least inclined to explain it to him.

He pushed back his chair, dropping his napkin on his plate. "I shall meet you outside shortly."

Mac forced himself not to run, taking the stairs swiftly. Climbing step after step stretched his leg muscles and set his heart drumming a quick rhythm. He'd prefer to swing over a saddle and ride hard until his pent-up emotion was fully let, but it would not do. It was better to play well with the others until more was revealed. He needed the distraction this position provided, assisting the captain with the tenant houses. He needed to be useful to the men. And above all else, he needed more time to make his decision.

He couldn't very well keep his father waiting forever, which he dutifully recognized. The moment the prize money was made available to him, he would have to act.

"I must go on this walk, Pippa," Mabel said, her voice drifting from the schoolroom and stilling Mac in his steps. He paused, his hand on the bannister, his head cocked to better hear.

"I'd rather stay here with you, but I am expected to accompany the guests. Papa would be disappointed otherwise."

"But it's unfair, Mae. Giulia has been gone for *ages*, and I am so bored with my wretched *French*. I don't know why I must learn French, anyway. I don't wish to ever speak it."

"Papa wants—"

"*Ugh!*" Pippa said. Mac could clearly imagine the young girl's scowl. A smile came unbidden to his lips.

Mabel's voice turned soothing, motherly. "Giulia has only been gone a fortnight, and she plans to return tomorrow, Pip. But you must remember that her wedding will take place shortly after, and she will not teach you much longer. If you don't wish for me to replace her, we must come up with an alternative."

"Why must Giulia get married? It is vastly unfair."

Mabel chuckled, and Mac echoed her silently.

"Because she would prefer to spend her life with Nick, Pippa. She loves him, and they make one another happy."

Hesitancy bit at Mac. He should leave, should cross the corridor and sneak quietly into his bedchamber before either Sheffield girl discovered him.

"Getting married will make them happy?" Pippa asked, curiosity lacing her tone.

A pause came before Mabel's answer, long enough to force Mac to peek around the wall and into the corridor, where he had a clear shot into Pippa's room. Mabel crouched beside her sister, holding the young girl's hands in her own and looking into her face.

"Getting married will make them happy," Mabel said, smiling.

What had that cost Mabel to say? The woman was unmarried herself. Did she wish for a union, to find a man to make her happy? Perhaps she didn't and was content with her life. Mac longed to inquire, to learn the answers to those questions. Mabel was adept at hiding her feelings behind a mask.

"But..." Pippa looked uneasy. "Do *you* want to be married, Mae? Will that make you happy? I'd much rather you stay here with me."

Mabel delivered a reassuring smile. "Don't fret, darling. There may be a way I can do both."

Both? Mac stepped back, his elbow bumping into the wood-paneled wall. Temptation to disappear down the stairs was high, but he wouldn't turn away now. He thumped his boots on the steps, making as much noise as he could rounding the corner to warn them of his arrival. Mabel stepped into the corridor.

He pulled back, feigning surprise. "Good morning."

She dipped her head. "Are they assembling for the walk?"

"Yes, soon." He glanced between Mabel and the room behind her where Pippa frowned up at him.

"Good day, Miss Pippa." He bowed.

She scrunched up her little nose. "Are *you* going to marry Mabel?"

Warmth bloomed in his chest, and Mabel's face turned scarlet. "Pippa," she hissed. "You mustn't say such things."

The little sprite sighed, exhausted with her elders and their games—or so it appeared.

"I will see you shortly," Mabel said, slipping past Mac and down the steps. Her scent drifted in a faint cloud behind her, delicately charming him. He wanted to inhale deeper, but Pippa's shrewd gaze was fixed on him.

"What are your intentions, Mr. Mac?" she asked, crossing her dainty arms over her chest.

"My intentions?"

She nodded.

Mac chuckled. He'd never heard such a grown-up question from such a small child. "I would like you to call me Mac. Most everyone does."

She nodded, but her eyes remained narrowed.

"Are you joining us on our walk today?" he asked.

"No," she said, sighing. "I must finish my studies."

"What a good, young pupil you must be." He stepped forward, crouching low, much as he'd seen Mabel do. "Do you like to ride, Pippa?"

She pulled back, slightly narrowing her eyes. "Yes, sometimes."

"Would you like to go for a ride with me later today?"

Her face lit up. "Yes! With pleasure."

"Good. I shall return for you later this afternoon. But only if you complete the tasks your sister has set out for you."

Determination set over her young brow. Would Mabel's daughters look so very much like her, as her sister did? Mac hoped so.

Pippa returned to her table to work, and Mac went to his room. He'd forgotten why he'd come up here in the first place. Mabel and her conversation had completely distracted him. But he didn't mind. She was worth the distraction any day.

CHAPTER 13

*M*r. Wright walked beside Mabel, keeping pace with her at the back of the group. From her position, Mabel had the fortunate situation of observing each member of their party. Charles led the way toward the pond, Miss Pemberton on his arm, and Mr. Pemberton to Charles's other side. The men appeared lost in conversation, and Mabel did not miss the look Miss Pemberton sent over her shoulder to her sister—faint irritation in the form of a raised eyebrow.

Miss Sophy followed closely behind them, hanging on Mac's arm, Mrs. Boucher toddling behind. The older woman had insisted on accompanying the Pemberton sisters but declared the summer heat to be far too strong for such a stroll. Her grumbles could be heard now. Surely the woman would turn around before they left the comfort of keeping the house within their sights.

Mr. Wright cleared his throat, offering his bent elbow for Mabel's support. She flicked a smile at him but could not leave her attention settled there for long. His dark hair and weathered skin gave him something of a roguish feel, and she didn't quite feel comfortable around him.

Papa could wish for a union all he desired, but Mabel wouldn't agree to marry just any man. And unfortunately for Mabel, it was difficult to consider anyone for matrimony when Mac was present. He was the man whom she judged all others against, and her rebellious heart could not imagine any other man measuring up.

But she owed it to Papa to at least give Mr. Wright a fair chance. Surely if she chose against forming a union with Mr. Wright after earnest consideration, Papa wouldn't press her.

Resting her hand upon his arm, Mabel noted how discomfited she became. It would have been wiser for Papa to allow her to meet Mr. Wright first, to gain something of a relationship with him *before* announcing his intention to form an understanding between them. For now she felt awkward around the man, as though he was constantly watching and analyzing her every move.

"Have you been in the navy long?" she asked, hoping to keep the conversation light.

"I joined when I was fourteen, ma'am," he said, a note of pride in his tone. "I moved around a bit, and two years ago I was fortunate to find a position on your father's ship. He is a good man, and I have been made better for working with him."

"That is kind of you to say."

"It is not only kindness." Mr. Wright slowed his steps, the space between them and Mrs. Boucher ahead stretching wider. "The last few years, Captain Sheffield has been the father I never had. I owe him a great deal."

"Is that why you have agreed to this scheme?" she asked, emboldened by their relative privacy.

Mr. Wright paused on the trail, the pond just beside them. Raising appreciative brows, he chuckled. "You aren't one to mince words, are you?"

"I am usually rather circumspect, actually. But this has been a trying few weeks, and I find that it has loosed my tongue."

"I am not averse to a woman who speaks her mind." He chuckled, and the sound was warm, soothing her troubled nerves. "To be frank myself, I find it rather more comfortable to be straightforward. I am used to being surrounded by sailors, you understand. None of them beat about any bushes."

Papa was much the same way. He was never much for polite society—likely the reason he was never troubled by staying away from Devon for long stretches of time.

"Might we start anew?" Mr. Wright asked, his dark eyebrows pulling together, a small crease forming between them. "I should like to be your friend without the threat of a betrothal hanging above our heads."

Wasn't this precisely what father wanted? But what did Mabel want? She tried to read Mr. Wright's deep brown eyes but came up empty. There was no evident malice, nor any particular warmth. He was seemingly genuine, and his request valid.

Mabel nodded. It would not hurt to form a friendship with the man.

A grin spread over Mr. Wright's lips, his face becoming handsome for the twinkle in his eye.

"Where does your family live?" Mabel asked. If they were going to attempt a friendship, surely she ought to learn about him. She'd been quick to dismiss Mr. Wright in Papa's study, repelled by the prospect of a stranger imagining he had any right to consider her his potential wife. But perhaps she'd been too hasty.

"London, but I never felt a need to settle near them. I've recently purchased an estate in Warwickshire. It is smaller than you are used to, but well maintained."

Had the man misunderstood her? She would like to become his friend, but speaking of the future, of his house as though Mabel was destined to one day see it, made her pulse race—yet not in a pleasant way.

"Is there any trouble?" Mac called.

Mabel startled, turning her attention to the path ahead. Evidently the party had rounded the bend and moved out of sight behind the small grove of trees that bordered the pond, but Mac stood at the corner in the path, watching her closely. Her cheeks warmed against their better judgment.

"Forgive our delay," Mr. Wright said, patting Mabel's hand where it rested on his arm. He tugged her lightly forward.

Mac stood in the center of the walking path, his legs planted firmly, and his hands clasped behind him—the steady footing of a man used to the swaying of ships. She expected him to step aside, but he failed to move as she and Mr. Wright approached.

Pulling on her arm, Mr. Wright came to a stop. "Is anything the matter, sir?" he asked.

Mac held his gaze, and Mabel glanced between them. Both standing tall—though Mac towered higher—chests puffed, unyielding. Like two lead dogs facing off. If Mac intended to assert his position as a long-time friend, he was surely mistaken. The only man with a right to assert any authority over Mabel was her father, and he was not present.

"It isn't seemly to be found dawdling," Mac said, his eyes never leaving Mr. Wright's face.

Mabel's back straightened as though his words had slid down her spine, bruising her pride. It chastened her as if she *had* done something she should be ashamed of—which wasn't the case. Slipping her hand free of Mr. Wright's arm, she stepped around Mac and continued down the path, leaving both men behind her.

Mac watched the swish of Mabel's skirt as she stepped away from him, her tall, elegant form highlighted by the rising sun. He noted a faint hitch in her step. Was she limping? The idea sent a rush of hot anger through him. Why would Mabel agree to so lengthy a walk if she had been injured?

"She is not what I expected," Wright said.

Mac's blood heated further. When Mac had glanced over his shoulder and noticed the missing pair at the back of the group, his hair had stood on end. If Wright's record at every port of call was to prove consistent, the man had spent his free time on land in the company of less-than-respectable ladies. And Mac was not about to allow Wright to add Mabel to his list of conquests. And now he spoke as though he'd had expectations prior to arriving? There was something afoot, and Mac wouldn't rest until he knew what it was. Wright wasn't here for a social visit—that was certain. "What did you expect?"

Wright's dark eyes glittered, and he fell in step beside Mac, traveling down the path toward the group. "The way her father described her, one would have expected an Amazonian." He lifted a hand. "She is tall, I'll give him that. But there is something pleasing about her manner of walking. She is the picture of grace, is she not?"

Wright was correct, and the observation was both disheartening and humbling. The man could not be entirely foolish if he found such value in Mabel. But appreciating the woman did not mean he deserved her.

"Are you intending to remain long?" Mac asked.

Wright shot him a side-long glance. "I do not plan to intrude upon your goals with the barley fields and tenant houses, if that is what you mean. But I will stay as long as she'll have me."

A weight settled upon his shoulders, pressing on Mac and slowing his pace. "As long as she'll have you? You speak as though there is an agreement in place already."

They were fast approaching the rest of the party and Wright cast Mac a look before stepping ahead of him. If he was trying to irritate Mac, he was doing a capital job of it. But if he expected

Mac to sit by silently and allow Wright to weasel his way into the Sheffield family, he had another thing coming.

Charles crouched, searching the ground for something as Desmond skipped a rock over the glassy surface of the pond.

"Thrice!" he called.

Charles rose and clapped Desmond on the back. "I'm certain I can make four."

Wright approached them, passing the women who stood behind, watching the men skip rocks. "Shall we place a wager on that surety? A shilling you can't make four."

Charles grinned. He turned toward the women. "Might I have your good luck wishes?"

Miss Pemberton stepped forward. "Good luck, Mr. Fremont."

Charles lifted the flat, round pebble. "Might you touch it for good luck?"

Her cheeks pinked quite becomingly, and she stretched her glove-clad finger out, brushing it over the top of the gray stone.

Charles turned and prepared his stance before sending the rock flying over the surface of the pond.

"One, two, three...four!" Miss Pemberton laughed, clapping her hands together. "You did it!"

Charles bowed to the group at large before taking Miss Pemberton's hand in his own and bringing her knuckles to his lips, bestowing a kiss on them. Mac glanced over the couple and caught Mabel's gaze. She refused to hold it, however, and looked toward her cousin, a troubled line forming between her eyebrows.

Mac longed to cross the distance and speak to her, to ask if she might unburden her troubles on his willing ears and do his best to soothe her worries. But the other guests of this haphazard house party stood between them.

"Shall we go again?" Charles asked, his grin widening as he turned back toward Wright. "I'm certain Mac could skip five. He was always the best of us."

Wright shifted, turning irritated eyes on Mac. "Oh? Shall we have another go?"

"I am rusty," Mac said. "There is no place to skip rocks on a ship."

"That merely levels the competition, does it not?" Miss Sophy asked.

Wright nodded. "What do you say, MacKenzie? A shilling to the man who skips the most."

Mac nodded before turning his attention to the hard-packed dirt in search of a good skipping rock. Would it be entirely ridiculous to ask Mabel to touch it for good luck? He located one that would do well enough, removed his gloves, and dug the stone from the earth.

He stood to find Wright proffering his open palm toward Mabel, and an amused glint in her eyes as she touched the stone there. The image soured Mac's stomach, and he pivoted toward the pond, doing his best to remove from his mind the picture of Mabel with Wright. The competition was set, and Mac was determined to beat Wright in every regard.

"Shall we begin?" Charles asked. "Mabel, will you count for Mr. Wright? Who shall count for Mac?"

"I would be happy to," Miss Sophy said, coming to stand behind Mac.

He lined up beside Wright, doing his best to ignore the women and focus on the task at hand. He reared back his arm, shooting Charles a glance.

"When you're ready, gentlemen...skip!"

Mac threw the stone with a familiar flick of his wrist. It had been years since he'd done this, but the motion was natural as though he'd just done it yesterday. Miss Sophy's voice counted in his ear, but he could not focus, so wholly did Mabel's voice claim precedence in his head.

"...four, five. Well done, Mr. Wright."

"Thank you, Miss Sheffield."

Mac watched the rings spread along the greenish water. "Congratulations, Mr. MacKenzie," Miss Sophy said, beaming. "Six!"

Mac turned back for the group, his brows lifting. She spoke as though he had won. Had he?

Wright offered a short bow. "Well done, sir."

Mac dipped his head. "And you."

"Shall we return now?" Mrs. Boucher asked, rapidly fanning herself at the back of the group. "That sun is determined to tire me."

"Just a little longer, Mrs. Boucher?" Miss Pemberton asked. "I should love to see where this path leads."

"I am certain I can show you where it leads," the companion responded, gesturing to the other side of the pond.

"But at least on that side we shall have the luxury of shade," Miss Sophy quipped. "Let us press on."

Mabel stepped around Charles as he approached to offer his arm to Miss Pemberton, and Mabel spoke quietly to Mrs. Boucher. The concern in Mabel's eyes spoke to her intentions. Mac stepped toward them, intent on offering the women his escort back to the house when a scream rent the air, and his attention was stolen by the Pemberton sisters ahead on the path.

"It was that wretched raven," Miss Pemberton screamed, turning around to face them, her arms raised and chest heaving in indignation. A line of white excrement pooled in her hair, running down the side of her face and dripping onto the front of her gown.

Mabel drew in a quick breath and Mrs. Boucher's hand found her heart.

"He has..." Miss Pemberton said, gasping for air. "*Ugh!* I must go back to the house *now*."

CHAPTER 14

The walk around the pond was cut blessedly short—
Mac could only abide so much time in the company
of Wright—and he now pulled his coat tighter together as he
made his way down to the stables. Miss Pippa had announced
upon his return from the walk that she'd completed her tasks
and was ready for their ride.

He had promptly changed into his riding clothes and
promised to meet her outside.

When Mac rounded the corner of the house, Pippa was
sitting on a mounting block set against the stable wall, her feet
dangling above the ground. Her hair was neatly plaited underneath a bonnet, the long, brown braids so similar to the ones
Mac used to tug at as a child—Mabel's. His heart constricted.
He swallowed, approaching Mabel's miniature and lifting her
hand in his, bowing over it.

"Your servant, madam."

Pippa lifted her nose, a smile pulling at her lips. "I've been
waiting an age, sir."

"Forgive me for the delay." Mac fought a smile as Pippa
hopped down from her mounting block seat and clapped her

hands together. The child mimicked adults so well, but her immaturity was difficult to hide completely.

A groom led Orion out through the open stable doors, followed closely by a light tan pony with a white mane. "Is this yours?" Mac asked.

Pride shone in Pippa's eyes. "Yes. Her name is Penelope and she is *such* a gentle beast."

Mac swallowed his mirth. The girl spoke as though she was an expert regarding horseflesh. The pony did indeed appear docile, but Mac wouldn't expect anything else for a girl of seven years.

They mounted their beasts and turned them toward the road when the front door opened to the house and Mabel stepped outside, her hand resting on the doorknob, eyebrows pulled together in confusion.

"Come, Miss Pippa," Mac said, turning Orion back toward the house.

"May I ask what you are doing?" Mabel asked, her gaze directed at her sister.

Pippa released a long-suffering sigh. "I have completed my studies and accepted this gentleman's offer to ride."

Mabel held her sister's gaze. "Alone? No chaperone?"

"I hardly need one, Mae. I am only seven."

Mabel's dark blue-violet gaze shifted to Mac, and his heart hammered in his chest. How dearly he wished to extend the invitation to her as well. He'd told Mabel that he'd like to take her riding, hadn't he? Well, it was true. But if he offered, would she turn him down? He swallowed his apprehension. "Should you like to chaperone, Miss Sheffield? We are planning a short ride."

She glanced down at her own, simple gown. "I'm not dressed for it."

Of course she would consider the niceties. Could she not be the familiar, devil-may-care girl he'd known when they were younger? No, of course she couldn't. She was a lady now. "We do not mind waiting."

"You don't want to leave the horses standing for—"

"We can circle the pond while we wait," Pippa said. "It is acceptable, I should think. We'll remain in sight of the house for the entirety."

That wasn't entirely true, but for the purpose of this situation, Mac held his tongue. Mabel's gaze flicked from Pippa to Mac, and she held it there. He could almost shrink under her scrutiny, but remained tall, his shoulders straight and eyes pinned to her.

She nodded before turning back into the house and Mac felt the satisfaction and anticipation of the prospect of time spent with Mabel alone.

Well, they would have Pippa for company, but that was even better. The girl could soften any situation.

"Shall we?" he asked Pippa, indicating the opening of the path around the pond. Pippa led the way down the narrow entry point. When the path widened at the place where the bird had defiled Miss Pemberton's hair earlier that day, Mac brought his steed level with Pippa's and gave her his full attention.

Pippa sighed. "Mabel thinks she hides everything from me, but I hear more than she thinks I do."

"Oh?" Mac said. "Perhaps you ought not to listen so closely then."

Her little nose scrunched up. "But if I don't listen, how will I know what is going on in the house?"

Mac chuckled, pretending to find the foliage to his right fascinating. It was no wonder this seven-year-old sounded like an adult. She mimicked those around her well. Mac was tempted to inquire what the girl had learned that was so interesting, but it wouldn't be right to encourage this behavior. "Is your play coming along well?"

"Oh, that," Pippa said, lifting her small shoulders in a shrug.

"I cannot practice without my friends, and they have not returned yet."

"I see."

Pippa's little nose scrunched up, her head tilting to the side. "Have you ever had a dream, Mac? I have one. I want to become an actress on the stage in London, where people will come from faraway places to watch me and tell me how lovely I am." She sighed. "I realize it isn't becoming of a lady, Mac, so you needn't remind me that it's impossible. It's only a dream."

"There is nothing wrong with dreaming, Pippa." Mac knew this well. He'd dreamed of a certain house since he'd first stumbled upon it as a youth. Camden Court. The estate had been beautiful then—not too large, built of stone and just on the edge of the northern Devon coast. The idyllic setting had struck his heart and he'd known from that moment that he wanted to raise his family there one day. That it was still for sale had tormented him for months, knowing full well he would never be able to both free his father from the Marshalsea and obtain the house he'd always longed for.

Pippa's voice broke through his melancholic thoughts. "I really need to see my friends again so we can practice, and of course we must begin building the scenery. But Mabel is too overwhelmed with Charles's difficult guests to consider calling on the Traynor girls." She clapped a hand over her mouth. "Oh! I should not have said that."

"You will not offend me, Pippa," Mac assured her, fighting a grin.

"But *you* are one of Charles's difficult guests, are you not?"

It took a great deal of control to temper his amusement. "I cannot speak to my level of difficulty, of course, but in truth, I am a guest of your father's."

Pippa's eyes brightened. "Then I have not offended you!"

"No, dear Pippa. You have not. Now, please, do tell me more

of this play you are planning, and what I might do to help you execute it."

———

Mabel pulled Star's reins and craned her neck to listen. She'd dressed quickly and followed the path around the pond, impatient to reach Mac and Pippa. Not that she truly believed a chaperone to be necessary, of course. But she did not wish to analyze her reasons closer; she was certain she would not like what she found.

Giggling drifted down the path and Mabel urged her horse forward, anticipation pounding her heart against her breastbone. She'd made it farther along the path than their walk had taken them that morning, most of the way around the pond and onto the shaded side, foliage and full branches blocking the beating sun overhead.

"If I agree to this scheme, then what am I to get from the arrangement?" Mac said, amusement tinting his low tone. She could perfectly imagine him now, his strong jaw lowered, the navy coat straining against his shoulders.

"Is fame and fortune not enough for you?" Pippa asked.

Mabel's desires were divided. She ought to make her presence known, but she would surely love to know more of this arrangement Mac spoke of.

His chuckle lifted on the breeze and traveled to her, and she felt wholly disconcerted. Something about his direct gaze the last few days had changed. He'd begun watching her closely, and it was both perplexing and invigorating.

But Mabel had eavesdropped far more often of late than in the course of her entire life, and it was unbecoming of a lady. Gathering a breath, Mabel clicked her tongue to move Star forward, around the bend and into view of Mac and Pippa.

Mac glanced up from where he sat, crouched low, his fingers

combing over the packed dirt. Pippa sat on the ground beside him, cupping her hands toward him, their horses tied to a tree near the pond.

"Mac is going to teach me to skip a rock!" Pippa said, jumping up. "I've never been very good, you know, and Jacob Tucker beats me every time."

Mabel lifted her gaze, catching Mac's. Did he find the same similarities between Pippa and Jacob Tucker, and Mac and Mabel as children, as she did?

"Have you found a good stone?"

"Yes." Pippa lifted a flat, oblong rock the size of a guinea and Mac took it from her, inspecting it. He directed a nod of approval at her, and Pippa's cheeks flushed with appreciation.

"Will you come down and join us?" Mac asked, turning and taking Mabel by surprise.

"Oh, I shouldn't. I do not mind watching from up here."

"But why would you watch us when you can join us?" He shifted his attention to Pippa. "Mabel used to beat me sometimes, too."

Mabel laughed. "You exaggerate, sir. I won *once*, and it was merely because of your less-than-honorable tactics."

Mac raised an eyebrow. "Are you accusing me of cheating?"

"Never." She could not contain her grin. "But you quite obviously tossed the rock into the pond with little effort and allowed me a win."

"A generous gesture I did not live down," he conceded. Rising, he crossed the path and approached Star. "The price of attempting to be a gentleman."

"A gentleman would have allowed me to win on my own merit or lose fairly."

Offering her a hand, gloveless and revealing all manner of calluses and scars—a hand which clearly knew work—Mac stepped closer. "Perhaps today you will win of your own merit."

She was tempted to accept his help, to get down and play

128

with Mac and Pippa. But it was far too difficult on an average day to mount a horse, and with her leg so sore from recent overexertion, today would be even more so. No, it made more sense to remain on Star. It had been difficult enough to mount the horse with a groom to assist her, she ought not attempt it without any help—especially with such a handsome audience.

"Forgive me, but I will remain on my horse."

He did not drop his hand, nor his gaze. "Have I done something to offend you?"

"Of course not."

"Then..." He glanced at Pippa, his eyebrows drawing together. "Would you prefer to continue the ride? I can return with Pippa another time."

"I am perfectly content to remain where I am, Mac. You mustn't fret so," she said, infusing her words with a measure of levity. "You remind me very much of a hovering nursemaid."

He cracked a smile but looked no closer to letting the matter drop. Really, all of this attention was growing tiresome and vastly uncomfortable.

"You vexing creature," she said, sighing. "If you must know, I would prefer not to dismount, for it would be a chore to obtain the saddle again."

He stared at her, uncomprehending.

"Mae has a weak leg," Pippa said from near the pond. "Sometimes it hurts her too much to climb into a saddle."

Mabel could have screamed, she was so angry. Her cheeks flooded hot and she pierced Pippa with a glare.

"A weak leg? I haven't heard of this." Mac moved as though to reach for her, but then stopped himself. "Does it pain you excessively?"

"Only sometimes. Unfortunately, today is one of those days."

He nodded. "I will not press you. Come, Pippa. We can return—"

"I am well enough, Mac. I can sit here all day with little trouble. It is the effort of *climbing* that bothers me. Please,"—she lowered her voice, beseeching him—"don't cease the lessons now."

"If you insist. But can I not help you?"

"Help me?"

"Yes, Mabel. For the sake of Pippa and my pride, I should dearly love a rock-skipping rematch." He laid a large hand over his heart. "I swear I shall not allow you to win."

But, her leg. If she got down, even with Mac's help, she would have to get up again before they set off. Either that, or lead Star around the pond once more, but the mere idea of so long a walk at present caused her leg to throb. But Mac's smile was wide and persuasive, his eyes sparkling. To say nothing of the prospect of trying to beat him at a game.

"Oh, very well. You've grown to be quite persuasive, you know."

He offered her a boyish smile, one she knew quite well. "You say that as though it is a bad thing."

"That depends upon your motives, I should think."

His large hands slid around her waist and she tightened her hold on the reins on impulse. Mac's hazel eyes bore into her. "Ready?"

She nodded, unable to trust her voice, and he lifted her from the saddle.

Mabel rested her hands on Mac's shoulders, gripping the reins as he lowered her to the ground as though she weighed no more than a bag of sheared wool. He took Star's reins and led her away, tying her to a tree near his horse, and giving Mabel a moment to catch her breath. She'd enjoyed being in Mac's hands far too much, enjoyed the way he made her feel smaller and daintier than any other man did.

"Who will begin?" Pippa asked, unaware of the tension in the air. Or perhaps Mabel was the only one who felt it. "Oh,

Mae, let me find you a stone. I'm rather good at searching, you know."

"Ladies first, of course," Mac said, catching Mabel's eye as Pippa dug around for another stone. He did not seem inclined to look elsewhere, and his steady gaze was unnerving, though not altogether unpleasant. Shivers of anticipation slithered up her spine and Mabel brazenly held his eyes captive in her own. It was undeniable. This man clearly felt the same tension she did, felt the line of rope that seemed to connect them growing taut when he looked at her.

"How is this one?" Pippa asked, breaking the spell. She raised a greenish stone and Mabel accepted the offering. It was not as flat as she would have liked, but it would do.

"Thank you, Pip. Would you like to begin, or shall I?"

"You," Pippa said. "I want to watch you."

Mabel spun the stone in her hand until she reached a comfortable hold on it, and then reared her arm back. She'd never been great at skipping rocks, but she could usually get two or three good jumps. Releasing the stone over the pond, she watched it bounce along to Pippa's count.

"One...two...three...four! Well done, Mae!"

"Beginner's luck, I'm sure," she said, stepping out of the way for Pippa to take her turn.

Pippa's nose scrunched up. "Beginner? But you've done this before."

"Not in quite a long time. Go ahead, darling."

Pippa stepped forward, her tongue darting between her teeth as her eyebrows narrowed in concentration. She tossed the rock into the pond with a loud plop and stared after it, dumbfounded.

"What did I do wrong?" she wailed, turning for Mac. "I did it precisely as you showed me."

He stepped toward Pippa and Mabel moved away to give them space as Mac explained how she needed to flick her wrist, not move her entire arm. Mabel watched him closely, his gentle explanations and kind instruction calming an enraged seven-year-old, giving her the opportunity to try again.

And again, and then again. Pippa threw stone after stone into the pond, each one plopping without a single skip. Her determined brow grew more and more frustrated until finally, she turned, giving Mabel a determined look. "I will remain here until I can get the rock to jump. I *will* do this. I must."

"So you might beat Jacob Tucker?"

"Yes," she said. "I will not allow him to mock me again. I *will* skip these wretched rocks."

"Not in your anger, you won't," Mac said, his voice soft. "You cannot do so gentle a thing as make a rock dance across the water when you are anxious and your spirits angry."

Pippa's face fell. "But I am always angry around Jacob Tucker."

Mac lifted his broad shoulders in a shrug. "Then perhaps you will never be able to skip a rock around him."

Pippa's little jaw dropped, shock reaching her eyes. "Do not say such horrid things, Mac."

He crouched low, coming to eye-level with the girl. "Master your emotions, Pippa. That is the only way you'll be able to remain calm in the face of your enemy."

"But I could never like Jacob Tucker."

Mac's gaze flicked to Mabel before returning to her sister. "I am not saying you should or shouldn't like the boy, only that you must control how you feel. No one else can tell you how to feel. And if you plan to skip a rock in the presence of your enemy, you must learn to remain calm around him, too. Despite how he might try to anger you."

She narrowed her eyes. "Mac, are you acquainted with Jacob Tucker? You speak as though you know him."

"Not personally, no. But I know his brothers and I imagine he is very much like them."

Pippa nodded in understanding. "Shall we practice more?"

"I think we will be late to dinner if we do," Mabel said. "But you can return tomorrow and practice then."

Pippa pouted. "I want to do this."

"Yes, and you will. Tomorrow."

Pippa gave Mac a look that said *Mabel is ever so controlling, is she not?* Then she stomped across the rocky earth toward her pony.

Mac helped Pippa into the saddle before crossing to Mabel. "Can I be of assistance?"

Her leg throbbed, the day's overuse wearing on her, and she knew she had no choice but to accept his help. Her body warmed, recalling the feel of Mac's capable hands on her waist, and she chastised herself for hoping he would help her again in very much the same way. But was it a crime to wish for a man's touch? Her virtue was intact. Mac had nothing but the desire to help.

Except, the way he looked at her now was so pregnant and full of emotion that she knew, in the recesses of her heart, that he *did* have more desire than simply to help her. The idea was equally thrilling and terrifying. He had clearly changed from the maddening boy she had known when she was young. And while she struggled to forgive the hurtful things he had said to her that day in the vale, she could acknowledge that youthful follies ought to be forgiven. Particularly when the gentleman was trying so hard to prove his changed heart.

And Mac, changed as he was, wanted to be Mabel's friend. She could grant him something so paltry as her friendship. She wanted to, dearly, and in the face of the uncertainty regarding Mr. Wright and Papa's wishes, it would benefit her to have a friend she could trust.

Reaching for Mac's arm, she placed her hand on his sleeve. "If you would be so kind, I would greatly appreciate the assistance."

She expected him to crouch, to cup his hands and create a foothold, so he surprised her by closing his hands around her waist, lightly pressing his fingers against her ribs as he found a secure hold on her and effectively discharged the air from her lungs. Lifting her, Mac placed her softly on the saddle and she hurried to hook her leg on the pommel and arrange her skirt over her legs.

Clearing his throat, Mac stepped back. "How is your leg?"

It was a novelty to be so thoroughly considered. It unnerved her, but she appreciated it. "I am well."

He regarded her closely before nodding. "Shall we round the pond or return to the house the way we came?"

"It would be faster to finish the path."

He watched her as though he knew this already, but it did not answer his question. Lifting his eyebrows, he said, "So, back the way we came?"

She smiled. "I would not be opposed to a longer ride."

"Nor I."

He left her so he might mount his steed, and Mabel drew in a steadying breath. She needed to be very careful, or she was in danger of falling very much in love with Mac once again.

CHAPTER 15

*L*eaving the horses and Pippa's pony in the stables, Mabel, Mac, and Pippa crossed the lawn, discussing the most important features of a good skipping rock when a carriage pulled into the drive. Pippa gasped, leaving Mabel and Mac behind as she ran toward it.

Mabel clasped her hands together to keep them near her. She couldn't handle touching Mac again, fearing the barest brush of her knuckles against his would ignite the longing which had taken root in her chest. It was alarming how fast and deeply she found herself falling for someone who had once rejected her so harshly. But perhaps that was why it was so easy to care for Mac —her heart had once been his, so it knew the path well.

Nonetheless, it wouldn't do to admire a man who did not hold her in the same regard. She could not put herself in a position to be so heartily rejected, for her heart could not survive another failure. He asked to become her *friend*, nothing more.

"Pippa is eager. I assume you know who that carriage belongs to." Mac sounded unsure as though his statement was, in actuality, a question.

"Yes," Mabel said, putting out the fire of unrealistic romantic thoughts in her chest and sprinkling water over the smoking remains. "We know the owner of that carriage quite well."

"And..." he pressed, lifting his eyebrows. "Who is it? Are you planning to keep me in suspense all evening?"

A smile flickered over her lips despite her best efforts to contain it. The horses came to a stop, and a groom hopped down from the back of the carriage, letting down the step and opening the door for Giulia. "This is a dear friend of mine who has been staying with us and helping me teach Pippa for the last year. She went to see her uncle when you arrived, so I'm sure you wouldn't have had the chance to meet her. Come, and I shall introduce you."

Pippa ran into Giulia's arms, nearly knocking the small woman over. But Giulia only laughed, the sound ringing out over the open drive.

"You've come back," Mabel said, waiting for Pippa to step aside before pulling her friend into an embrace.

Giulia returned the hug, then leaned back and appraised Mabel, a small line forming between her eyebrows. "You look weary. What is troubling you? Your leg or your guests?" She lifted her face and stilled, seeming to notice Mac for the first time.

Mabel stepped back to introduce the pair, and they exchanged greetings.

"I will leave you to your reunion," Mac said, dipping into a regal bow. He offered Mabel a warm smile before turning for the house. Had the man always looked so charming when he did that?

The sun lit his back as he walked away, highlighting his tall form and the back muscles straining against his coat as he moved. She struggled to tear her gaze from him. Memories of the feel of his hands on her waist, his eyes fixed on her so earnestly, were enough to drive her mad. She longed for a repetition of the short ride along the pond path, wanting to claim Mac's full attention, his touch.

"I would dearly like to hear more about that particular guest," Giulia said.

A blush rose up Mabel's neck. Ignoring Giulia's knowing look, she strung her friend's arm through her own. She had been so quick to disregard her earlier resolve to not fall for the man. It appeared she would need to strengthen that resolution. "Come. I'll have Carson set another place for dinner. You have plenty of time to rest and change."

"Unless customs have changed in the last few weeks, I only have a half-hour."

Mabel tugged on Giulia's arm, watching Pippa's hair sway as she ran ahead of them. "That is plenty of time to change and rest, is it not?"

"Enough of this misdirection, Mabel. What is troubling you, and how might I help?"

They climbed the steps to the front door, and Mabel helped Giulia into the foyer as Pippa mounted the stairs toward the schoolroom and disappeared out of sight. "It's nothing. I overused my leg today and it wants rest, which I will presently grant it. Let's get you settled again, first. Were you able to see your Mr. Pepper before leaving?"

"Yes, only just before leaving Halstead Manor. The poor man returned from visiting his sister a quarter-hour before I left. I was tempted to remain there for dinner, but I was eager to see Miss Pippa. And you, of course." She added the last part with a saucy smile.

"You ought not to call her that, you know. She requested Charles's guests refer to her as Miss Pippa, and they have so far indulged her. I fear it is getting to her head. The little sprite is becoming more grown-up every day."

Giulia laughed. "It does not surprise me." She sighed, hesitating, her dark brown eyes softening. "I shall miss seeing you both daily. Indeed, I missed it immensely these last few weeks."

"We will still be neighbors, and we will always have our weekly visits with Hattie and Amelia."

Giulia lifted a dark eyebrow as they reached the landing and turned down the corridor. "Meetings you have been absent from the last two weeks."

"I could not get away. Managing Charles's guests and my father's return has been more intensive than I anticipated."

"Well, I am here now, and I will endeavor to lighten your load."

"Must I remind you that you are here for less than a fortnight? You must enjoy this time, not work through it."

"What I *must* do," Giulia said, stepping into the bedchamber she was to use for the next two weeks, "is keep my mind busy. Otherwise, I might expire from sheer anticipation." Her brown eyes glowed, the light of joy and love evident within them.

"Your wedding will arrive before you know it. But in the meantime, I can think of plenty to occupy your mind."

Gram sat across from Mrs. Boucher at the small card table, grimly silent as they focused on their game of piquet. Dinner had long since been over, but the men remained behind, still consumed with port, cigars, and talk of politics—if Mabel speculated correctly.

The Pemberton sisters sat close together on the sofa, their heads bent in quiet conversation.

"Do the men typically remain behind for so long?" Giulia asked, settling comfortably on the settee beside Mabel.

"No, they—"

"I cannot think *why* they have not joined us yet," Miss Sophy said, her voice traveling across the rug and forcing Mabel's jaw to clench. "They have previously been quite eager to follow us into the drawing room after dinner. I wonder what has changed this evening."

"Perhaps they are reminiscing about their time spent together on the ocean," Giulia said, a benevolent smile stretching over her face. "You know how men can linger over port."

"Indeed," Mabel agreed.

Miss Sophy sighed, dropping her head in boredom. "I do hope they will come soon."

Mabel fixed a patient smile on her face, turning to Giulia. "What news of Halstead? Is your uncle well?"

Giulia nodded. "And eager for the ball to be over, I believe. Though the whole of it was his idea. I tried to convince him that the ball last year was sufficient, but he would hear nothing of it."

Mabel reached across the cushion and grasped her friend's hand. "He is proud of the union and has likely been looking forward to it *since* the ball last year. I would guess your uncle has been most eager for the betrothal."

"You are to hold a ball?" Miss Sophy asked, her eyes sparkling, eyebrows lifted. "I did not know you had enough society in Graton to support it. How very exciting."

A beat of silence passed before Giulia turned her attention toward the Pemberton sisters, and she could not hide her amusement from Mabel. "How long do you plan to remain here?" Giulia asked.

"We are at the mercy of our brother," Miss Pemberton said.

Her sister straightened. "But we have every reason to expect that our visit will be of a very long nature."

Miss Pemberton's cheeks grew rosy. She shot Miss Sophy a reproachful look before directing her attention to Giulia. "We would be most delighted to attend your ball if it would not be too troublesome. In truth, I quite prefer country balls. I understand why the matrons of London strive for a crush, but they are not in the least bit comfortable. I much prefer lighter company and a relaxed environment."

"All of Mabel's guests are welcome at our ball, of course." Giulia shifted. "Did I misunderstand you, Miss Sophy, or do you mean to imply that you are intending to remove to Devon permanently?"

Mabel's hand tightened on Giulia's, but her friend did not spare her a glance, so wholly was she fixed on the Misses Pemberton.

"That will entirely depend upon others," Miss Sophy said. "As my sister mentioned, we are not at our own leisure."

Giulia's gaze flicked to Mrs. Boucher, and Mabel followed it. The Pemberton women didn't need their brother to lend them consequence. They hired a companion for that.

"Drat these cards," Gram spat, tossing the last of her cards on the table.

Mrs. Boucher settled back into her chair, a smug smile pinching at her round cheeks. "Shall we go again?"

"Yes, we shall." Gram's displeasure sat on her lips, her beady eyes closely watching her companion gather the cards into a pile.

Heavy steps congregated in the corridor outside of the drawing room, and the women who made up the younger set all seemed to pause at the same time, their ears cocked toward the door. The Misses Pemberton both straightened in their seats.

Giulia leaned toward Mabel, lowering her voice. "I expect a full explanation when we have the benefit of privacy."

"Regarding?" Mabel asked, swallowing. Giulia was far too perceptive for Mabel's tastes at present. And she hadn't missed the way Giulia had caught her watching Mac earlier. But did Giulia wish to know more about Mac, or more about the Pemberton sisters?

The door opened to admit the men, and Giulia leaned closer,

lowering her voice. "Why the Misses Pemberton would believe they are entitled to a lengthy stay under this roof, of course."

Charles led the procession of gentlemen and came to a stop at the side of Mabel's settee, his gloved hand resting on the armrest. "What sort of entertainment shall we have this evening?"

"Is your young cousin awake?" Miss Pemberton asked, her voice obtaining a tinny, cheap quality which it had lacked just a few minutes before. "I should dearly love to visit with the girl if it can be managed."

Mabel stilled. Miss Pemberton had not wished for a moment of Pippa's time since her arrival in Devon, and the sudden change could not be genuine. In fact, Mabel could not recall one moment when Miss Pemberton and Pippa had interacted before now. The woman would have requested Pippa's company when they arrived in the drawing room an hour since if she'd desired it for Pippa's sake.

"My dear, I am certain Miss Pippa has retired already," Miss Sophy said. "Surely she could not be awake at this hour."

Charles glanced to Mabel, his eyebrows high. The man would do anything to please Miss Pemberton, and it was growing tiresome. What had the young woman done to earn his affection? Of course, she *did* lay claim to every good quality befitting a young gentlewoman, but she was so very dull besides. She was pretty, yes, but tedious. And the manner of screeching which had torn from her throat when the bird had seen fit to dirty her hair was enough to ruin her good image in Mabel's mind completely.

Just the same, the way Charles watched Miss Pemberton, his eyes alight, was enough to force Mabel to swallow her tongue. "I am certain she is asleep. Perhaps tomorrow evening."

"Yes," Charles agreed, his smile never resting for long on anything other than Miss Pemberton. "Tomorrow she shall join us directly after dinner. Perhaps we can play a round of spillikins then. Does she still favor the game, Mabel?"

Mac stepped around the sofa, Mr. Wright on his heels, and paused behind the Pembertons. His hazel eyes seemed to bore into Mabel from across the rug, so intently did he watch her.

She swallowed. "Indeed, she dearly loves the game. She is quite good at it, too."

"*You* are quite good at it, from what I recall," Charles said, sparing a pleased look for Mabel before turning his attention back to Miss Pemberton.

The man was clearly besotted. Mabel could not choose his bride, but neither would she wish to be in the way of his happiness. She ought to do her part to help him, she supposed. "I am not sure—"

"Why wait for tomorrow?" Mac asked, the deep timbre of his voice forcing the breath from Mabel's lungs. "Shall we not play tonight?"

CHAPTER 16

*M*ac would have given nearly anything to have skipped the portion of the evening sipping port with the likes of Wright and gone straight to the drawing room with the women instead. The man fawned and flattered Captain Sheffield grossly. Mac ought to fetch a mirror so Wright might realize what a cake he was making of himself. But he had a feeling the man wouldn't catch on to his own ridiculous nature. Perhaps if they were to play spillikins, however, the evening would not be a waste. Not if it meant spending more time with Mabel.

Miss Sophy clasped her hands together. "Oh yes, let's play!"

"Capital idea, Mac." Charles turned toward the door. "Carson, send for the spillikins."

A table was brought forward and chairs set up around it. Mac watched Miss Sophy lead her brother to Mabel's side and direct him into the chair beside her, shooting him a telling expression with widened eyes. What was the minx playing at? As if Mabel didn't have enough to contend with, with Wright's watchful eye. Did Miss Sophy think to make Desmond a possible suitor for Mabel as well?

Charles opened the wooden box containing ivory spillikins sticks and tossed them onto the table in a heap.

"Oh, it is too bad of you," Miss Pemberton said, leaning closer to Charles as he settled back in his chair. "You've made it a difficult round, I do expect."

"So we might spend more time playing," he said, sending her a faint wink. She blushed rosily and it took all of Mac's self-control not to scoff audibly.

"Who shall begin?" Miss Sophy asked.

Mabel sent a glance past Charles's shoulder. "It should be Miss Pemberton, I believe, since Charles threw the sticks."

"Is that how you play here?" Miss Sophy asked, her dark eyebrows lifting. "I suppose I have no qualms with it, but in our house, it is always the youngest who begins."

"Would that make it you, Miss Sophy, to start us off today?" Mac asked, unable to curb his tongue. "If we were to play by the Pemberton rules, I mean."

"Well, I am not sure it matters since we are in the Sheffields' home. But yes, now that you say that, I suppose it would be me who chose first, if we were playing by my family's rules."

Mabel shifted in her chair, her gaze flicking to Desmond beside her. Clearly her strong sense of proper hosting required that she allowed the game to follow Miss Sophy's rules, so her guest would be most comfortable. Mac could almost see the dilemma dancing on her eyebrows. "Perhaps we ought to—"

Mac would not allow Miss Sophy to have her way now. It was so paltry a disagreement, but it still mattered to him. "I think we should obey the Sheffield rules." He sat back in his thin, ladder-back chair and eyed Miss Sophy. "As you said, we are in the Sheffield home, after all."

She dipped her head in acquiescence. "I wouldn't dream of anything else."

Miss Pepper coughed lightly beside Mac and he spared her a

glance as Miss Pemberton proceeded to choose a thin, ivory stick from the messy pile.

If he was correct in his assumption, Miss Pepper was doing her utmost to stifle her amusement, and he liked her for it. "I was told that you are soon to be married, Miss Pepper," he said, hoping to draw her into conversation. The table was so round and the group around it so large that smaller conversations had already broken off.

"Indeed. The wedding is in a fortnight." She stood in order to reach the spillikins sticks and selected one before sitting back down. "My uncle is to throw us a ball in two days' time. I hope you might be able to join us." She leaned back, tucking an errant strand of her wild, dark hair back into her coiffure and then indicated the table at large. "I did mention this to Miss Pemberton and Miss Sophy earlier, but every one of Mabel and Mr. Fremont's guests are welcome at our ball, of course. It is by no means meant to be a grand affair, but there will be dancing and plenty of delicacies. My cook makes an extraordinary lemon tart."

"They are delicious," Mabel agreed, nodding. "I believe I shall attend just for one of those."

"How do you find reasonably priced lemons here?" Miss Pemberton asked, impressed. "We are so out of the way, are we not?"

"We grow them," Giulia said, her smile unwavering. If ever there was a woman capable of maintaining the peace, it was this one. It must be an immense relief for Mabel to have such support.

Mac glanced to the hostess in question and paused, finding her in conversation with Desmond. It became Desmond's turn in the game, and he paused to choose a stick before returning to speak to Mabel, and Mac's gut clenched. Whatever could they possibly have to speak about so intently?

"I do look forward to it," Miss Sophy said, her shoulder

drawing so close to Mac's arm that he felt it. Swallowing his irritation, he shifted further away from her. "How glad I am that I thought to pack a ball gown."

"Indeed," Giulia said. "Fortunate."

Wright, seated on Mabel's other side, chose an ivory stick before sitting back in his chair, his gaze sweeping over the table occupants before settling on Mabel. She failed to notice, however, so rapt was she listening to Desmond.

The remainder of the evening passed with equal frustration. Mac watched Mabel speak to Desmond or Wright, or sometimes both, from the other side of the table, with no way to insert himself into their conversations. Mabel was a perfect hostess, kindly listening and softly speaking to both men as though she actually did care about what they had to say. She was the soul of diplomacy.

"Mabel!" Mrs. Sheffield called from her chair at the card table near the fire. "Where is Mabel?"

Mabel immediately pushed back her chair and rose. "I am here, Gram. Are you ready to go upstairs?"

"I do not need a new *chair*, Mabel. I want to go to bed."

"Wonderful. Allow me to assist you." She inclined her graceful head to Mrs. Boucher and offered her arm to Mrs. Sheffield, helping the older woman rise. Casting a sorrowful look over the table, she said, "I'm not sure if I'll return. Pray finish the game without me."

Giulia rose. "Let me help you."

The women bid the rest of the room goodnight and took their leave, and Mac watched them go, wishing he could join them.

"You have been quiet this evening," Miss Sophy said, leaning close and lowering her voice. "Is something troubling you, Mr. MacKenzie?"

"No," he said, offering her a smile that felt more like a grimace.

"We are old friends, are we not?" she pressed, her mouth forming an unattractive pout. "You can trust me."

"That is a relief," he said, pushing his chair back. "If you will all excuse me, I have an early morning tomorrow."

Miss Sophy's pout grew, but the remainder of the table didn't seem to mind. Charles and Miss Pemberton seemed to notice least of all.

Mac slipped upstairs to his room and closed the door behind him. Pulling the chair closer to the low-burning fire in the fireplace, he lifted the letter that had arrived earlier that day from the desk and read it again. Father's tiny scrawl took up the entirety of the page and crossed diagonally twice. He had much to say about the conditions of his home and the rats which had taken up residence within the room he slept in; apparently, the prison cat had gone missing a few weeks before and now the rodents were roaming free and unhindered. And Father was begging for speedy assistance.

The tale had likely been embellished to gain sympathy, but guilt nipped at Mac regardless. He would have enough to pay his father's creditors the moment the prize money was awarded. Surely that had to be soon. It had been tied up in courts for eight months now.

But the lines at the end of the letter puzzled Mac, and he squinted to make out the words again through the layering, overlapping words.

The only bright spot to my days are the dignified conversations with those men whose positions are in greater turmoil than my own. One man in particular has alleviated my suffering with his association. Though I mourn for him, his friendship has greatly relieved my suffering. There is no bonding agent like shared grief, is there? In any case, I hope you can soon relieve me from this wretched place. Soon, even my dearest friend will depart.

The passage was as cryptic as it was perplexing. Had Father meant to confuse Mac or to persuade him to quicken his liberation? Mac was not sitting on a fortune, biding his time as he considered his options. He needed the prize courts to approve their acquisitions.

Mac believed he'd made a good deal of his money during his years serving as Captain Sheffield's lieutenant, but he wasn't the only man in that role, and they would have to split the prizes accordingly. Every man on the ship would get their cut—even if some did not deserve it as much as others.

Slipping quietly from his room, Mac let himself down the stairs and knocked on the study door. When the deep, familiar voice bid him enter, he opened the door and let himself into the room.

"Ah, MacKenzie," Captain Sheffield said, gesturing him forward. "Come in."

"Have you thought more about my proposal?"

"Sparing the vale?" the captain asked. His white eyebrows lifted, and he pushed the reading spectacles up on his nose. "I did consider it, but that's the best place to put the cottages."

Mac swallowed his frustration and lowered himself into the chair across from Captain Sheffield. "But the south field is so far from the vale. Surely there is a better, closer location for the houses."

The captain removed his spectacles, folding them and setting them on his desk. Pinching the bridge of his nose, he leaned back in his chair. "By the time we fill those houses with men, I hope to plant every space of earth between the south field and the vale. There will be nowhere else to build."

"That is a mighty goal, Captain."

"The more fields we farm, the more men we can bring to work."

"Did you have other men in mind? I only heard you mention Rogers, Halpert, and Jemmings."

"Aye," Captain Sheffield said, "but I return to sea in two

months' time, and I am certain to find more men who might fit our situation well."

A beat of silence passed, and Mac held his captain's gaze. "You cannot help every man, sir."

"No, but I can do my best to help as many as possible."

"And the three families coming here now to farm these lands will greatly benefit. I'm certain they would have ended up in the workhouse without your assistance, Captain. These men and their families have much to be grateful for. But the fact remains that you cannot help *every* man who leaves the navy with nowhere to go."

"But I wish I could," Captain Sheffield said softly. "Perhaps in time..."

"Perhaps we ought to focus on those we might help now and worry about expanding in the future. We can't even bring Rogers, Halpert, or Jennings' families in until the cottages are finished."

Captain Sheffield puffed up his rosy cheeks before blowing out a long, slow breath. "This is why I brought you on, son. I need your level-headedness to maintain control when I leave."

This was news to Mac. He did not mind participating in the venture and directing the building of the houses and farming of the lands, but he did not intend to remain indefinitely. He had other things that required his attention. His father could not remain in the Marshalsea forever. Indeed, he could hardly leave his father there for the rest of the summer. "Everything should be in order well before that day, sir."

"But if it's not, I'm counting on you, MacKenzie." He lowered his voice, though no one was nearby to listen in on their conversation. The raucous laughter of guests playing spillikins could still be heard down the corridor. "Charles is a bright lad, of course, but he doesn't have a managing hand. I'm not blind to the way my Amabel runs this estate and all which that entails. But she won't remain here for much longer, and I need you to teach Charles how to take over in her place."

Mac's body went still, but his mind was assaulted with images of Mabel doing precisely that: managing the house, the family, the guests. She was incredible. He was glad her father noticed. But... "If she is not planning to remain here much longer, where is Mabel planning to go?"

"I have yet to finalize the union, so I trust you to keep this to yourself," Captain Sheffield said with a narrowed eye.

"Of course, sir."

"Wright has offered for her. He plans to take her to his estate in Warwickshire at the end of the summer."

The ground felt as though it had fallen away and swept Mac with it. His breath suspended, he struggled to make sense of what his captain had just said. He swallowed the bile that rose in his throat. "And Mabel, she is amenable to this scheme?"

"She needs more time, but I think she'll be satisfied with it in the end." Captain Sheffield chuckled. "You should have seen her face when I initially proposed the idea."

"I can well imagine it."

"But she has softened toward Wright, do you not agree?"

Arguments and displeasure butted against his lips, struggling to free themselves, but better sense prevailed. "I have not noticed."

Captain Sheffield nodded. "I suppose you wouldn't have. She is a proud girl, my Amabel. I think she will make Wright a good wife. And, to be frank, it will be better for Charles. If he does wish to wed, his wife won't be wanting another woman about the place who is used to being mistress."

"Is your mother not mistress?" Mac asked.

"In name, she is. This will be her house while she yet graces us with her company. But she's deferred to Amabel these last many years, and that will not stop until a new mistress is in place." Chair legs scraped against the wooden plank floor as Captain Sheffield stretched his legs. "I have hired two men to help with the foundations. We can break ground tomorrow."

"I have some business to arrange in the morning, but I will meet you in the vale when it is concluded."

Captain Sheffield didn't question Mac; he simply nodded.

"Actually, I was wondering," Mac hedged. "What have you heard from the prize court?"

A scoff ripped from the older man's throat. "Nothing. It should have been sorted by now, but it's that dratted *Triumph*. They're reviewing the records detailing how many slaves were freed."

"But that was only one of the prizes. What of the other ships?"

"It's coming," Captain said. "I plan to have it by the end of the month. We haven't run into any trouble on those, if that is your fear. The courts merely have so many cases to review they haven't reached ours yet. The war made many men rich. Not that I have any complaints to make on that score," he added, grinning before his face melted into a grimace. "Have you need of the blunt earlier? Is it your father?"

Mac's jaw clenched. His father being taken from his estate while his mother collapsed in his arms, tears running down her face, flashed through his mind. He could have handled the humiliation alone. His father was a reckless fool who ran up too many gambling debts that not even the sale of his family estate could cover. But his mother?

She hadn't deserved any of it.

She deserved to be cared for in a home she would not fear losing, with servants who respected her, free of creditors banging on the door, waiting on the doorstep for hours until Father returned home. Mac could give her that comfort and peace...but not if he wanted to free his father. Mac was not the captain of a ship. He had only been a lieutenant. His portion of the prizes would only cover one of his needs. His father's freedom, or an estate.

Captain Sheffield cleared his throat. "If it's just money, I can—"

"No," Mac said, shaking his head. "I can wait. My father can wait. He's safe in the Marshalsea, at least."

Captain nodded. "Very good. And you must know I plan to pay you for your services here."

"I am not in the market for charity, Captain, and neither do I need it." He swallowed against the discomfort such a lie procured. He *did* need the money—or he would, at least, if the wretched prize courts didn't come to a satisfying conclusion soon.

"Of course not. But 'tis honest work you'll be doing, and honestly you'll come by your earnings." He stood. "We can discuss the parameters of the arrangement tomorrow. I'd best be off to bed now."

Mac followed suit, watching the captain walk away while the choice rumbled about his mind as if it had not yet been made. But even if he convinced himself it was proper to set up a home for his mother, she would never abide such a scheme. She had a blinding love for Mac's father that he would never understand. Her goodness was unparalleled.

No, that was untrue. He *could* think of another woman with such kindness in her heart, and she was walking ahead of Mac right now.

CHAPTER 17

*M*abel's heart refused to slow. She had heard Papa and Mac prepare to leave the study and lifted her skirts, hoping to make a quick escape, but she was not swift enough. The door closed behind her, and she slowed her pace, hoping her retreat appeared natural.

She hadn't intended to listen in on the men's conversation when she'd gone to speak to her father, but their voices were powerful, penetrating the door, and were clearly discernible from her position in the corridor.

When Mac had asked if Papa had heard from the prize court, Mabel had shoved aside all of her governess's lessons on politely *not* eavesdropping and leaned in closer. Had she been living under a rock? Mabel had known that Mac's father had gone away, and his mother had gone to Bath, but the MacKenzie estate remained empty, and Mabel had assumed that was by choice. How had she not heard?

Never would she have imagined the family to be in strait-ened means, that his father was in the Marshalsea. She yearned to turn now, to close the distance and wrap her arms around his waist. The time surrounding Mac's leaving Graton and going off to join the navy had been difficult for Mabel—she'd believed she was forever saying farewell to her one true love, a love who had wholly rejected her. But she hadn't known that he was leaving because his parents had been put in such horrifying circumstances. How difficult it must have been for him to leave his parents at such a trying time.

She scoffed quietly. Mabel had pitied herself because Mac had called her *tall*. Her mouth bent into a frown, and she lifted her skirts, pretending not to hear the heavy footsteps follow her up the stairs. Would it be too much to wish Mac would simply let her be so she might go to her room and pity him in silence? If she turned about now, Mac would surely see the distress in her eyes.

"Mabel?"

Oh, dear. Perhaps she could continue on, pretending she hadn't heard him. He had spoken so quietly, her name barely touching his lips.

"Mabel?" he called again.

A chill ran down her neck. She paused at the top of the staircase, her hand resting on the bannister. Glancing over her shoulder, she caught his hazel gaze as he approached her slowly in the dim candlelight, her heart speeding the closer he grew.

"How is Mrs. Sheffield?" he asked, coming to pause on the landing beside her.

"Asleep, I hope."

"And you?"

"Awake."

Mac chuckled, and Mabel's breath caught. This kind, compassionate, dear man had the weight of the world on his shoulders, and she never would have guessed it before. He wore his struggles quietly, and that made her heart ache all the more. She did not know a more even-keeled person, especially one who was so wholly responsible for the welfare of his parents.

"I meant to ask if you are well," Mac said, his mouth tilting into something of a smile as his eyes bore into hers. "It cannot have been easy for you to take on so many guests with such little notice, and yet you've remained perfectly composed. Are we beginning to wear on you?"

"Not *beginning* to, no." Mabel couldn't contain her smile. "You've worn on me from the first."

"*Touché*, Mabel."

It was on the tip of her tongue to remind Mac of his place, but the way he said her name made her heart jump in her chest. She was not strong enough to ask him not to repeat it, not when she wanted to hear it again.

"Have you concluded your business with my father?"

He nodded. "There wasn't much business to attend to. I was merely visiting with him."

"And was your visit satisfactory?"

Mac searched her face, his own just higher than hers. She enjoyed looking up at him and wondered if her height was as obnoxious to him now as it was when they were younger. "I learned some things which I found utterly distasteful, and others which interested me greatly. So I suppose it was an enlightening visit if nothing else."

Interesting. She could say the same about what she had overheard. Though she would never admit so aloud. "And what did my father say that was so distasteful?"

He opened his mouth to speak, but then closed it again. Seeming to weigh his words, he leaned closer, eyes sparkling with emotion but lacking levity. "That you are going to marry Wright."

Her breath caught. "I have agreed to nothing yet."

"Good."

"But the idea does not repel me as much as it does you." She swallowed, unable to refrain from provoking him. "Pray, do you have cause to be so disapproving?"

Mac stepped closer still. "Wright is not the sort of man one wishes to align themselves with."

"My father would beg to differ."

"Your father sees the good in people."

"So you admit there is good in Mr. Wright?'

A small smile tipped one side of his lips. "He is not *entirely* evil, no."

Mabel narrowed her gaze, and Mac rubbed a hand over his face. "I would not defame his character had I not just cause. But the man is lazy. He only works hard when he knows he is being watched. We only served on the same ship for just under two years, but it was time enough to give me a thorough understanding of the sort of person he is."

She lifted her eyebrows. "You will allow me to make up my own mind on the matter."

"I trust you," Mac said, his voice softening. "But not him."

He was so close now that Mabel could feel warmth emanating from him, his chest rising and falling so near he almost touched her. She struggled to form a coherent thought. Swallowing hard, she focused on the smooth curve of his jaw, his striking honey-colored eyes. "Then you will recall that you have no say over whom I marry, or whom I esteem."

His eyes glittered dangerously in the candlelight, darkening. "You esteem Wright? You have only known him for a matter of days."

"I did not say that I esteem him, only that it is no business of yours whether I do or not."

His voice lowered. "Unless I make it my business."

Mabel tilted her head to the side. "And how do you propose to do that?"

Mac's chest rose and fell rapidly in time with Mabel's, and his gaze dropped to her lips.

Was he going to kiss her? She grew dizzy, roaming every inch of his face and wishing she could cup his cheeks, to pull him closer and comfort away his worries—the worries she shouldn't know about, but did. Her hand came up and rested on his chest of its own accord, fulfilling her desire to close the space between them, and his quick intake of breath shot through her heart.

"Mac..."

"Yes?"

"I just..." She watched her hand rise and fall with his heavy breathing, the steady pounding of his heart beating under her palm. She yearned to have his hands on her waist again, his warmth cocooning her, wrapping her in safety. But that was selfish to ask so much of him, and the last thing Mac needed was her misunderstanding his kindness. She'd done that once, and it had cost her dearly. She'd poured her heart out only to be rejected.

She would not make the same mistake twice.

Fear overcame her. Dropping her hand from his chest, Mabel took a step back and sucked in a slow, deep, calming breath, willing her brain to clear and her breathing to slow. "I heard that you are planning to begin Papa's project tomorrow."

There was a beat of thick silence before Mac spoke, his voice hoarse, rough. "Yes, in the late morning. I have business to conduct at first light."

"What sort of business would take place so early?" she asked, her voice deceptively light. She hoped he could not sense her heightened nerves.

"It is nothing, really. I suppose I ought to cancel it, but I cannot bring myself to. How are you holding up in regard to the work tomorrow?"

"I am glad for my father. He is looking forward to this farming venture."

"As am I."

Mabel stepped back again. "Then I suppose I won't see you

until tomorrow night. Charles told me that he expects the work to take all of the daylight hours." The prospect of a day free of Mac was equally a disappointment and cause for relief. She needed to get a steady handle on her feelings, and space could help her accomplish that.

Mac nodded, but his penetrating gaze did not leave her face. Could he see the flush of her cheeks in the dim light?

"Until tomorrow night, then." He bent in a distinguished bow more fitting for a ballroom than this quiet, dark corridor.

Mabel dipped in a curtsy. "Goodnight, Mac," she whispered.

"Goodnight."

She forced herself to walk calmly to her bedchamber and slipped through her door, leaning against it and willing her heart to slow. The steady tread of Mac's boots on the stairs leading up to the next floor punctuated the quiet, and Mabel leaned closer to the wall to listen as his steps faded into silence.

Her eyes drifted closed, and she dropped her head back against the thick, oak door. Perhaps she ought to marry Mr. Wright just to rid her mind of Mac. He would never want her. He'd flirted plenty when they were younger, leading her to believe he felt something for her beyond a passing friendship.

She wished things were different this time, but they couldn't be. Not when she knew Miss Sophy harbored the same feelings for Mac that she did. Mac was clearly the same flirt he'd been in their youth—with no intention to settle down. She would not be fooled again. This time she would guard her heart and not allow herself to fall victim to his caring charms. The man was hazardous, and she was very much in danger of falling deeper in love with him than before.

Daylight broke through the open window and fell upon Mabel's face. She lay in bed, her eyes squinting against the warm rays of light. Swinging her legs over the mattress, she leaned forward, rubbing the sleep from her eyes. It was far too early for anyone but servants to be up and about, and the prospect of having her home to herself was too enticing to pass up.

Mabel rang for her maid and dressed quickly in her dark green habit, tugging the waist lower and pinning her hat on her head. Her leg had throbbed something fierce the night before, but the long rest had done much to soothe it, and she was determined to get a long, bracing ride in before the efforts of the day rendered her useless in the saddle once more.

"Thank you, Payne. I shall return in an hour or so."

"Of course, miss."

Mabel slipped downstairs, crossing the dewy lawn without the slightest hitch in her step. She could almost believe during these mornings that she was normal, that her leg had miraculously healed. But then she would grow sore and tired over the course of the day, and by the time she went to bed again, would remember with bitter clarity that her leg would never fully heal.

Though she had done her best since the accident to come to terms with her lot in life, sometimes she still felt keenly the way it had changed and affected her.

The groom was waiting beside Star, holding both her reins and the reins of the light brown hack he intended to ride, standing at attention. When he noticed Mabel approaching, he led Star to the side of the stables and the mounting block nestled against the planked wall.

Mabel thanked him, grasping the saddle and lifting herself into it, then arranged her skirts to cover her ankles. She ran a hand down her leg, massaging her calf, hoping the slight ache would remain so, and not increase after her ride.

"Where to, ma'am?"

"I've yet to decide, Wagner. Let us begin northward."

Wagner nodded, waiting for her to move forward before

mounting his saddle and following behind. The cool, crisp morning air was already beginning to thaw, the higher the sun grew in the sky. Warmth permeated her habit, soothing her skin as much as it calmed her soul.

She led Star along the north of the house, meandering at a canter. This sort of head-clearing ride was exactly what she needed to rid her mind of the clouding expectations troubling her. Whether she wanted it to or not, Mac's warning against Mr. Wright had nestled in her thoughts, planting a seed of doubt deep within her.

It was unfair of him to color her opinion of another suitor—her only suitor, in fact. She didn't count Mr. Pemberton. His sister may have wanted him to throw his hat in the ring, but the man himself clearly did not intend to do any such thing. What right did Mac have to try and persuade her opinion?

None.

Leading Star through the grove of trees, Mabel glanced over her shoulder to assure herself that Wagner was still following. She caught the nose of his horse coming through the trees before spurring Star on. She wanted to reach the vale alone.

It had been years since she'd allowed herself to come here. After her conversation with Mac last night and the way he'd looked to her lips, she had been utterly convinced the man was about to kiss her. But she'd thought that once before, and she'd been wrong. He'd laughed in her face when she had admitted so aloud, and it had ruined her; she would never believe a man's flirting to mean anything significant, not again.

Which was unfair. A man should not flirt with a woman—or a young girl of sixteen, as she'd been when Mac had begun using flowery praise to speak to her—unless he meant what he said.

Star broke through the woods and into the vale, and Mabel gasped, her heart squeezing from the impact of the vision before her. The larkspur was in full bloom, a sea of dark violet stretching forth and filling the small valley surrounded by a grove of full chestnut trees. The flowers were so vivid they looked almost to be a deep blue. And standing tall in the center of it all, was Mac.

CHAPTER 18

*W*hen Mabel rode into the vale on her horse, Mac's heart leapt to his throat. Loose strands of hair whipped around her face, her lips parting as her gaze swept over the flowers and landed on him. He had been stunned when he'd entered the vale and found the flowers in full bloom, and it lifted his heart to watch Mabel have the same reaction.

It was the very thing he needed after meeting with the solicitor at Camden Court that morning and realizing how very far away his dreams were. He didn't know why he'd gone to the estate, to walk the empty halls and imagine a life there, when it could never be his.

And it hurt even worse that the property remained closed up and uninhabited. If the owners would drop the price, they'd likely find a family willing to obtain it. As it was, the estate needed so much work it was unlikely to sell at such an inflated value.

But Mac needed to remove the idyllic house on the northern Devon seaside from his mind. His family was more important. Once he received his prize money from the ships they'd captured during the war and freed his father from the

Marshalsea prison, he would find a smaller estate they could afford, work the land and build a life for themselves. If he even had enough blunt left over for that after paying his father's debts. He swallowed hard.

Shaking away his plans for the future, Mac fixed his gaze on the tree line and the woman paused before it. Mabel slid down from her horse and left the beast standing at the edge of the field. Crossing over the sea of flowers, she paused just a few yards from him.

"What are you doing here?" She sounded breathless, her cheeks and the tip of her nose rosy from the morning chill.

Mac clenched his hands at his sides, doing his best to appear unaffected when in actuality he'd had a trying morning and his nerves were shot. He wished to cross the distance and pull Mabel into his arms, to gain comfort from her, but he couldn't do so. He would not use her in such a way. Last night when she'd moved closer, when she'd rested her hand on his chest, he had wished above all things to close the distance between them. But Mabel hadn't wanted that. She'd pulled away, after all. Hadn't that made her wishes perfectly clear?

Mabel held his gaze like the steady lighthouse on the shore, calling to him, calling him home. The startling realization washed over him like warm sunlight on a ship deck—he loved her. Mac *loved* this woman.

The last time they'd been together in this vale, Mabel had opened her heart and bared her soul for Mac, and he'd shot her down. Of course, he'd cared about her then, but he hadn't loved her—not like this. With the overwhelming stress of his father's debts just coming to light and his uncertainty in life, he had been too devastated, too caught up in his own grief, to consider her feelings. And if he was perfectly honest with himself, he'd been too full of shame to consider accepting a lock of her hair, of making a promise he didn't know if he could keep. With the life he'd had before him, he'd never have deemed himself worthy of

164

her. But now, could things be different? Doubt filled his chest. They couldn't be. Not yet.

Mabel's eyebrows arched, and Mac realized he was staring. But how could he help it? He'd just discovered the most important truth in his life. And he could do *nothing* about it. Prize money from ships captured during the war was not a guarantee, not until the prize courts decreed them valid and distributed the money. If his prizes were denied, Mac would be a pauper. He couldn't just ask Mabel to give up everything here for a *chance* that they'd be content. He needed to know first that he could provide for her.

He cleared his throat and tried to clear his mind with it. "Your father is meeting me here. I suppose I am early."

"Did you not say you had business to attend to this morning?" Mabel's gaze ran the length of Mac's shirtsleeves, pausing at his open waistcoat and bared throat.

He swallowed. He'd forgotten that he'd left his coat near Orion, but he hadn't thought he'd see any women today. All he'd planned to do was work through the pain and frustration of a life moving the opposite direction from how he wished it would.

"I did have a meeting this morning, but I completed my business earlier than expected."

Mabel took a step closer. The breeze lifted loose strands of her hair and they danced along behind her, the skirts of her habit swaying to the rhythm of the wind. "It is quite early to conduct a meeting. May I ask the nature of this business? Surely you are not doing anything illegal." She paused, a playful smirk on her lips. "Are you smuggling, Mac?"

"No." He chuckled, and her answering smile, though small, warmed him. "Though, I did travel to Camden Cove."

Her eyebrows lifted. "So far?"

"It is only seven miles. Not even an hour's ride."

"*Nearly* an hour, though. You must have left before dawn."

Mac nodded. An overwhelming desire to relieve his burdens filled him, to tell Mabel everything and see what she could make of it. If anyone could take his mess of a life and make something lovely from it, it was her.

"What took you to Camden Cove?"

"A house," he said. "It will come to nothing, of course, but there is an estate there I fancy, and I considered buying it for a moment."

"Oh?" She tilted her head to the side, a crease forming between her eyebrows. "If you think nothing will come of it, why did you go to see it?"

He kicked the dirt beneath his boot, his gaze trailing along the wild-flower strewn earth, hoping to avoid answering that question. He didn't know why he had gone.

The flowers swayed in the soft morning breeze, their light, sweet aroma tickling his nose. The sea of larkspur spread out like a flawless violet-blue carpet, the exact color of Mabel's striking eyes. Grief struck his heart. The vale would not remain such an untouched place after today. Mabel's vale would be gone. Perhaps then she would understand loss, and he could tell her of his troubles. "I hoped it might be different, I suppose."

She followed his gaze to the flower-blanketed earth, confusion clouding her brow. "Mac, why are you meeting my father *here?*" she asked, uncertainty lacing her tone. "I thought you were beginning the farming venture today."

He glanced up. "They did not tell you?"

Panic gripped Mabel's stomach. "Mac," she repeated, noting the fear in her tone. "*What* did they not tell me?"

He held her gaze, his eyes bent and sorrowful.

Understanding hit her before Mac uttered the words aloud. When Papa had explained his plans to bring families to Graton to farm the neglected, untouched fields on Gram's land, Mabel hadn't realized that he'd lumped Larkspur Vale in with the rest of the barren fields.

Because this field wasn't barren. This field was lovely, useful. It had been a haven for Mabel for much of her life; she had only recently avoided it for the unpleasant memories it brought to the surface. Her sights fixed on Mac. Unpleasant memories involving *him*.

He cleared his throat. "This is where they plan to build the cottages."

"But, the larkspur..."

"I tried to convince them of the merits of using a different field for the cottages, but they would not be deterred."

"You?" she asked, stricken. "What do you care for this place?"

"I don't—I mean, I just know what it means to you."

That was true. He'd caught her here enough times to know what it meant to her. The memories she held close to her heart were of being alone in this vale, reading a book or taking a nap, far away from the realities and responsibilities that consumed her at home. The time following Pippa's birth and their mother's death had been so lonely for Mabel, needing to be the adult while she was still hardly older than a child herself, and she had found solace here.

A month after her mother's death, Mabel had wandered to this vale, this place that was an oasis within the woods, and had seen more flowers than had ever before covered the ground—a veritable sea of violet-blue larkspur the color of Pippa's and Mabel's eyes. Papa had an explanation for it—he always did. The wind, he'd said, had carried the flowers to cover more ground than usual. It *had* been a particularly windy season, of course, but Mabel had known better. She'd known that her mother was responsible—the flowers a gift from heaven.

And now they were destroying them.

Mabel squeezed her eyes closed. Was her mother full of sorrow up in heaven, too?

Large, warm hands came around her arms, and her breath fled when Mac pulled her against his chest. She gripped his shirt, fisting it in her hands and measuring the steadily increasing beat of his heart against her own. Papa was so absent that she couldn't expect him to know what this place meant to her, but Charles? Was her cousin so caught up in himself that he had not thought of her?

Grief clawed up her throat, threatening to break free. Mabel focused on her breathing, forcing herself to remain calm as her cheek rested against Mac's firm chest. It was a leveling thought that the only person who considered what this vale meant to Mabel was the man who had once broken her heart there.

He'd ruined this place for her. After that incident, Mabel had not been able to return. She'd tried to visit it once after he left, but it had been uncomfortable, tainted. It'd no longer held the magic—only memories of the uncomfortable.

So she'd begun looking for her mother in other ways. In Pippa's face, in the looking glass, in the painting in Papa's room. She did not need the vale. It would always mean something to her, but it was no longer her special place. Yet even with the tainted memory, she'd always known it was here, that she could come back if she chose to. Just like she had that morning.

Mabel released a shuddering breath, gripping Mac's shirt tighter. He tightened his arms around her, his embrace both soothing and protective.

But this was how he always had been. Kind, attentive, flirtatious. A man with a teasing glint always dancing in his eyes and a playful smile on his lips. A man who made her feel special, petite, appreciated. She would never forget the shock in his eyes, the playful grin slipping from his lips when she had confessed her feelings for him. His cheerful nature had been erased, replaced with panic, and he'd stammered his refusal of her lock of hair, telling her she'd been mistaken, that she was too tall, that he had never thought of her in that way.

If she tilted her head back now, confessed her feelings, would Mac's face distort once again into panic and disgust?

She released his shirt, pushing against his chest and stepping back away from the circle of warmth and contentment he created for her.

"Mabel, are you—"

"It means nothing to me now," she said, feeling the bitterness of the lie on her tongue. She wiped away the moisture lingering on her lower lashes, careful to suppress the emotion hovering at the edge of her composure.

Mac stared at her, his confusion quickly melting away, his eyes growing hard and unyielding. He could see through her, undoubtedly. "Nothing? It means nothing at all?"

Tearing her gaze from his, Mabel stepped back, taking in the entire expanse of open, wild land. The vale was large enough for a multitude of small cottages, and the new tenants would likely enjoy the odd larkspur here or there as long as the men did not uproot each flower. Now that the shock of the discovery wore off, she could see how it would be an idyllic place to raise a family for these displaced sailors. She knew intrinsically that her mother would have sacrificed it without hesitation.

She ignored Mac's question. "If I must give it up, this is a worthy cause."

"You mean it," he said, his voice soft. "And here I was worried you would be sad to sacrifice this place."

"I am sad that things must change. When is change ever easy? But at least I can find solace in the fact that it is a worthy reason to destroy the vale. It will change these families' lives for the better, will it not?"

"Indeed." Mac dropped his head to the side, his mouth set in a firm line. "I only wish we could accomplish that without needing to ruin this place."

Mabel shrugged, hoping she appeared at ease when instead her body tingled, the feel of being in Mac's arms impossible to shake. "I'd best be getting back." She glanced over her shoulder to find Wagner resting on his horse beside Star. He looked away as though affording them privacy, and Mabel's cheeks grew warm.

"Mabel, wait."

She paused, turning back toward Mac. The sun behind him framed him perfectly, creating an ethereal glow around his bent frame. He straightened, reaching toward her, offering her a small bouquet of larkspur, and her heart stuttered.

She took the flowers, brushing her fingers against his, and dipped her head to smell them. The faintly sweet scent charmed her. "Thank you."

He nodded.

"Good day, Mac."

He didn't say anything else as she fled. Wagner hopped down from his horse and bent to help Mabel into the saddle, and she turned her face away from Mac to hide her wince from his watchful eye. Once she was securely seated, she turned Star back toward the woods, careful not to crush her flowers.

"Will you be wantin' to go any farther, ma'am?"

"Not today, Wagner," Mabel called, as she led into the woods. "That is enough for now."

CHAPTER 19

*G*iulia sat at the writing table in the drawing room, scanning the papers neatly set out before her, the afternoon sun highlighting her wild, brown hair. The concentration on her brow pulled her eyebrows together, and she chewed on her lower lip. It was a familiar image and Mabel stored it away for the future when her friend was moved into Halstead Manor after the wedding and would no longer complete mundane tasks in this house such as letter writing or going over preparations for a ball.

"Is there truly nothing I can do to be of assistance?" Mabel asked, leaning over on the settee to better see her friend. "I feel useless."

Giulia quirked an eyebrow. "You are coming as a guest, Mabel. You shouldn't feel useless, exactly, but understand that I will not be putting you to work. I expect you to enjoy yourself." She flourished her hand through the air. "Find a handsome man and dance all night."

"I shan't be doing any dancing if this wretched leg is still bothering me tomorrow." She leaned down, squeezing her calf. Pain shot clear up to her hip and she grimaced.

Giulia's dark eyebrows pulled together. "Do you need to skip the literary society today? I can tell Hattie and Amelia why you've decided not to come if you wish to rest for tomorrow. They will understand."

"No, I have not seen either of them in a fortnight beyond passing in the church yard. And that does not count, not truly. I won't skip the literary society to save my leg." She sent Giulia an arch look. "I might be happy of the excuse to sit out the dancing tomorrow anyway, if I am to be honest."

"In that case, we ought to be leaving soon."

Mabel stood, her leg aching with each clumsy step toward the door. Her ride earlier to the vale had been foolish, only adding to her pain. But there was little she could do about that now. Gathering the folds of her habit's skirt, she lifted the hem from the floor so it wouldn't collect dust, resting her other hand on the wall. "Shall I request the horses be brought around?"

Giulia's focus remained on the sheets of paper before her, but she nodded absently.

Mabel asked for the horses to be saddled, then waited for her friend to join her by the front door.

"Are you going somewhere exciting?" a saccharine voice said, preceding the figure who stepped into the lit entryway. The early afternoon sun shone through the window above the door and lit the marble floor in a tilted square, and Miss Sophy inched forward, narrowing her eyes against the bright rays of light.

"Not yet," Mabel answered. "Is there anything I might do for you before I leave?"

"I had wondered if we might plan a drive to the seaside."

"Our beaches here are not what you'd find in Brighton."

"Of course they aren't, but the outing would be enjoyable, yes? And I should dearly love to see what sort of beaches Devon has to offer. Even if they aren't as lovely as what I'm used to."

They were certainly lovely, but they lacked the bathing machines and resorts along the coast. Mabel gave the woman a tight smile, grateful to see Giulia heading toward them. "I will see what I can do. We will be attending Giulia's ball tomorrow, so perhaps the day following."

"Or the day following that," Miss Sophy said, "so we are not forced to rise early after a night of dancing."

Giulia glanced between them. "What is this?"

"Plans to visit the seaside," Miss Sophy said.

"What a lovely idea." Giulia grinned. "The distraction is well-timed for me."

"Indeed," Mabel said, smiling between the women. "Well, we must be off. We will see you at dinner."

Miss Sophy dipped her head, and Mabel and Giulia returned the action. They were outside and halfway to their waiting horses when Mabel leaned close to her friend and lowered her voice. "Ought I to have invited her?"

"No."

Mabel paused. "You are quite decided in that opinion."

Shrugging, she smiled unapologetically. "This is not just tea with friends, Mabel. The literary society is a safe space for the four of us, and while I commend your bend toward inclusivity, it is not warranted in this situation. Did not Amelia consult with you and Hattie before inviting me to join your ranks?"

"Yes."

"Then there it is." Using the mounting block, Giulia lifted herself into her saddle.

Mabel followed behind, allowing Giulia to go ahead of her so her friend might not see the strain on her face. Her leg throbbed acutely, but she gritted her teeth and waited for the waves of pain to pass. It only needed a rest. She would return home later and put it up for the rest of the evening and by morning she would not feel a thing.

For the last four years, she had managed the ache in her leg well enough, and it only bothered her when she stressed it. But recently the pain had seemed to increase in both strength and frequency, becoming increasingly more difficult to ignore.

"What do you plan to wear tomorrow?" Giulia called over her shoulder. "Please tell me you will wear your mother's garnets. I have been longing to see them on you since you showed them to me."

"Garnets seem a mite fancy, do they not?"

"Are you trying to say that my ball is not reason enough to rig yourself out in your best gown?"

"When you use lowborn cant like that, Giulia, I cannot understand a word you say."

Giulia laughed. "No excuses, darling. Your father is a sailor. You perfectly understood me. Besides, do you not have a suitor to impress?"

"I don't know what you mean."

Giulia laughed harder as she directed her horse across the open field toward the Green's barn where they were meant to meet up with Amelia and Hattie. Dismounting from their horses, Mabel and Giulia led them inside and stabled them.

She glanced to the long ladder which would take them up to the loft where the foursome met weekly, and her throat grew tight. Stepping on a rotten plank and falling to the hard-packed dirt below was how Mabel had broken her leg in the first place. Returning here had never caused her much distress before, but her leg hadn't pained her in this manner in some years. Not since the original injury had taken place, if she thought about it.

"Is something troubling you?" Giulia asked, her dark eyebrows drawn.

Mabel shook her head, leaving her horse in the stall. "It looks like we are the first to arrive. Shall we?"

Giulia agreed, but the concern didn't leave her face.

Fourteen painful rungs later, Mabel made it to the top. "What are *you* planning to wear to the ball?" she asked.

"Mabel? Giulia?" a soft voice called from below before Giulia had a chance to answer.

"We are up here." Mabel glanced over the loft edge, waving to Hattie.

"Oh, Mae, it has been absolute ages since I've seen you!" Hattie called. She quickly stabled her horse and then climbed the ladder. "I want to hear everything. Giulia tells us that you have three handsome men at your house. *Three.* Is this why you've been absent so much of late?" She dusted out her skirts before crossing the floor and pulling Mabel into an embrace. "Oh how I've missed you."

"I saw you in the churchyard just a few days past."

Hattie pouted. "And you hardly said three words." She plopped onto one of the sofas, leaning her head against the back of the cushion. "Please, I want to hear about these men. Are they all very handsome and eligible? Who do you find most attractive?"

Mabel's mind's eye brought forth an image of Mac standing beside Mr. Wright, Mr. Pemberton languidly resting behind them. There was no comparison; Mac was certainly the best looking.

"Who is it?" Hattie's eyes were bright, sitting up as Mabel came to sit beside her, Giulia taking a seat across from them on the other sofa. Amelia climbed the ladder then and their little group was complete.

"Who are we speaking about?"

"The handsome men staying at Mabel's house," Hattie said.

Amelia's red eyebrows lifted, striking on her pale skin against the black, high-necked gown she wore. She had buried three husbands in her short life and had vowed to never again wed. Her severe wardrobe was a manifestation of this promise.

"If you do not wish to share your knowledge, I am certain we can convince Giulia to."

"By all means," Mabel said, lifting a hand toward her friend. "I should like to hear your opinions after all."

Giulia straightened. "Very well."

Amelia sat beside her, her delicate posture nearly rigid.

"There is a lieutenant from Captain Sheffield's ship," Giulia began. "He is called Mr. Wright now that he's sold out, and while his face is worn from the sun and the sea, he looks as though he'd make a nice husband. But perhaps not as preferable when compared to a Mr. Pemberton, who spends his days discussing sport and sipping drinks. He is never fully lucid, as far as I can tell."

Mabel sat back. Never fully lucid? Did she mean to imply that Mr. Pemberton was always in his cups? If that was the case, wouldn't Mabel have noticed it?

"And then there is Captain Sheffield's other lieutenant, who also sold out of the navy and has been traveling with Charles's party. He looks like a brute of a man, but it is my belief that he has the heart of a lamb."

"Intriguing," Hattie said, tapping her chin with one finger. "Will they all attend the ball?"

"Yes," Giulia said. "I have invited the entirety of the Sheffields' house party, including Mr. Pemberton's sisters."

"Why do you say that with such disdain? Surely they are not too bad."

"Oh, you shall see for yourself tomorrow night."

Mabel whipped her head around. She had taken a dislike to the Pemberton sisters, but she had no idea Giulia felt the same way.

Amelia turned her attention to Mabel. "You are being unusually quiet. Has one of these men caught your eye?"

"Actually, you'll know the second lieutenant," Mabel said, hoping to avoid needing to answer that question. Giulia wouldn't have realized, perhaps, that Mac grew up in Graton with the rest of them. "Liam MacKenzie."

Amelia's eyebrows lifted. "He's come back?"

"Indeed."

"And how long does he plan to stay?"

Mabel sighed. "As long as Papa needs him. Mr. MacKenzie is heading up the project to bring in new tenant farmers for Gram's land. They broke ground today in the vale, actually."

Quiet settled over the loft, each woman growing still. Even Giulia, though a relatively recent addition to their group, knew of the connection Mabel had to the vale—in part. She'd never shared her experience with Mac with another soul, but they all knew of her love for the flowers and her belief that they came from her mother.

"Does your father understand what it means to you? Does he not know of your mother's love for larkspur?" Amelia asked.

She considered the flowers in a vase now on her dressing table. "Papa does not possess a sentimental vein, I am afraid. I'm certain the portrait in his room is reminder enough of my mother, though we do not speak of her much. Occasionally I do find him watching me with an odd expression, and I sometimes wonder if it is because he sees her in my countenance."

Hattie inched closer on the sofa and strung her arms around Mabel, burying her face in Mabel's shoulder. Sitting back, she squeezed Mabel's hand. "He does love you. There is no mistaking that."

"I did not question it." She laughed awkwardly. "You are the most supportive friends, but come, let us talk about something less depressing. The ball, perhaps?"

Giulia's gaze narrowed. Drat her perceptiveness. But she seemed to sense that Mabel needed the topic of conversation to shift away from her. "I have commissioned my cook to bake as many lemon tarts as she can. We've used up all of the lemons on our tree and will have to suffer without them for some time, but I do feel it will be worth it."

"Of course it shall," Hattie agreed. "I plan to wear a new

177

gown my sister-in-law sent me from London and as much as I'm loath to admit it, it is exquisite."

Amelia laughed. "Surely you can admit that the woman has virtues as well as faults."

"That is hard when all I see are her faults," Hattie said. "It would be easier to like her if she was not so insufferable."

"Yes, what an insufferable creature," Amelia agreed. "To send you lovely ball gowns all the way from London? Absurd."

Hattie's gaze flicked to the ceiling. "Well, I thought so. 'Tis plain she is doing her utmost to buy my love, is it not?"

"Perhaps she is merely doing her best to be kind," Mabel said.

"And Charles?" Hattie asked, clearly changing the subject. "Is he much improved since returning?"

"He has grown darker." Mabel glanced at Amelia, curious how her friend would take this news. "And it is my understanding that he is soon to be engaged. Though you must all promise not to tell a soul until it has been made official."

"When shall we meet the woman?" Amelia asked. Mabel watched her face for any indication that she was bothered by this revelation, but her face was void of anything but basic interest.

Mabel swallowed her frustration. The woman had allowed Charles to trail behind her, watching her wed thrice while he sat in the background, utterly in love with her. If nothing else, shouldn't Amelia feel some measure of relief that Charles was about to find his own happiness? He certainly deserved it.

"You will meet her at the ball tomorrow. Her name is Miss Pemberton, and she brings with her a sister by the name of Miss Sophy, and a hired companion called Mrs. Boucher."

"A formidable woman with a stare that will straighten your back on impact," Giulia added.

Hattie scrunched her nose. "She sounds like my old

governess. It's glad I am that I do not have to worry about companions or other uncomfortable creatures anymore."

"Not unless you visit your brother and his wife in London, at least," Mabel couldn't help but quip.

Hattie broke out in laughter and Amelia and Giulia quickly joined in. Sitting back against the ratty sofa cushion, Mabel stretched her leg to cease its throbbing and did her best to appear unaffected. Glancing to the top of the ladder peeking out over the edge of the loft, she swallowed hard. She needed to make her excuses and leave now, or she was afraid she would be sleeping in the loft that evening.

The pain pulsed so continually in her leg that she allowed her eyelids to drift closed, gripping her hands into tight fists hidden in the folds of her gown.

"Mae, what is it?" Hattie asked beside her. "Are you quite exhausted? Perhaps we should be getting home."

Mabel offered her friend a smile, hoping to deflect her friend's concern. "The house party cannot end soon enough, but that is all I will say on the matter."

"You must be so glad to have your father around."

"I am," Mabel said. "His leave will end far too soon, of that I am certain. So I am enjoying having him home while I can."

"Let's go home," Giulia said, standing. "We shall see you all tomorrow."

Mabel waited for her friends to rise and move toward the ladder before she attempted doing the same. Pushing herself to her feet, Mabel clutched the armrest of the sofa, breathing through her nose.

Her eyes drifted closed, the chatter melting into a far-away din. Pain shot up her leg in waves. She needed to get down now and onto her horse or she was not going to be going anywhere. Pushing off from the armrest, she stepped forward, aches erupting with each step.

Hattie was the last to go down and Mabel made it to the

head of the ladder, slipping down the rungs one at a time, gripping the smooth wood and praying her leg wouldn't give out from under her.

Her friends' conversation moved toward the horses and Mabel paused, gripping the ladder and catching her breath. Her leg had only bothered her this badly once before, and it was after she'd overused it for many days in a row, the pressure and strain culminating until she could not step without shooting pain slicing up her leg and into her hip.

She exhaled. Only two more rungs to go and she would be safely on the ground once more.

She tried to remember how long it had taken to feel whole again the last time she had experienced this level of pain when a voice called her name just behind her.

"Mabel?"

She startled, turning to see what Giulia needed, and her knee buckled beneath her. A loud pop rent the air. Releasing the ladder rung, she watched the packed dirt floor rise until her face collided with it, and everything went dark.

CHAPTER 20

*M*ac shrugged his arms into his coat, the warmth from the day disappearing around the edge of the world.

"'Twas a good day's work," Captain Sheffield said, clapping him on the back as they moved toward the horses tied up at the edge of the vale. All of the workmen had gone home, and Charles and Desmond had headed back to the house to change for dinner, leaving Mac, Wright, and their captain at the vale to finish marking the boundaries for the third cottage.

Captain Sheffield sighed, swinging into his saddle. "There is nothing like a full day of hard labor to remind a man that he isn't young anymore."

"Speak for yourself," Wright said, grinning. "I have never felt better. And you, sir, have never looked better. This country air is doing wonders for your health, I am sure."

Mac chuckled to cover a scoff. Wright was a ridiculous flatterer. "Then I suppose we'll see you again tomorrow at sunup?"

"Of course," Wright said quickly. Irritation flashed in his eyes, but he turned away before Mac could answer his look in kind.

They made it through the woods, the captain in the lead, when Mac urged Orion faster, passing the other men on horseback and making a break for the house. He heard Captain Sheffield laughing behind him, but only urged his horse to go faster. Just knowing Mabel was at the house waiting for him strengthened his desire to be there. Working in her vale that day, despite her adamance that she was not bothered by the destruction of her special place, had made him feel close to her. Imagining her wry smile, the way her entire body maintained rigid control even while her eyes danced with amusement. She was incredible, and she was…being carried into the house?

Mac directed Orion toward the front door, sliding from the saddle before his horse had come to a full stop. Tossing the reins to Captain Sheffield, he crossed the drive in large steps, following the footman up to the foyer.

"What happened?" he demanded.

Mabel, his strong, steadfast Mabel, was pale, her face drawn.

Miss Giulia Pepper spoke to the footman and he nodded before heading toward the stairs, Mabel still in his arms. Mac's stomach recoiled. If Mabel should be in anyone's arms, it should be *his*.

He caught up with the man carrying Mabel. "Where are you taking her?"

"To her bedchamber, sir," the young footman responded. Mabel didn't spare Mac a glance.

He looked to Miss Pepper following close behind. "Is she hurt? Have you sent for a doctor? What the devil is going on here?"

Miss Pepper paused at the base of the stairs, forcing Mac to halt beside her. "Mabel fell from a ladder and her leg pains her. Yes, I sent for a doctor to see to her, and no, I do not believe there is cause for alarm."

"How would you know if there is cause or not?" he asked.

She took a sustaining breath, her mouth pinched in disapproval. "I have some healing experience, and I have already looked at the injury myself. It is nothing a good deal of rest cannot heal."

"I will feel better once the doctor has looked at her," Mac said. As confident and collected as Miss Pepper appeared, she could not truly know how Mabel fared. She was not a doctor.

She leaned back a little, appraising him. "You are quite concerned, sir."

He tore his gaze from hers. The last thing he wanted right now was a judgment cast upon him for *caring* about Mabel.

"She needs her rest, Mr. MacKenzie."

He glanced at the short woman over his shoulder before ascending the stairs behind the footman. The young man was clearly struggling. He paused on the landing and Mac cut him off.

"Allow me," he said.

Mabel looked stiff in the arms of the powdered-haired footman. The young man was strapping and tall, but he looked to be struggling, regardless. How far had he carried her? From the stables to the house was a goodly distance.

"I can take her the rest of the way," Mac said when the footman wouldn't relinquish Mabel.

The footman glanced between Mabel and Mac, seemingly unsure. But Mac was tired of waiting. He was not a man to sit by and allow others to make up their minds. If something needed doing, he did it. And in this case, he needed to carry Mabel the rest of the way, so the idiot footman didn't end up dropping her on the stairs.

"I can walk," Mabel said feebly.

Mac slid his hands under her back, easing her away from the servant. "Don't do anything foolish," Mac muttered, pulling Mabel close to his chest. He probably smelled of sweat and dirt, but he didn't care. He hoped she wouldn't care either.

"The only foolish thing I've done was allow that blasted

footman to carry me inside when I can walk perfectly fine," she said weakly. "I'm certain the whole of the house now thinks I'm on death's door, but that could not be farther from the truth."

He would decide that for himself. Taking the stairs one step at a time, Mac tried not to think too much on the feel of Mabel in his arms, her body soft and yielding, long and slender.

Clearing his throat, his fingers tightened on her and she sucked in a tight breath. He paused immediately. "What is it?"

Her gaze flicked away. "Nothing."

"Mabel, be honest with me, please."

Be honest? The man wanted her to be honest with him? Perhaps she ought to tell him that while she was doing her utmost to give Mr. Wright every opportunity to prove that she could be content as his wife, he was falling short of the mark because she compared each and every thing he said and did to Mac. And, unfair as it was, nothing anyone could do quite measured up to Mac in her stupid, nonsensical eyes.

"It really is nothing," she said.

"If it was nothing, would I be carrying you upstairs right now?"

Resisting the urge to scoff, Mabel glanced about for anything to settle her attention on besides Mac's handsome, startlingly close face. The feel of his hands holding her, his heart beating rapidly against her shoulder, was enough to drive a woman mad.

"You are carrying me because you are a stubborn mule and could not allow a footman the pleasure of being the hero," she said. He tugged her leg closer again and she stifled the gasp this time, but the way he pulled her in was both heady and painful.

"I can see the strain in your eyes, Mabel," he said, lowering his voice. "Can you not just tell me how badly you've hurt yourself? How far you fell?"

"I only missed the last few rungs of the ladder. I fell hard on my bad leg and it was something of a chore getting home. It is nothing, but Giulia would not allow me to walk inside."

"A wise woman."

"Thank you," Giulia said from behind Mac. Mabel lifted her head to look over his shoulder and found her friend trailing just behind them, lifting her skirts to follow them up the last few steps and down the corridor. "I have *some* experience in the matter."

Mabel leaned closer, whispering. "You would do well not to make an enemy of my friend, you know. She can be quite a formidable opponent."

Mac glanced down, holding her gaze, and she stilled, trapped in his fiery gaze. "So can I."

He stopped in the corridor and Giulia came around him to open the door to Mabel's bedchamber. "If you could just lay her on the bed, that would be much appreciated."

Mac's steps seemed to slow as he went into Mabel's room, looking about him like a distracted child. Bending, he carefully set her on the mattress, slipping his hands from underneath her, his fingers dragging slowly away. Her breath caught but she tried to disguise it with a poorly executed cough.

"That will be all," Giulia said, standing sentinel near the head of the bed.

Mac remained, feet planted firmly on the wood-planked floor, his gaze fixed on Mabel. "What can I do for you?"

"Understand that I am far from death's door, sir. All I need is a decent night's rest, and I shall be recovered by tomorrow."

His voice lowered. "Is this typical?"

She tried to appear unaffected by his concern, but she was wholly aware of the tall, handsome man standing above her, worried for *her*. "I do not typically fall, no. But when my leg aches, it usually requires nothing more than a night's rest to restore it to functionality."

"I deeply hope that will be the case. I should like to request the first dance at Miss Pepper's ball tomorrow."

Warmth bloomed in Mabel's chest, spreading through her body and down her limbs.

"Can I plan on that, Mabel?" His voice was low, husky.

She glanced to Giulia before directing a nod at Mac.

He bowed. "Goodnight, ladies. If there is anything you stand in need of, please do not hesitate to call on me. I am your servant."

Mac walked from the room and Giulia followed him to close the door. Spinning back, she lifted an eyebrow. "If you think you are going to refrain from telling me what all of that was about, then you are sorely mistaken."

"I do not know—"

"That cannot be true," she said, coming forward and lifting Mabel's hem to get access to her half-boots. She worked on untying the laces. "If you'd like to talk, then I am here to listen."

Mabel's eyelids drifted shut. She *did* wish to unburden herself, to share her worries and fears. How was it that Giulia knew precisely when Mabel would require a listening ear? Managing her inner turmoil over Mac's consistent presence these last few weeks had felt like she was walking a very thin line. She'd been careful to remain properly distanced from his kind smile and the heady warmth he ignited in her, constantly reminding herself that he did not mean anything beyond friendship. Sure, he cared for Mabel. But he did not love her.

The fall from the ladder, the final breaking point in her equilibrium, had pushed Mabel beyond her scope of self-control. She wished to unburden her heart and hoped that in confessing she could release these feelings for good.

"I once thought myself very much in love with Mac."

"Mac?"

Mabel's cheeks warmed. "Mr. MacKenzie."

Giulia shot her a wry smile. "I realized that. I was only surprised. How long have you been on such intimate terms?"

"We've known one another for most of our lives," Mabel said, doing her best to sound nonchalant. "Years ago I shared with him how I felt, and it was mortifying. Needless to say, he did not return my regard then, and I know he does not now. But it is difficult, at times, to remind myself of that when he is near."

"But he has singled you out, asking you to dance with him tomorrow night. Surely that must mean something?"

Mabel gritted her teeth as Giulia slid her half-boot free, pulling at her leg. Pain sliced up her thigh.

"But perhaps you won't be dancing tomorrow after all."

Mabel tried to smile. "Usually a night's rest is enough—"

"This is not a usual situation though, is it?"

Mabel noted the grim smile on her friend's face but didn't reply. Exhaustion tugged at her eyelids, pulling them lower.

"Let's hope the doctor will arrive soon so you might go to sleep."

Little, quick footsteps beat down the corridor. Pippa crashed into Mabel's room, taking one fearful look at her sister before bounding across the room and jumping into Mabel's bed.

"Oh Mabel, I hate that you're hurt!"

"Then you might appreciate that your bouncing her about is not going to help her heal very quickly," Giulia said, rounding the bed and taking Pippa's hand, tugging her. "Come, Pippa. Let's leave Mabel to rest." She glanced up and caught Mabel's eye. "I will send up your maid."

"Thank you, Giulia."

She paused in the doorway, Pippa now pulling on her arm. "Of course. I hope you know that I will still be here for you in whatever way I can."

"I know." Mabel smiled, but her whole body felt as though it was sinking into the feather mattress, the world dimming about her as she looked at her friend. Regardless of Giulia's intentions, things would change once she married and moved away. They could change even more if Mabel married Mr. Wright, if she accepted his hand and allowed him to take her far away from Devon. Maybe an escape was precisely what she needed. She could bring Gram and Pippa with her, and they would be happy anyway, as long as they were together.

The idea had merit but did not settle well in her heart. Devon was where she belonged, where her mother was buried, and her family land remained. If she was to leave this place, to ask the same of her grandmother and sister, she needed to be wholly certain that it was the right choice.

She was inclined to think that anything that took her far away from Liam MacKenzie was a good idea, but it would mean marriage to a man she did not love.

The doctor would be arriving any moment, and Mabel snuggled down into the blankets to wait. Perhaps she would consider the idea later in greater detail, but for now, she needed to focus on healing.

CHAPTER 21

$\mathcal{M}$ac pierced the shovel into the soft, damp earth and released it, careful to make sure it would remain upright before stepping away and hitting his hands against his pant legs.

"Calling it a day?" Wright asked, tossing his own shovel aside. Had no one ever taught the man that leaving a shovel lying in the grass was foolish? Anyone could step on it unawares, ending up with a wooden handle in the face.

Mac crossed the roped-off perimeter of the cottage they were leveling the ground for and picked up the shovel, striking it into the earth as Wright walked away. It was too bad Captain Sheffield faced the trees now. He really had a knack for missing Wright's more idiotic moves.

"Are you looking forward to the ball?" Charles asked, coming behind Mac and slapping him on the back.

Mac watched Wright's distinctive swagger as he crossed the torn-up vale, saying something to the captain and then throwing his head back in laughter.

"Mac?" Charles said again.

He scrubbed a hand over his face. The ball. He'd forgotten. He hadn't spared a thought for anything that day beyond the house they were building, or visions would creep into his mind of Mabel, lying in her bed with her leg bandaged and paining her. She had told him last night she expected to be recovered after a much-needed rest, but he was unable to cease his worrying.

He cared about Mabel, that was certain. He always had, even when they were children and the stakes of life were so much lower. But now? Now his body ached at the thought of her discomfort, his mind worried over the prospect of her pain.

Charles took his contemplation as an answer, evidently, and chuckled. "The things we do for our family, eh?" His voice sounded strained, uneven.

"What bothers you?"

Charles looked over abruptly, holding Mac's gaze. "It is nothing, really. Childish worries. I held a long-time fondness for Amelia Mason, you might recall? She is Amelia Fawn now."

Mac remembered. Charles had fallen madly in love with Amelia—Mrs. Fawn—when they were young, and she had written him off immediately, marrying another man instead. Charles had been gutted. But he'd rallied and done his best to move on.

The other men in their party had all found their horses and were leaving for the day when Mac finally reached Orion. "Do you expect to see Mrs. Fawn this evening?"

"Yes," Charles said. "But I have every hope of believing Miss Pemberton is about to make me a very, very happy man. So it matters not what Mrs. Fawn thinks, does it?"

"I suppose not." Mac obtained the saddle, turning Orion about to face the path through the woods. "That cannot make it any easier to face the woman, however. Or so I would imagine."

Charles blew through his lips. "No. To be honest, I am more

concerned over seeing her again than I gather I ought to be." He shook his head, disgust bubbling from his throat. "Miss Pemberton deserves better than the likes of me."

"Is that why you have not offered for her yet?"

He glanced up quickly, eyes widened. "I hadn't considered that before. But maybe there is some truth to what you say, and I have yet to allow myself to think too much on it."

"Well," Mac said, offering his friend a smile, "let us return home quickly, dress in our dratted britches and go dance with our women."

Charles's head tilted back, and he shot Mac a considering look. "*Our* women? Who do you have your eye on?"

Mabel's name danced on the end of his tongue. Would it be unwise to share his feelings with the man who felt very much like her brother? If any person had a right to learn of Mac's intentions, it was Mabel's father. But Charles was a close second.

A small scream pierced the waning afternoon and both men turned toward the sound, Charles's question forgotten in an instant as Mac spurred Orion on. Another scream followed the first and he urged his horse to go faster, darting through the trees until he approached the clearing where he had skipped rocks with Pippa and Mabel a few days before.

Pippa stood on the edge of the pond, her hands fisted by her sides and an angry red mark on one cheek. "I told you to come down here and fight me!" she hollered. "Stop hiding in the trees like a coward!"

"I'm no coward!" a voice yelled back.

"Yes you are!"

A high voice said, "Pippa, maybe—"

Pippa turned toward the soft voice and Mac followed the sound as well to find two young girls standing on the other side of the path, huddled close together, uncertainty lacing their features. They looked familiar, their blonde curls swaying in the breeze as he searched his mind to place them.

Ah. The young girls who had been playing with Pippa in the schoolroom that day when Mabel and Mac had interrupted their play practice. He swung down from Orion, looping his reins over a nearby branch.

Pippa's head whipped around and she caught Mac's gaze, a triumphant smile stretching over her lips. Charles dismounted behind Mac and came up beside him, his eyebrows drawn together. "What is this about?"

"Jacob Tucker hit me with a branch!" Pippa said.

"I did not!" the accused argued from within the safety of the tree branches. "I just let go of the branch and she walked into it."

"On purpose!" Pippa shrieked. "He let go of it on purpose!"

Charles stepped forward. "It is time to return home, Pippa. This screaming is unbecoming of a lady and you must desist immediately."

Her mouth opened to argue, and Mac stepped forward. "Perhaps we ought to get your friends home, Pippa?"

Her eyes darted to where her two young friends stood, and her cheeks pinked. The boy in the tree sniggered and Pippa pivoted toward him. She was going to be trouble when she grew up if Mac wasn't missing the mark here.

"It's getting late, Pippa," Mac said, offering her his hand. "Should we return to the house?"

"Probably," she said with a defiant little shrug. She gestured to her friends and they followed along.

Mac hooked Orion's reins over his arm and led the horse as Pippa and her friends fell in beside him. They started back toward the Sheffield house.

"Am I correct in my understanding that the three of you are preparing to put on a performance?" Mac asked, eyeing Pippa and her quiet, solemn friends.

Pippa's face lit up. "Yes! You already know about it, Mac. That is why we came out here, actually. We needed to practice."

"And the Tucker boy?"

Her little nose wrinkled up, and he noticed her friends' noses mimic its actions. "He followed us. And I'll get him for it."

Hooves clopped behind them, bringing Charles up to their group. He had the Tucker boy on his horse and shot Mac a disgruntled look. "I'm going to see Jacob home. Can you take the girls?"

Mac saluted his friend and they separated in opposite directions. He would have to ask Charles the nature of that boy's relationship with Pippa. He shot the little sprite a side-glance. Or he could ask *her* now.

"What do you plan to do?"

Pippa glanced up, startled. "What do you mean?"

He lowered his voice, darting his glance between each of the rapt girls as they began walking again. "How do you intend to get your revenge on your enemy?"

She looked to her friends before standing taller. "We have a plan."

"Can you share it with me?"

"No."

Mac almost missed a step but caught himself. "Pippa, if you are planning something dangerous—"

She laughed. "It's not dangerous."

He lifted his eyebrow and she returned a look of pure confidence. "Does Mabel know of this plan?"

"Yes. To a degree."

What sort of answer was that?

"Our play is nearly ready. I hope you will be there. You *did* promise," she said, her eyes bright.

"I wouldn't miss it."

She nodded, appearing satisfied by this interaction. "Katie, June, let's go," Pippa said, taking off in a sudden run. The quiet girls looked to Mac before the taller blonde whispered to her sister and then they ran, following behind their leader.

Mac chuckled, watching them go down the path. The house was in view and they went straight toward it, so he jumped into the saddle and urged Orion forward, passing the girls as they entered the clearing. He would need to inform Mabel of this development. She would know how to move forward.

He rode onto the gravel drive in front of the house and pulled Orion to a stop, his gaze riveted by the woman standing in the doorway, her hand resting lightly on the frame. Mabel. She was beautiful. Her hair swept behind her and her ball gown billowing in the slight breeze.

Their eyes locked and Mac had to work to swallow. He was inordinately pleased that she was dressed for the ball, that there was a chance he'd have the opportunity to dance with the woman he loved.

His heart jumped, the truth of that statement spreading warmth through his body. It felt good to acknowledge how he felt. Now he just had to make sure he had something to offer her before Wright swooped in.

Pippa reached her, barreling into Mabel and nearly knocking her over. The smile that lit her face transformed her from a woman of dignity and poise to something far lovelier. How could Mac have refused the lock of hair she had offered him in the vale all those years ago? He hadn't loved her then, not in the way she'd wanted him to. He could kick his younger self for not recognizing her value as he did now.

Still, his mind had been so consumed; the grief he'd felt, little more than a boy himself, over his father's carelessness and the way it had torn his family apart and forced him into a life at sea had blocked all other feelings and emotions. When Mabel had presented him with a lock of her hair, he'd been angry, revolting against the situation that had forced him to leave his beloved Devon. Her offered token had pained him, and he had lashed out.

Mabel had not deserved that. Not then, and never again. He watched her shoo Pippa and her friends into the house, glancing up with a questioning look. Did he look a fool hovering on his horse in the middle of her gravel drive? He didn't care. His heart was brimming with regret and love. Love for such a strong, incredible woman.

Forget Wright and Desmond. Mac had known her first, and he was just as eligible now with his career behind him and the prizes hopefully heading his way. He could—but no, he could *not* offer for her, could he? Not until he had taken care of his obligations first.

But he would. He would free his father from the shameful bond of the Marshalsea, set up a home for his mother, and then offer for Mabel.

He just needed to ensure that another man did not win her heart first.

Mabel led Katie and June Traynor into the parlor where their mother sat waiting for them and saw the women off before returning to her bedchamber. She had spent the entire day abed and boredom had gnawed at her for sitting so idly, but her leg appreciated the rest. She could now walk with minimal aching, though dancing would certainly be out of the question that evening.

A lowering thought, considering the promise she had made to Mac to possibly partner him in the first set. She had spent many afternoons as a girl dreaming of dancing with Mac in a glittering ballroom like the one in Halstead Manor, and her dreams would almost become a reality that night.

Lifting her mother's garnets from the dressing table, Mabel

noted the stark contrast the deep red made against her milky throat, and she lowered them back to the table. This was not the sort of attention she wished to draw to herself. Pulling the single strand of white pearls from her mother's jewelry box, she fastened them around her neck and stepped back. They contrasted her mauve silk gown nicely and were the right amount of elegance to help her feel made up without overdoing it. A woman who planned to sit out the entire evening did not need to glitter on the dance floor, anyway.

At least she would have Amelia to sit beside—the woman wore her widow's weeds like a badge of honor and hadn't danced a set since her third wedding if Mabel remembered correctly.

A tiny sob in the doorway drew her attention and Mabel shot a rueful glance over her shoulder. "Pippa, I told you that you are too young to come to the ball."

"But I *dearly* wish to come! Does that mean nothing?"

"It means that you will be much disappointed, and ought to recall that you are only seven. When you are fifteen, you can attend every ball your heart desires."

"But fifteen is so far away," she said, popping out her lower lip. "It is unfair of you to leave me here alone."

"You won't be alone. You will have Hope in the schoolroom, as you always do, to watch over and keep you safe."

Pippa scoffed, and Mabel turned back for the looking glass so she might hide her mirth from her sister. But the glint of longing in Pippa's eyes tugged at her heart, and Mabel held out her arms, which her sister ran into.

"You know, I have an idea," Mabel said, drawing out the words, her chin resting on top of Pippa's head.

"What is it?" the small voice replied.

"An outing to the seaside has been proposed," she said, feeling Pippa's body stiffen in her arms. "And if you are very good for Hope and complete all of the tasks Giulia has asked you to do, I see no reason why you cannot accompany us."

Pippa lifted her head, her eyes sparkling. "Oh, yes, Mabel. Please let me come. I will be so good!"

"I am certain you will," she said ruefully. It was easy to be good when such a tantalizing treat was on the line. "Now run upstairs and eat your dinner. I must see to our guests."

Pippa nodded, jumping up and skipping from the room.

Mabel shot one last glance in the looking glass before rising and smoothing out the skirt of her gown. She lifted her mother's ivory lace shawl from where it rested on the end of the bed and draped it over her shoulders, tugging it close as though the length of fabric was actually her mother's arms coming around her in a comforting embrace.

Rubbing her hand down her leg, she massaged as she moved, hoping to keep the throbbing at bay for the evening. While resting for most of the day had done much to allow her use of her leg once again, it was far from healed. If only she had never broken the dratted thing to begin with. But she could not change the past; she could only do her best to manage it better in the future.

Their guests were all gathered in the foyer and Mabel searched the group for Giulia but came up empty. Gram sat on a chair against the wall, both hands wrapped in lace gloves and resting on the top of her walking stick. She looked positively gloomy and it brought a smile to Mabel's lips. The woman was so crotchety, but Mabel didn't blame her. She would be irritable too if she could not hear half of what was being said to her.

Miss Pemberton hung from Charles's arm, resplendent in a gown of pale blue silk, her hair done up and strung with beads of pearls. Beside her, her sister fanned herself with one gloved hand while the other smoothed out her thin gown.

"The carriage should be waiting," Mabel said to her cousin. "I am going to remain behind and ride with Giulia."

"And Gram?" Charles asked.

"Gram may come with us."

He nodded.

A throat cleared behind her. "May I escort you to the ball, Miss Sheffield?"

She turned, bestowing a benevolent smile on Mr. Wright. "Your carriage will be ahead of mine, sir, but I thank you for the honor of your request."

He dipped his head in acknowledgment. "Then may I have the privilege of the first dance?"

"I am afraid the first set has already been claimed," Mac said, stepping forward. His imposing figure towered over Mr. Wright, and the shorter man's face grew tight.

"I shall see you at Halstead," Mabel said, stepping forward. "I plan to wait here for Giulia."

"Splendid." Miss Sophy snapped her fan shut. "Shall we be off?"

Mr. Pemberton offered his sister his arm, and they led the way outside. Charles led Miss Pemberton out behind them, followed by Mr. Wright and Mrs. Boucher. Gram started to rise but Mabel put a staying hand on her shoulder. "Would you like to ride with me and Giulia?"

Gram nodded, sitting again.

Mac hovered before the door, his hat in his hands. "Shall I remain behind? I might accompany you." The man was striking in his crisp black jacket, the stark white cravat at his throat tied perfectly. His hair was still damp, and she watched a water droplet fall onto his shoulder and trail down his arm.

Mabel swallowed hard. Mac was not making it easy to fall out of love with him. He looked as though he intended to step toward her, and she moved back, beside her grandmother. "We will see you there, Mr. MacKenzie."

He nodded and left, allowing Mabel the space to breathe. She leaned against the wall, her hand coming to rest on her heart.

"That MacKenzie boy has grown into a handsome lad," Gram said, startling Mabel. Her periods of awareness came at the oddest times.

She followed Mac's sure, smooth steps out to the carriage and watched him slip inside. "Indeed, Gram," she whispered. "He has become exceedingly handsome."

CHAPTER 22

*M*abel stepped into the bustling ballroom, Gram on her arm, and glanced about for a place to settle. An abundance of candles lit the room from the enormous chandelier overhead with extra candles set before mirrors against the walls. It appeared as though every person who lived in or around Graton was in attendance, their laughter and conversation filling the room with more light than the candles could muster on their own.

Mabel, having left Giulia in the corridor to steal a quiet moment alone with her betrothed, did not need to greet her hostess and sought out a good place to plant herself and Gram for the duration of the evening.

"Come, Gram," she said, leading her grandmother around a group of women toward a set of empty chairs against the back wall and then helping her to sit.

"Do you feel that draught?" Gram asked, looking about as though she would see it, her mouth bent into a frown. "I don't wish to catch cold."

Mabel found the culprit—a nearby window cracked open just a smidge. "I will correct it for you."

"You aren't leaving me, are you?" Gram asked, her feeble hand clasping Mabel's wrist.

Shaking her head, Mabel laid a hand over Gram's and squeezed. "I am only going to shut the window, and then I will return."

Gram nodded and Mabel slipped her hand free, encircling her wrist where Gram had clutched her. If she was to follow her father's plan and marry Mr. Wright, what would become of Gram? Would she accompany them to Warwickshire, or refuse to leave Sheffield House? The woman did not truly need Mabel the way she thought she did. Any number of young, responsible women could take Mabel's place in caring for Gram. But that did not mean Gram didn't rely on Mabel, to say nothing of how Mabel relied on Gram.

Had Papa considered his own mother when he had made the plan to wed Mabel to his lieutenant?

Clasping the wooden casing to the window, Mabel shoved downward, but it would not budge. Setting her fan on the ledge, she got a better grip on the window and gave it another push. But still, the thing would not move.

"May I be of some assistance?" a soft, masculine voice said behind her. *Mac.*

Mabel's heart thumped in her chest, beating so loudly she could feel it hammering against her breastbone. Mac's quiet voice was enough to send her into the vapors. She needed to get a handle on her feelings, or she was bound to say something she shouldn't.

She turned, and words failed her. Why was he looking at her in that way? His eyes glittered, so serious and unwavering, and she swallowed. "I was hoping to cut off a draught, but this dratted window won't close."

"Allow me?"

She stepped aside and Mac gripped the window, giving it a push. Even with his effort, it would not move. He shot her a rueful glance. "I would have been far more obliged to the window had it done my bidding."

"Perhaps you need to try again," Mabel suggested.

Mac stilled, holding her gaze. "I had that same thought. Sometimes when something does not go the way we planned the first time, we merely ought to try again."

Her breath caught, and Mabel longed to tear her eyes away from the tall, handsome man before her. He held her captive within his gaze and she couldn't look away. He wanted to say something—she could feel it.

Giulia's and Nick Pepper's entrance was announced, gathering the attention from the room and slicing the cord that had bound Mabel to Mac. She drew in a breath, turning to join the occupants of the ball in congratulating the happy couple.

A thunk sounded behind her and she turned to see the window closed, Mac standing triumphantly beside it. "I only needed to try again."

"So it would seem."

He picked up the fan that she'd left on the windowsill. She reached for it, and he hesitated before placing it in her hand.

She gestured to her grandmother and he nodded, clasping his hands behind his back before stepping beside her. "How is your injury?"

"Better," she said. Biting her lip, she gave him an apologetic smile. "But I cannot dance tonight. I fear one day of rest was not enough, as I had hoped it would be."

"Never mind that," he said with a dismissive wave. "I would be happy to have your company for the duration of the set instead. Might I sit beside you?"

Her body warmed at the question, her pulse quickening. "Of course." Her voice was unsteady, and she busied her fingers arranging her shawl about her shoulders.

Gram's craggy voice startled her. "What did that man say to you?"

Mabel's cheeks warmed. Hadn't Gram just recognized him earlier that evening? Leaning close to Gram, she said, "That man is Mr. MacKenzie, Gram. He has requested the next set, but I am unable to dance. So he will join us here."

Gram gave Mac a shrewd side-glance and he smiled at her. She had mentioned him by name just an hour before; her mind must really be leaving if she could forget Mac so quickly.

"May I join you, ladies?" he asked.

"Certainly," Gram said with a gesture to the chair beside Mabel. Mac took the seat and his shoulder brushed against hers, sending a wave of shivers up her arm.

The next dance was announced, and couples filed from the surrounding crowds, forming the set with broad smiles and antsy feet. Mr. Wright stood at the end of the line, Miss Sophy his partner, and they had the looks on their faces of two people doing their utmost not to laugh. Charles was some way down the line across from Miss Pemberton, and while Mabel could not see his face from where she sat, she imagined him to be very much anticipating this dance.

"Do you long to be out there?" Mac asked, pulling her attention from the group as the song began.

"No. I do love to dance, of course, but when my leg aches this way it is not in the least enjoyable. I do not find myself at a loss for being unable to join my friends when I know it would hurt excessively." And it did. She'd overestimated herself, and just sitting here was painful enough. Mabel never should have left her house today; not after her fall in the barn.

"Has your leg pained you in this way for long?"

She trained her gaze on Miss Sophy at the end of the line so she would not be forced to endure the pity on Mac's face. His tone spoke of sorrow and regret, and both of those were useless, given the situation. "It has only been four years since the initial injury, sir. I'm sure if I'd had a physician attend me, I would be better off now, but as it stood, we had no one in the neighborhood and my father's farrier stepped into the role."

Mac's voice grew incredulous. "His farrier?"

"What else could we have done? Dr. Mason was not yet practicing here and the man who we relied on in those situations was not in town at that time. He had gone to visit his sister in London, and I had no choice but to receive the help I was given."

"Some help that was," he muttered.

Mabel turned in her seat the slightest bit and her knee brushed against Mac's. She righted that blunder and moved her knee back a little, but Mac's eyes darkened a fraction. "You need not look so angry, Mac. My father came home on leave shortly after my injury and required every physician he could conjure to come and see what could be done about my leg, but by then it was too late. I had to choose between limping for the rest of my life or allowing them to break the bones again in an effort to set them properly—with the caveat that it might be an impossibility. They could *try*, but there was no promise of success."

"So you refused."

"Yes, Mac. I refused. The limp is not lovely by any means, but I would rather the one I know than perhaps something much worse."

"What did your father want you to do?"

"My father wants me to be happy. He allowed me to make the decision for myself and supported me when I did. He has never mentioned it again, and neither have I."

"You are a strong woman."

Mabel stilled. No one had ever called her a strong woman before, and the words, coming from Mac's lips, managed to steal her breath. She glanced down, tracing the hems of the gowns in front of her with her eyes to give her something to focus on. Last time Mac had treated Mabel with care and regard, she had fallen in love with him and he had turned around and rejected her. She was dangerously close to repeating those offenses and it was utterly terrifying. She wanted him to mean the things he said, and that made it infinitely worse that he couldn't.

He was merely a nice man. And she would do best not to fall for his kindness again.

Mac could not imagine the sheer amount of pain Mabel must have endured when the farrier—the *farrier* for heaven's sake—had failed to accurately set her leg. It was a miracle she could walk at all, given the circumstances. He recalled the first time he'd noticed her limp when they had taken that walk around the pond, and how slight it had been just days after his arrival in Devon.

Mabel must have put an inordinate amount of strain on herself the last few weeks to have begun limping the way she was. To say nothing for falling from a ladder. She had told him she was distracted, but he would have bet money her bad leg gave out from beneath her due to the stress she had recently put on it.

"How is the work progressing in Larkspur Vale?"

Her question caught him off guard and he had to remind himself of their very public setting. He longed to shove aside all thoughts of others and pull her into his arms, to soothe her and make certain she never took another step ever again if it pained her; her large, round eyes blinking up at him broke through his daydream and landed him on level ground.

The sound of the music rushed into his ears all at once and he shook his head.

A concerned line formed on her forehead. "Are things going poorly already?"

"No, not at all. I have reason to believe we will complete the cottages ahead of schedule, in fact."

"Then why do you look so stormy, Mac?"

"Do I?" He leaned back in his seat, rubbing a finger over his jaw. He could not help looking stormy, he supposed. But it was a little embarrassing she was able to see through him so easily.

Her answering smile was stunning. "Yes, sir. You do."

"Well, perhaps it is because I would rather be dancing."

Mabel's face shuttered so quickly, Mac wanted to throw something. He rubbed the back of his neck. "No, I did not mean—"

She raised her eyebrows. "By all means, sir. I do not expect you to sit out with me when you'd rather be dancing. I do not hold you accountable to your request, particularly after I am unable to comply—"

"No, Mabel. I only meant—"

"Really, Mac," she said, her voice stern, but a smile bravely fought to remain on her lips. "I am not so weak as to be offended."

"Good. Because I do not plan on doing any such thing. I *meant* that I would rather—"

Her eyes closed and she lifted a hand in protest. "Do not concern yourself—"

Mac grabbed her lifted hand and pulled it down, holding her fingers tightly within his. She paused, glancing to him, startled.

"If you would allow me to speak, Mabel, you would understand that I did not mean I would rather dance than sit here with you. I meant that I would rather be dancing *with you*, holding you in my arms, than sitting out and watching your friends enjoy themselves."

She was silent, searching his face.

He dipped his head, holding her gaze. "In the case that you should not dance, however, I would much prefer to spend the whole of the evening in this chair, beside you, than anywhere else in this room."

Her eyes widened further, and he hoped he hadn't gone too

far. But how many hints could a man drop? Should Mabel not realize by now that he was implying his feelings for her had grown, developed? Soon he would need to speak to her explicitly about the matter and take her answer as it stood.

But, not yet. He could not speak his heart until he knew for a surety he could support her.

"Is that little Amelia?" Mrs. Sheffield asked, lifting her fan and waving to a woman dressed in black.

"Yes, Gram," Mabel said loudly, shifting closer to her grandmother. Mac felt the distance and wished he had it in his authority to slide her closer to him once again.

But *little Amelia* was coming their way, her gaze darting between Mabel and her grandmother, and Mac. Her deep red hair was pulled back in a conservative style, the black ball gown done up in what appeared to be the most recent fashions. He knew Amelia but couldn't recall her new surname. Mrs. Ferris... no, that did not sound right.

"Good evening," she said, dipping into a curtsy.

Mabel gestured between them. "Mr. MacKenzie, you remember Mrs. Fawn?"

Ah, that was it. Mac rose immediately and caught Charles's gaze over the top of the woman's head. Charles watched her move despite his dance partner requiring his attention. He bumbled along the set, doing his best to smile at Miss Pemberton, but Mac could see clearly on his friend's face how difficult it was for him to tear his gaze away from Mrs. Fawn.

Mac bowed. He indicated the chair beside Mabel. "Please, take my seat."

"Thank you, sir." She took the offered chair, but her scrutiny remained on him. "It has been a few years. Is this a long visit?"

Mac clasped his hands behind his back, planting his feet firmly. "No, unfortunately."

Mabel's head swung around, her beautiful eyes startled. "Are you leaving us soon?"

"When the cottages are finished, I'll no longer have a reason to remain." He watched her, hoping to see a spark of emotion—anything which might reveal her disappointment at his confession. He'd provoked her with purpose, and it appeared to have been for naught. Her face looked carved from stone, so still and emotionless it was.

He tried not to feel hurt by her lack of emotion, but she brushed him away like a stray piece of lint on her sleeve.

"I will leave you to visit together." Mac dipped a bow, waiting as the women acknowledged him with a nod—Mrs. Sheffield, with cool indifference—then walked away.

CHAPTER 23

*A*melia was silent until Mac moved out of earshot and then leaned in. "I would very much like to know why you have not mentioned him before now."

"I did," Mabel reminded her friend. "I spoke of him at the literary society."

"Hmm." Amelia did not look convinced. She followed Mac's retreat, her eyebrows pulling together. "But you did not say how handsome he has grown. Since when have you kept secrets from me?"

"Am I not allowed that luxury?"

"No, you most certainly are not," Amelia answered, chuckling, amusement dancing in her eyes. "Not unless you really must."

Mabel hesitated. This was the second time in as many days that a dear friend of hers had asked to be admitted into her confidence. She was not typically so tight-fisted with her secrets, but Mac seemed like so much more than a confidential piece of information. This mattered so much more.

"I can see you wrestling with the idea of speaking about it, so please, forget I said anything. If anyone might understand the need to hold things close to one's heart, Mabel, it is me. Some things are simply too painful to speak aloud."

A sudden shift occurred between them, and Mabel leaned back, taking in Amelia's gentle acceptance. What sort of things had Amelia kept from her? Mabel did not know the details of each of Amelia's marriages, nor the particulars of her husbands' deaths, beyond what was generally known. Amelia had always been rather private, and Mabel had always respected her friend's desires to keep things to herself.

Now, Amelia was willing to do the same for her. But Mabel was different. She had relied on her friends after her mother's death, and when she became upset following her father's many returns to sea. She could rely on them now, too.

"I only feel that I must guard my heart from Mr. MacKenzie's sly, clever tongue."

Amelia's face hardened. "What has he said to offend you?"

"No, it is nothing like that. I only fear that if I do not take great care, I may fall in love with him again." She lifted her shoulder. "And if I do that, I am bound to be heartbroken."

"Again?" Amelia asked softly.

Mabel nodded, shooting her friend a wry smile. "I tried to send him off to the navy with a lock of my hair. He soundly refused it."

Shock spread over Amelia's face. "Well, I never…"

"I did not tell a soul. I was utterly mortified."

"I don't doubt it." Grasping Mabel's hand, Amelia squeezed it.

"He was so charming then, I had believed…but that is neither here nor there. I am merely horrible at knowing when a gentleman is being kind, and when he might mean more than kindness."

Shaking her head, Amelia frowned. "Do you want my advice?"

"Yes."

"Stay away from him. I saw the way he looked at you, Mabel. He is clearly interested in you. And if you know that to be false, or merely friendship poorly disguised as more, then you are better off keeping your distance." She searched Mabel's face. "If you can, I would suggest doing your utmost to avoid being around him as often as you can. He mentioned he won't be here much longer. If you put distance between you now, it will surely make that parting easier to bear."

Mabel nodded, sucking in a breath. "I did not wish to hear that."

"I'm sorry, Mabel."

"No, don't be. It is sound advice." She turned, giving Amelia her full attention. "Thank you for being honest with me. I could not ask for a more supportive friend."

"Friend? I like to think of us as sisters."

A smile came to her lips and she nodded. She had long since thought of Amelia and Hattie as her sisters and now felt the same way about Giulia. She often thanked God for putting these supportive women in her life. She would not have been able to bear the difficulties of life without them. "Where is Hattie? I have not seen her yet."

"Dancing," Amelia said with a nod toward the center of the room.

"Mabel," Gram said. "Mabel!"

"Yes?" Turning, she placed a hand on Gram's forearm. "I am still here."

"Are they serving anything stronger than lemonade? I must have something. I'm parched."

"Allow me to fetch you something," a deep voice said behind her. Mabel turned to find Mr. Wright smiling broadly down at them. She introduced him to Amelia and thanked him for the offer, and he left to procure something stronger to appease Gram.

"And who is *he*?" Amelia asked. "There was no mistaking the way he looked at you, either."

"That," Mabel said, drawing in a sustaining breath, "is the man my father would like me to marry."

Mac downed the remainder of his drink in one gulp. He watched Mabel from across the ballroom, Wright dancing attendance on her. The idiot had been hovering around the Sheffield women for the last hour, and Mac wanted to march across the polished wooden floor and demand to know why Mabel allowed Wright to linger near her. But that would be odd, so instead, he glowered from afar.

"You are bound to burn a hole in the man if you keep watching him that way," Charles said, swirling his own glass.

They leaned against the wall, Mac watching Mabel, and Charles gazing in the same general direction.

"Miss Pemberton looks lovely this evening," Mac said.

Charles's reply was noncommittal. "Hmm."

"You disagree?"

"No. She does look lovely." Charles took a sip, his voice lowering. "And it is entirely unfair. I should be ecstatic to have such an amazing creature interested in sharing a life with me, and yet, I cannot fathom asking anyone but Amelia Fawn to fill the role."

"You cannot force her to love you," Mac said, doing his best to be gentle.

"What shall I do, then?" Charles turned, folding his arms over his chest, and looked at Mac. "Is it fair to Miss Pemberton to marry her when my heart belongs to another woman? I have tried to forget Amelia, to replace her, to distance myself...*nothing* has worked."

"I cannot answer that, Charles. Only you and Miss

Pemberton can decide for yourselves if it is fair. But if the arrangement is satisfactory to both you and Miss Pemberton, then I see no reason why you cannot still marry her."

Charles did not reply. His brow furrowed, and he nodded absently.

"Where is your uncle this evening?" Mac asked.

"You didn't hear? He was called to London. An urgent missive arrived."

"What was the nature of the missive?"

Charles shrugged. "He plans to be home by the end of the week, so it could not have been too extensive."

Mrs. Boucher crossed the perimeter of the ballroom, selecting the empty seat beside Mrs. Sheffield and lowering herself into the chair. Miss Pemberton and Miss Sophy remained on the dance floor in the midst of a country dance, and Mac watched their companion strike up a conversation with Mabel's grandmother. The two had become friends if Mac took their measure correctly.

"What do you plan to do once the houses are finished?" Charles asked, pulling Mac from his trance.

He straightened, shooting his friend a half-smile. "I need to free my father at the first possible moment, and then set to finding an estate we can afford with whatever I have left. I've often wondered..."

"What?"

Mac shook his head. "I should be horsewhipped for allowing the thought a moment's time."

"You cannot say such things, for now I must know what you were about to say."

The dance came to its conclusion and the Pemberton sisters were led toward the Sheffield party and their companion. Amelia Fawn still sat beside Mabel—the woman had not left her post all evening—but other women came and went, and that side of the room appeared a veritable hotbed of company.

"Of course if it is truly of a sensitive nature," Charles said, lifting a shoulder, "then forget I pressed you at all."

"No, it is merely uncharitable. I would prefer *not* to help my father, but it is the lowest of filth who would leave their parent to rot in prison when they have the means to free him."

"Perhaps, but you are human. No one expects perfection of you, Mac."

"Or they would be sorely disappointed."

Charles pushed off from the wall. "I am going to ask her to dance."

"Miss Pemberton?"

Charles's determined, narrowed gaze found the object of his desires and clung to her. "Mrs. Fawn."

A warning went off in Mac's chest, and he held out a hand to halt his friend. "Hold for a moment, Charles, and think about this. How many times have you asked her to dance before in your life?"

"Countless."

"And how many of those times has she accepted the request?"

Charles's mouth shut. He swallowed, his throat bobbing. "None."

"Yet Miss Pemberton, who stands just two paces away from Mrs. Fawn, might overhear this request, yes? How shall that make her feel?"

"She is unaware of my feelings for...but I do see what you are getting at." He sighed, rubbing a hand down his face. "Perhaps I ought to ask Miss Sophy instead. I must do *something* to busy myself, Mac, or I will go blasted mad, and I've already asked Miss Pemberton twice."

"Then you ask Miss Sophy, and I will inquire of her sister. We will pass this evening as swiftly as we can."

With that battle plan in place, the men moved out, picking their way through the crowded ballroom toward their targets.

They passed Miss Giulia Pepper on the arm of a tall, blond gentleman—her intended, Mac had earlier learned—the two of them positively beaming. He hoped to one day look as pleased as this man did, and hoped it was Mabel hanging from his arm, looking as smitten as Miss Pepper did now.

Someday. Someday was sure to come, once everything was put in order.

They approached the group, Wright's overbearing voice breaking through the din of voices and assaulting Mac's ears.

"I know just the place for a seaside venture, and I should be most happy to escort you there," Wright said, his attention fixed on Mabel.

"A trip to the sea sounds most delightful. What place is that, Mr. Wright?"

"You've probably not heard of it. It is a small oasis of a place, really, called Camden Cove."

Mac's teeth clenched, his blood rushing up past his ears so loud he could not make sense of what else was being said around him. Of course Mabel had heard of the place; anyone from Graton would have. But how had *Wright* heard of it?

If this interloper thought he could slide into Devon and pretend he was a local, he was bound to be disappointed.

"Mr. MacKenzie," a sly, feminine voice said at his elbow.

He turned, stunned to find Miss Sophy there, her hand sliding up his arm and wrapping around it like a declaration. Her other hand closed over the first. Did she not realize they were in a crowded ballroom full of Graton's gentility?

Her voice, silky and slick, dripped over him like an unpleasant rain. "I have heard you make mention of Camden Cove before, but I cannot recall why. Would you care to remind me?"

"I cannot think what you are referring to."

She pouted, her lip jutting forth, and pressed herself into him. Mac felt as though all eyes in the ballroom were on them.

He tried to disentangle himself from her grasp, but she was unrelenting, gripping him fast. Panic bloomed in his chest, pounding his heart hard. He stepped back, but Miss Sophy only stepped with him, laying her head on his arm.

It was happening *again*. The wily woman was entangling herself with him in such a public place on purpose, putting him in a predicament. He must either be utterly rude to her or give rise to gossip about the nature of their—truly nonexistent—relationship. Glancing around for something or someone to help him, Mac found Mabel watching him and he froze.

Her eyes were wholly transfixed on his arm and Miss Sophy's secure hold there. Mrs. Fawn said something to Mabel, and she snapped her head around, but the furrow upon her brow would not yield. Standing, Mabel smoothed out her dress, taking Mrs. Fawn by the arm, and they slipped away together quietly, Mabel's limp more pronounced now than ever before.

Yanking his arm free, he heard Miss Sophy yelp softly. But he did not care. He'd been such a fool to imagine her changed. He'd let his guard down, convinced she did not think him the prize she once had. He was a fool.

He tore away from the group, following the direction Mabel and her friend had gone, but she was nowhere to be seen. Heading for the exit, he bumped a man in the shoulder and, turning to apologize, found a startled Desmond.

"You," he said through his teeth, "ought to remind your sister that I am not the catch she thinks me."

Desmond's eyes grew wide. "Sophy, was it? What did she do this time?"

Seething, Mac clenched his hands to keep them down by his sides. "I am tired of her games. Her previous attempts to trap me when we were in London were feeble and foolish, and I thought them in the past. *You* told me you would speak with her, and I thought that was enough." He recalled his surroundings and leaned forward, lowering his voice. "But if she makes another attempt, Desmond, I will not hold myself accountable for finding it necessary to cut her acquaintance."

"Of course, Mac." Desmond seemed to age in a single minute. "I had thought she wouldn't repeat those actions here. We've talked...well, never mind that. Please, forgive me for bringing her. I had thought I could trust my sister to hold to her word. She cornered you, then?"

"No. She merely hung off my arm like a harlot."

"Here?" Desmond asked, glancing about.

Mac nodded.

"Gads, Mac. It certainly was untoward of her. I will speak to her again. You have my word."

"Your absence would be of more value than that."

It took a moment for Mac's meaning to take root, but he could see when recognition dawned on Desmond's face. "Perhaps we've remained in Devon long enough."

"Perhaps."

Letting out a sigh, Desmond rubbed his eyelids. "My sisters are set on the trip to the sea, Mac. And Lydia feels as though Charles will propose to her any day now."

"Then maybe you should nudge him in that direction. I will not tell you what to do, but I would appreciate it if you got your sister's affairs in order and made a hasty retreat."

Desmond nodded. The men held one another's gaze before bowing slightly and continuing in opposite directions.

Mac escaped from the ballroom. He could not force anyone to do his bidding, but when he and Charles had met up on the continent and the Pemberton siblings had joined them, it was clear Sophy had been after one thing: Mac's hand in marriage. Her futile efforts to attract him were only followed by poorly executed attempts to trap him into proposing once they reached London. But he had extricated himself from their group, traveling with Charles and Desmond to Devon instead.

Of course, he hadn't known she was going to follow them.

He'd done a decent job of avoiding her since arriving at Charles's house, and her respectful distance had lulled him into thinking she was past those horrible plans—that she'd been informed of Mac's precarious financial situation.

He had been wrong. And worse, Mabel had witnessed Miss Sophy's vulgar behavior.

He needed to find her, *now*, and assure her that Miss Sophy meant nothing, that the way she touched him was in no way a proclamation.

That Mabel, and no other woman, held Mac's heart.

CHAPTER 24

*M*abel slipped quietly into her bed and let out a long, soothing sigh.

"Thank you, Payne," she said quietly as her maid snuck out of the room. She had escaped for the latter half of the ball after witnessing the revolting scene between Mac and Miss Sophy and hid in the library with Amelia until it was time to depart. She had contemplated sending for Gram and sneaking out early, but this had been Giulia's special ball, and not even Mac's idiocy could make her leave before it ended.

And besides, she'd had Amelia by her side to keep him away when he eventually found them at the end of the evening and tried to speak to her. She was no fool. She understood that Mac had not *asked* Miss Sophy to hang on him as though she was a trollop. Indeed, he had looked rather distressed for the duration of it.

But the fact remained that Mac had a tendency to charm women, and Miss Sophy was likely another of his witless victims.

Her leg throbbing acutely, Mabel reached under the blanket and massaged her thigh, then her calf. She had gone too far, allowed herself to continue using a leg that instead needed rest. She sank further into the mattress, recalling to mind the moment Mac had glanced up while Miss Sophy draped herself over him and caught her gaze. He'd been panicked then, of course, but there was something more, something she could not quite put her finger on.

She fell asleep to rebellious dreams of dancing with Mac, with a leg that did not bother her in the slightest.

Sitting up in her bed, propped against a multitude of pillows, Mabel was entirely at her ease. Payne had just left to fetch breakfast, and Giulia sat in the chair beside her bed, pulling a needle through a linen handkerchief.

"I expected you to put up more of a fight," Giulia said, lifting an eyebrow as her attention remained on the handkerchief.

"I might have, but a break from our guests' company will do me a world of good, I should think." A break from *Mac's* company, specifically. She stretched her leg beneath her blanket and a thread of pain sliced up her thigh. No, she most definitely would not be stepping foot outside of her room for the duration of the day.

"And what of the plans to visit Camden Cove?"

Mabel lifted a shoulder. "They may go without me."

"Miss Pemberton and Mr. Wright were speaking about the outing at breakfast this morning." Giulia lifted her eyebrows. "They seemed awfully cozy."

"Miss Pemberton, you said? Not Miss Sophy?"

"Oh, you're right. It was Miss—"

The door swung open, hitting the wall with a resounding bang, and Pippa skipped into the room, jumping on the end of Mabel's bed and landing near her legs.

Sucking in a breath, Mabel put her hands down on impulse

to keep her sister from jumping into her lap. Giulia stood quickly, reaching for Pippa.

"Don't get too close, darling. Mabel's leg is hurting today."

Pippa turned around, widened eyes on her sister. "Again? Was it all the dancing, Mabel?"

She suppressed a laugh. "No, Pippa. Believe it or not, I did not dance at all last night."

Her young sister's face pulled back, disturbed. "Why would you go to a ball and not dance? Were all the gentlemen hideous?"

Mabel and Giulia shared an amused smile before Giulia tugged Pippa a little further away to sit on the end of the bed. "No, they weren't. Just the opposite, in fact. There were plenty of handsome gentlemen who longed to dance with your sister, but she refused them all."

Pippa's expression grew even more disgusted. "Then why did you not dance?"

"Because I was hurting, Pippa. My leg would not have supported it."

"Your sister needs to rest so she might heal," Giulia said gently.

Pippa frowned. "How long must you stay in bed?"

Mabel shrugged. "As long as I need to." She rather hoped it was long enough so that the Pembertons might be absent when she finally escaped her bedchamber, but that was likely a longshot.

Mrs. Henderson appeared in the doorway and dipped in a curtsy. "Might I have a word when it is convenient?"

"Of course. Please, come in."

Giulia rose. "Come, Pippa. Shall we get started on our lessons a little early today?"

Pippa's nose scrunched and her shoulders drooped. "If we absolutely must."

Giulia took her hand and led the girl from the room while

Mabel did her best not to laugh. She dearly wished Pippa could stay a seven-year-old forever.

Straightening against her pillows, Mabel gestured her house-keeper forward. "What is the trouble, Mrs. Henderson?"

"There is no trouble, dear. Not exactly." She glanced at the ceiling for a moment as if looking for what she meant to say.

"Well?"

"It is only that I feel I need to say something to you, but I do not wish to be impertinent."

Mabel's hands fisted the blanket. "Is someone in danger?"

"No, ma'am."

"Please, speak your mind."

Mrs. Henderson took a step closer, glancing over her shoulder before settling her gaze on Mabel. "I was not witness to this myself, ma'am, but heard it directly from Peter after he finished serving breakfast."

"Yes?"

She cleared her throat. "It would appear that a certain guest has felt it her duty to step in and concern herself with matters of the house as though she was the mistress."

Mabel bristled. She could well imagine who this guest might be, and why she wished to do that. But the truth remained that when Charles married, his wife *would* take on that very impor-tant role. Perhaps, in Mabel's absence, they might all practice, as it were.

"Miss Pemberton?" Mabel confirmed.

"Yes, ma'am."

"Then I believe it is wise to treat her as though she was the lady of the house. She very well might be by the end of the summer. Perhaps we could think of these next few days as something of a trial to show Miss Pemberton precisely what her life will be like should she become mistress in truth."

Mrs. Henderson did not appear the least pleased with this plan, but she agreed. "The menus, then?"

"Take them to her for approval. And any sort of snag you come upon in the course of your day, please take the issues to her to be resolved. I am certain she will do so with great satisfaction."

"Shall I, um...would you like me to inform you of how she gets on?"

"No, thank you. I believe I will take full advantage of this break and simply rest, Mrs. Henderson. I have full faith in you."

That seemed to harden the older woman's courage. She gave a clipped nod and left the room, closing the door behind her. And Mabel slunk into blessed relaxation.

Mac watched Mrs. Sheffield stack her playing cards once again, hitting them against the table with jarring thunks. Candlelight flickered against the window, casting a dancing shadow over the elderly woman as she began another game with Mrs. Boucher. The entire day had come and gone without one blessed glimpse of Mabel, and Mac was growing antsy.

Miss Pemberton had slid into the role of hostess with alarming finesse, ordering the servants about as though this was her home and Mabel was gone for good. It gave Mac the desire to meet one of the men outside for a bout of friendly fisticuffs, but he had no takers. Not that he'd asked. He was fearful of actually hurting one of his friends with all of his pent-up energy.

Sweeping the room, his gaze landed on Wright leaning against the pianoforte at the end of the room as Miss Sophy picked out a song in between bouts of tinkling laughter. Well, there was one man he wouldn't mind venting his frustration on. But despite his avid dislike of the sailor, Wright had yet to give any actual cause for Mac to swing at him.

Pity, that.

"When shall we plan to venture to the sea?" Miss Pemberton asked Charles, who sat nearby.

"The moment Mabel is well enough for the trip, we shall go."

Miss Pemberton nodded smoothly. "Of course. We would not wish to go without her, naturally."

"I was surprised to find her absent at dinner," Mac said. "Is her leg bothering her again?"

Charles nodded, concern evident on his brow. "I am only glad we could convince her to rest. It is difficult for her to allow others to take her responsibilities."

Mac recalled the moment he had caught her gaze in the ballroom, the irritation and hurt on her features. Surely Mabel was in need of this rest and not simply using the injury to stay away from Mac and the other guests. They had outstayed their welcome days ago, if not weeks, and he assumed she was eager to have her house back to the way it was before their large party descended on her with no notice and a carriage full of men.

But Mabel had borne it all with equanimity and poise. She upheld the strength and dignity he had grown to expect from her, and she had not flinched when plans changed or new guests were added to her household, or when she discovered her special vale was to be dug up and turned into tenant cottages for her father's cast-off sailors.

Mac had watched Mabel over the last few weeks accept each and every hurdle or discomfort and move forward accordingly. Including the ridiculous man her father had brought home for her to marry.

Wright leaned over further on the pianoforte, saying something to Miss Sophy, who giggled wickedly and swatted at the sailor's arm.

Truly? *This* was the man that Captain Sheffield deemed good enough for Mabel? No. No man was good enough for Mabel.

Not even Mac. But he would spend every day of his life

trying to be the man she deserved, if she let him. If he could get his life in order fast enough to offer before someone else did.

Mac tapped his heel, anxious to leave the room but uncertain where he would go.

"Mabel? Where is Mabel?" Mrs. Sheffield called.

Charles sat up immediately. "She is in bed, Gram."

His grandmother looked at him as though he had grown antlers on his head. Her eyebrows drawn together, nostrils flaring, she spoke in frigid accents. "What the devil do you mean, my Mabel is in Bedlam? Certainly you are mistaken."

"No, no Gram," Charles said, lifting his hands as he crossed the room. "She is in bed," he said again, enunciating each word loudly. "Her leg pains her, and she is resting upstairs."

She seemed disturbed but allowed Charles to help her stand. "I don't like this, Charles. I don't like it when Mabel is not here."

Rising, Miss Pemberton crossed to them and offered her arm to Gram. "Might I help you to your room, ma'am?"

Gram's mouth pinched. "No."

Startled, Miss Pemberton looked to Charles, her cheeks pinking.

"Gram," Charles said stiffly. "Miss Pemberton has offered to help you."

"And I don't want her help," Gram said, perfectly at ease. "I will have Mabel, or I will have no one."

Miss Pemberton's voice grew louder. "Surely you have a servant we can fetch, ma'am."

Mrs. Sheffield watched Miss Pemberton through narrowed eyes, stepping around her with slow, cane-assisted steps.

Mrs. Boucher got to her feet at once. "I will see you upstairs, Mrs. Sheffield."

Mrs. Sheffield shot Mrs. Boucher an appraising glance but nodded and accepted the woman's offered arm before they both left the room.

"Please do not take offense," Charles finally said, running his hand through his chestnut hair. "Gram is quite aged and particularly set in her ways."

"I am not offended by that old bird," Miss Pemberton said kindly, though her expression said otherwise. "I am certain I could have been just as comforting as Mabel, had I been given the opportunity."

Charles looked at her oddly before shaking his gaze away. "Of course."

Mac leaned back in his seat and closed his eyes. He understood Mrs. Sheffield's dismay at finding her granddaughter missing. He felt very much the same way. Perhaps if the two of them put up enough of a complaint, Mabel would appear again, and soon.

CHAPTER 25

$\mathcal{A}$ week had passed since the ball, Papa had still not returned from London, and Mabel had healed more with each day. She now suffered more from boredom than any unruly leg ailments and deemed today to be the day she would venture to finally leave her bedchamber. Charles had told her of their plans to travel to Camden Cove and was determined not to go without her. She had put him off for days now, hoping he would change his mind. But alas, he was undeterred.

She had the sense that Charles was not quite happy with their current situation. But he would not speak when she pressed him, so she ceased her attempts to discover what bothered him. Perhaps at some point during the day she would get to the bottom of it.

Payne finished pinning Mabel's hair up and stepped back, allowing her to survey her appearance in the mirror. She gave her maid a nod of approval and the woman began cleaning up discarded night clothes and unused hairpins.

Sliding her bonnet over her head, Mabel picked up her gloves and headed downstairs, leaning heavily against the bannister as she tested her leg—but it held up against the strain of descending the stairs. The extra few days of rest had been exactly what she'd needed.

Carriage wheels and horse hooves sounded on the gravel outside as the Sheffields' guests filed out to fill the carriage. Giulia stood near the door helping Pippa tie her bonnet strings, and Gram sat on the chair situated beside the wall.

"You are coming with us?" Mabel asked Gram, delighted.

"No, but I wanted to see you."

Gram started to rise, so Mabel put a hand under her elbow to assist her. Her beady, wrinkled eyes bore into Mabel's. "I have missed you this last week. I don't wish to be parted from you again in that way."

"You will not," Mabel said. It hadn't occurred to her that by avoiding their guests, she was also avoiding her grandmother. But Gram's resolution was jarring. What had kept her from visiting Mabel's room? "I would have welcomed you any time, Gram. I was well—I just needed to refrain from using my leg. It was vastly boring."

Gram's eyes flicked behind Mabel, a frown marring her face, and Mabel turned.

Miss Pemberton stood in the open doorway, Giulia and Pippa stepping outside behind her. The blonde woman tilted her head. "Ah, Mabel, I am so glad to see you recovered." She crossed the room, a tight smile stretching her lips flat. "I am certain Gram is just as grateful for your presence."

Gram? The woman had taken to using a family name? That lifted Mabel's eyebrows and she tried to temper her surprise. "Is everyone waiting in the carriages? I fear I have been awfully slow this morning."

Miss Pemberton nodded. "Nearly everyone. We only were waiting on—"

"Here!" Mr. Wright called, coming down the stairs at a fast

clip. "Forgive me, I was writing a letter and lost track of the time." He came to a quick stop before the woman and bowed, his smile revealing crooked, white teeth. "Might I escort you outside?"

"That would be lovely, sir," Miss Pemberton said, taking one proffered arm.

Mr. Wright looked at Mabel expectantly, but she stepped back. "I will be out momentarily."

He accepted this with a nod but watched her a moment longer before leading Miss Pemberton away.

"Gram," Mabel said, taking her grandmother's hand in both of hers and raising her voice to be heard. "Please come with us. I am certain there is a comfortable seat available, and the sea air will be mightily refreshing."

"Not today, dear." Gram patted her hand before extricating herself from Mabel's grip. "But I will not refuse your company this evening."

"You will have it," Mabel promised.

Gram turned away, her cane clicking on the marble floor as she made her way toward the drawing room. How had Mabel ever thought she could take her grandmother with her if she married and moved away? This woman refused an easy ride's journey to the restorative coast. She would never remove to an estate in Warwickshire.

Mabel tugged on her sleeves, pulling them down over her gloves. Her pulse sped as she left the safety of her house—of Gram's house—and stepped down onto the gravel drive. Mac stood at the head of the first carriage, rubbing the horse's neck as he spoke to the driver. It had been a week since Mabel had caught sight of him, and her heart jumped up and lodged in her throat. His smile was easy, effortless, crinkling the edges of his eyes. His bottle green jacket was molded to his torso as though it had been sewn directly onto him, revealing the curve of his back and thickness of his arms. A life of labor for the past six years had changed Mac, and it was hard to look away.

Amelia's advice to avoid Mac had been sound, and Mabel had cowardly done so all week by remaining within the safety of her bedchamber. But now, how was she supposed to keep away from him in a party such as this? Her first act, of course, could be ensuring that they did not ride in the same carriage.

"Mabel!" Pippa called, bouncing toward her. "I am so impatient to be going! Are you ready? I have been ready for an age."

"Yes, dear Pippa. I am ready to be off. Where are you sitting? Shall I come sit beside you?"

Her little nose wrinkled. "I'm afraid that will be impossible." Her eyes widened. "But you may sit across from me!"

"Very well." She allowed Pippa to take her hand and pull her toward the second carriage, away from Mac and the Pemberton family and Charles. Mr. Wright caught Mabel's eye just before she slipped inside her carriage. If he was hoping for a private moment with her, he was bound to be disappointed.

Climbing into the carriage and settling into the seat opposite her sister, Mabel swallowed the guilt that nipped at her. She had promised her father she would give Mr. Wright a fair chance—to see if any sort of amicable relationship could form between herself and the man. But she hadn't done any such thing. Instead, she'd thwarted his efforts to spend time with her, and disappeared from his presence whenever given the opportunity. The poor man had spent significantly more time with the Pemberton sisters than the woman he had come here to marry.

Marry. The word itself sent a volley of shivers down Mabel's spine.

Giulia stepped into the carriage, taking the seat beside Mabel and smoothing down her skirts.

"Are you not going to sit beside Pippa?" Mabel asked, grinning. Why else would Pippa have acted as though the seat was taken?

"Good morning, ladies," Mac said in the doorway, his slow smile causing her stomach to flip over. The way he tilted his head a little to see into the carriage, looking at her from under his eyelashes, sent a warmth through Mabel's chest.

A chorus of good mornings met Mac and he ducked his head further, climbing inside. Pippa was all but bouncing on her seat, grinning up at the beast of a man. "We are going to finish our lessons today, yes?"

He smiled and creases formed at the sides of his lips. "What lessons are those?" His gaze flicked to Mabel before settling back on her sister. "You don't mean the pirate…"

"No, not that," Pippa said hurriedly. "I mean the skipping, Mac."

"Oh, yes, the skipping. Well, I hate to disappoint you, Pippa, but the sea is not a great location for skipping rocks."

Jutting out her lower lip, Pippa scowled, her eyes unfocused. Brightening, she turned back to him. "But you will still teach me?"

"Yes, I shall still teach you. Just not today."

Satisfied, she leaned back in the seat. A shadow fell over the open doorway and Mr. Wright appeared, resting a hand on the door. "Is there room for one more sailor among you?"

"Of course," Giulia said at once. "Pippa, move over, dear."

Mac halted her. "You sit in the middle, Pippa." He maneuvered around her until he was sitting across from Mabel, his knees pressing against hers. Her gaze rested there, where they touched, unsure of what she ought to do. This was entirely the opposite of creating space between Mac and herself. And blast her wretched heart, but she liked it.

The carriage rocked as Giulia crossed to the other side, squeezing beside Pippa. Mr. Wright claimed the seat beside Mabel. The door was closed by a servant and within moments they were rolling forward. Mabel looked out of the window at the tree line in the distance and the glimmer of the morning sun on the pond—anything to keep her mind from the man whose knees were pressing into hers, and the other one whose shoulder was brushing hers.

Why did men take up so much dratted space? Surely taking the tallest man and tallest woman and seating them across from one another was faulty planning. But—well, Mac had done it on purpose, hadn't he? The moment the thought took root in her mind, Mabel looked at the man in question and found him regarding her thoughtfully, his eyebrows pulled together faintly and fingers drumming against his thigh.

Swallowing, she felt as though he pressed against her knees again, and she could not move her gaze from his, held captive as she was in his hazel eyes. It was out of her control.

And the way she felt about this man was entirely out of her control, as well.

⸻

Why had Mabel been avoiding him? If Wright hadn't weaseled his way into their carriage, perhaps Mac could have found a way to ask her. As it was, she was entirely silent for the duration of the ride to the ocean, her eyes glued to the window for most of it, broken only by the occasional attempt at a conversation from Wright.

Was the man an idiot? By his third failed attempt at engaging Mabel in conversation, Wright should have known to cease trying. But he was not a man to give up, evidently, and the frustration showed on both his and Mabel's faces.

"Do you think we will arrive soon?" Pippa asked wearily.

"Very soon," Mac said. He had traveled this road twice since coming to Graton this summer and knew Camden Court was just around the bend, the sea just beyond that. He watched Mabel's face as she looked out the window, eager for her reaction when she set eyes on the moss-covered stone house.

The occupants of the carriage swayed to the side as they rounded the bend, and Mabel turned to watch out the window. Mac's gaze fastened on her lovely face; the gentle curve of her neck was milky white, and a loose curl danced along her skin, blowing in the slight breeze. He was faintly aware of Wright speaking to Giulia, but his attention was so wholly focused on Mabel, he could not tell what they were discussing, and neither did he care.

This was it. The house was just outside their window, down a tree-lined path overgrown and dripping with foliage.

Mabel's eyes lit, her brows lifting so faintly Mac would have missed it had he not been watching for that very thing. Had she not seen this house before? Surely she'd been to Camden Cove. It was not a private beach by any means, but the path that led from the house down to the water was on Camden Court's land. It could have been Mac's land, but he would not allow himself to think on that.

Mabel's breath hitched, her lips parting, and Mac's chest warmed. Her gaze sought his and he stilled. Had he been pressing his knees to hers again? It wasn't intentional, but he found himself doing it occasionally. What was he supposed to do, though? With legs as long as his, he was cramped in any carriage.

Clearing his throat, he turned to Pippa. "I believe we shall be seeing the ocean from that window in just a moment."

She bounced on the seat again and Miss Pepper put out a staying hand, reminding Pippa to sit still. She was just a child, though. Mac didn't see the harm in her eagerness. He had felt much the same way when he was a boy. The carriage pulled out from behind the overgrown trees and up a small rise, and the ocean appeared as though from thin air. A small volley of gasps sounded in the carriage.

"Oh, it is lovely," Miss Pepper said. "It has been ages since I've been to the seaside."

"Then we must make this a day to remember," Wright said. "I admit to being partial to it myself. I could never tire from the view."

"Nor I," Mabel agreed. "There is something quite heavenly about the majesty of the ocean, is there not?"

Wright turned an appreciative smile on Mabel, and Mac very much wanted to hit the man.

"My play takes place on the ocean," Pippa said proudly.

Mabel's eyebrows shot up. "Oh? And when do we get to see this play?"

Pippa shrugged. "We aren't quite ready yet. But give me a few weeks and we shall be."

"That is about how long it will take for us to finish building the cottages," Mac said, looking at Wright. It could possibly go even faster if *all* of the men worked hard.

Pippa was bouncing beside him as the carriage rolled to a stop. "Can we perform our play at the celebration Mabel? Please, can we?"

Mabel looked startled, her eyes going unfocused as though she was working through the idea in her mind. "I suppose that would be all right. We must ask Mrs. Traynor first, of course."

"She will agree!" Pippa said, confident.

"What celebration is this?" Miss Pepper asked.

Pippa turned to her as the door opened and the groom let down the step. "Papa wants to have a celebration when the cottages are complete to welcome the new families." She turned to Mac. "Can we perform at the celebration? Do you mind?"

He considered the part he played in Pippa's theatrical, and how very silly it would make him appear. But the hope shining in her widened eyes was enough to force him to forget any potential embarrassment and nod instead. "I do not mind at all. Now, shall we go hunt some crabs?"

Pippa's face brightened and she clapped. "Yes, please!"

The group exited the carriages, stretching their muscles after the hour-long ride. They spread out to look over the expanse of water beyond the cove, the sun rising in the sky and shining out over the sea. It was a lovely day—albeit, a little windy. But when was the coastline ever without wind?

Mabel came up beside Mac, tightening the ribbons on her bonnet. "The view is breathtaking."

He watched her, outlining her beautiful profile, and imagined he could sit and watch her all day as she looked out at the sea. "Yes, Mabel. It is absolutely breathtaking, indeed."

She drew in a quick breath and faced him, her cheeks and nose pinking against the wind. Swallowing, she dipped a curtsy and turned to catch up with the rest of the party.

He followed, his long strides covering the ground between them fairly quickly.

Miss Sophy turned back, catching his eye as he approached them. She looked away with haughty disdain, and relief coursed through him. Ever since her brazen behavior at the ball, Mac had been doubly mindful when around her. But it had appeared that Desmond had spoken to his sister as he'd promised, and she had given Mac a wide berth since that night.

Not that she would *ever* be successful in her endeavors. He'd been perfectly clear with Desmond, and he would make himself plain to Miss Sophy if need be: she could compromise herself however she wished. Mac would never offer for her.

"It is rather windy, is it not?" Miss Pemberton asked, holding her bonnet tight at the back of her head.

"This is how it is here," Charles explained. "Our beaches are not for everyone."

"They are beautiful to me," Miss Pemberton said.

Mabel glanced between the pair and Mac would have given a guinea to know what was causing her brow to furrow.

The sun beat down on them as they followed the pathway

down to the beach, the women lifting their hems as they trekked across the sand. Mabel paused and bent to pick something up, and the grin that spread over her lips as she straightened went straight to Mac's heart.

"I've found a shell," she said, holding it out to Pippa. Her sister's eyes lit, accepting the offering, and immediately Pippa ran off, searching the ground for similar treasures. Miss Pepper stepped ahead and strung her arm through Mabel's, and they walked toward the sea.

Charles paused. "Shall we eat first, or put it off until later?"

"If we wait an hour or so, I know just the place to take our food where we can escape both the sand and the wind," Mac said.

"Superb." Charles nodded. "Now, who is going swimming?"

A chorus of laughter met his ludicrous question and Miss Sophy said, "I should like to search for shells. Who will join me?"

"I already have shells," Pippa said, displaying a handful of broken mussel shells for the group in her small, pudgy hands.

"How nice for you," Miss Pemberton said tightly. "I will come, Sophy. Charles? Will you join us?"

Charles? Had the man actually given her leave to use his Christian name? It was startling, for Mac had thought Charles to be wavering in his opinion of the woman. But it was true that when they'd talked at the ball, Charles had seemed likely to press forward with his plan to marry Miss Pemberton if she was amenable to the scheme.

Perhaps they'd talked about it already. It *had* been a week since the ball. But working from sunup until sunset had made the days fly particularly quickly all week. Mac was eager to complete the cottages in the case that the prize money came through and he would have to leave to attend to his father's business.

"I would love to accompany you," Charles said, clasping his

hands behind his back and following Miss Pemberton and her sister toward the ocean.

"Mac, will you show me the crabs now?"

"Most certainly." Turning to Mabel and Miss Pepper, he asked, "Will you come with us?"

CHAPTER 26

The rocky shoreline which lined both ends of the cove gave the illusion that they were cut off from the world, privately enjoying a beach that was just their own. The jagged edges of the dark rock spilled down into the ocean and spread out toward the sandy beach, creating an area of shallow pockets of water full of sea life. Mabel walked the perimeter of the rocky surface, searching for unique shells or bits of colorful rocks with Giulia.

Mac led Pippa further out, pointing out crabs in the deeper crevices or the occasional living thing that would peek from beneath the clear water.

"A crab!" Pippa squealed. "Mac, look! Another one!"

Mac's booming laugh traveled through the wind and wrapped around Mabel's heart. His eyes glittered as he squatted on the wet rock, reaching into a crevice to pull out the creature. He held it toward Pippa, fearlessly grasping the thing between two fingers.

Pippa reached for the crab and Mabel held her breath, sensing Pippa's eagerness. She didn't want her sister to get hurt.

Pippa held the crab, her face alight with pleasure as she grinned at Mac in adoration.

"For such a tall, imposing-looking man, Mr. MacKenzie is very sweet with Pippa," Giulia said.

Mabel nodded, watching them interact. Mac was so patient with Pippa, so gentle. He spoke to her as though she mattered. He did not treat her like an obnoxious hanger-on, and Mabel loved that about him.

He looked up, glancing at her as though he could read her thoughts. Saying something to Pippa, Mac turned and led her back toward the beach, the crab still firmly in her small hand.

"Are they coming toward us?" Giulia asked, awed.

"It appears that way."

Mac guided Pippa along the rocky, unsteady ground until they reached Mabel and Giulia. "Pippa would like to introduce you to her new friend," he said, a smile tipping one side of his mouth.

Pippa grinned, revealing the gap on top where her tooth had recently fallen out. "I'm holding a crab."

"I can see that," Mabel said, smiling. It was smaller than Mabel's hand, dark brown with a hard, shiny shell. Its pincers snapped slowly. "It's a darling little thing, isn't it?"

"Would you like to hold it?" Pippa asked.

Mabel took a step back. "Oh, no thank you, Pip. I am quite content to watch it from this distance."

"But he won't pinch you. See? He hasn't hurt me."

Giulia and Mac both grinned, and Mabel felt quite outnumbered. "Oh, very well. Hand it here."

Pippa held the crab out and Mabel took it from her, her heart pounding in her chest. A sharp pinch struck her between her thumb and finger, and she yelped, dropping the crab on the rocks. It scurried away, crawling sideways onto a lower rock and then into the shallow water.

"Oh, no!" Pippa said, following the crab. "You could have hurt him, Mae!"

"Never mind that he hurt me," Mabel muttered, the soft place on her hand throbbing. She shook her hand out and Mac stepped forward, concern etched on his brow.

"Come," he said, gently taking her by the shoulders and leading her toward the sandy beach. They got away from the slick rocks and he dipped his head to look her in the eye. "May I look at it?"

She swallowed, unable to speak with him standing so near she could smell him, the scent of his shaving soap surrounding her and making her head fog. He continued to watch her, waiting for an answer, and she nodded.

Taking her hand in his, Mac pulled at the tips of her fingers, loosening the gloves one small tug at a time. Her heart hammered in her chest, her pulse jumping erratically as she watched his large, strong fingers work with gentle care. After loosening each finger, Mac slipped the glove from her hand and tucked it under his arm, turning her hand over to check the area the crab had pinched.

There was an angry red mark, but no broken skin.

"It was here?" Mac asked, brushing his thumb softly over the injured place.

"Yes."

He brushed it again, then looked at her. "You'll likely have a bruise later. They don't often break the skin, but it can feel as though they had."

She nodded again, feeling rather unintelligent as the ability to speak seemed to have left her. But Mac, touching her this way, made her feel so delicate, so cared for. She never wanted it to end.

"You have lovely hands, Mabel."

She glanced up quickly and regretted it at once. He stared

into her eyes, his own resolute. He was going to say something important—she could feel it.

"Mabel, I realize that we have a rocky past, that I was not exactly kind to you that day in the vale. I know I can never fully apologize to you, but I should like to do my best to make up for my foolish actions as a boy, to show you how very much I have changed."

This was no declaration. It was an apology? Mabel was unsure what to think of it, what to make of his words.

"I have tried to show you how I've changed this last month," he said, pulling her closer, refusing to release her hand. His skin on hers was intoxicating, and the smell of his shaving soap intensified, mixing with the salty air, making it utterly impossible for her to back up. "And I would like to continue to do so if you would allow me." He swallowed, but then his mouth bent into a firm line. "I would like to ask your father for permission to address you, Mabel."

He...what? Mabel could not breathe. The sand below her feet was unsteady, and she felt as though the sound of waves crashing on the shore intensified at once, blending with the birds overhead and the laughter down the beach. The sea roared in her ears while Mac's face swam before her.

He could not mean it, could he? Swallowing, she found her voice. "You wish to beg permission to address me? Can you not simply address me now?"

His brow furrowed. "No—of course not."

She pulled her hand from his grip and stepped back, needing a bit of space in order to breathe. She was not the fainting type, but she had come awfully close a moment before. And his words were dangerous, inconstant as they were. He either wanted her, or he did not.

"I do not have time for games, Mac."

"No, I shouldn't think you do. I just mean that my prospects are not—"

"Your prospects?" He meant *marriage?* Mabel stepped back again, the world spinning before her. His hand came under her elbow to steady her, and she sought his gaze, hoping to find the truth there. "How can you speak of such things to me?"

Mac scrubbed a hand over his face. "I realize I should have waited until I knew for certain. There are too many variables I must sort through before I can offer for you."

"*Offer* for me? Mac, what the devil are you talking about?"

A smile fought its way onto his lips, and she found her gaze glued to them, unable to look away. They looked so soft, and she had a sudden, unreasonable desire to brush her finger along them to see if they were as soft as they appeared. "Your language is not befitting a lady, Mabel."

"And?" she asked, unable to fight the blush that warmed its way up her neck.

"And I am utterly enthralled by you."

The breath whooshed out of her lungs. Mabel could not take any more of this. She removed herself from his grip, so certain that she would be able to think clearly once more if she was given proper space to breathe.

"Is everything all right?" Giulia called, returning with Pippa along the rocky shore. "Does your hand hurt, Mae?"

"I am well," Mabel called back. Struggling to stand this close to Mac but not touch him, not allow him to continue touching her, Mabel turned from him and made her way down the beach. She did not make it more than a few paces before she halted mid-step. Mr. Wright stood just a few yards away, his hands hanging limp by his sides and a hard expression on his face.

He had just witnessed the entire episode.

Mac had bumbled things with Mabel. He'd been such a fool to say anything before he knew what sort of debts he needed to pay for his father, how great his portion of the prize money was going to be, and how much blunt he would have left over when it was all sorted.

But she had been in his arms—nearly—and it had felt so natural, so right. He'd wanted to close the distance and embrace her, hold her close to himself and tell her how much he loved her.

But what if the prize money did not pass through the courts? If Mac was left with the money he had now, he would be penniless by the time he freed his father—*if* he could come up with enough money for that.

No. He'd done the right thing. He would not offer Mabel anything less than a good situation. He merely needed to ensure he had one of those, first. Mac would not do to Mabel what his father had done to his mother.

"Is it much further up?" Charles asked, panting.

"No, it is just up ahead."

Mac led the group up the slope and toward Camden Court. There was a small clearing where the property opened up, surrounded by trees to abate some of the wind, but still in perfect view of the vast ocean. It was one of the reasons Mac had wanted to purchase the estate. It was a blessed thing the house was empty now so they might make use of its land.

Charles motioned to the servants near the carriages and they sprang to action, untying the baskets from the boot of the first carriage and carrying them to where Charles and his guests were gathering. Mabel hung back, using Miss Pepper and Pippa to shield her from the gentlemen. When Mr. Wright had come upon them, he'd looked angry, but Mac did not care. The man did not deserve Mabel, and his current pouting only further proved as much.

Miss Sophy straightened her bonnet and then ran her hands down the front of her gown. "It is wretchedly windy here. I do wonder how I am going to manage eating a bite. Surely it will fly away before it reaches my lips."

"You will see," Wright said. "This little inlet here will block most of the wind. If you would only take a few steps back."

"You know a great deal about this place," Miss Sophy said, tipping her face to bestow a saccharine smile on him. The servants spread a thick blanket over the dry grass and began setting out the baskets, leaving the food within them to keep it from becoming sandy. Though they'd moved inland, the breeze still carried a good deal of sand where it wished.

Wright took her hand and helped her to sit on the corner of one blanket as the servants laid out another one. "Well, I should know something about this estate. I have considered purchasing it."

Mac stared, unsure if the earth actually slipped out from beneath him or if it only felt as though it had. His stomach dropped to the ground, spinning and souring as it went. *Wright?* Purchase Camden Court? How the devil had he even heard of the place?

"But you have a house in Warwickshire," Mabel said, sounding as stunned as Mac felt. Her eyes were round, widened, and she looked about them as though seeing the place in a new light. Was she imagining it as if she was mistress here? Devil take it. Mac *wanted* her to be mistress here, but only if he was master.

"I had imagined my bride would appreciate living closer to *her* family estate," Wright explained.

Mabel's face went white. Was she truly considering the prospect of marrying that wretched man? Mac's blood heated and he clenched his fists, anger pumping through him. More baskets were brought out, but he could not partake of their contents. He could not do anything but refrain from attacking Wright, and it was a dangerous position to be in.

Turning from the group, Mac rounded the path and found his

way to the road. A brisk walk and a few minutes away from the party would give him time and air to clear his head.

Camden Court could already be in his possession if he'd wanted it to be. When he'd met the solicitor here a few weeks before to discuss the parameters of the sale, he'd learned that no one had shown any interest in the estate in well over a year. He'd thought he'd had time. Foolishly, he'd hoped the prize money would come in larger than they'd expected—that he would be blessed with enough to free his father and purchase Camden still.

But as Captain Sheffield's lieutenants, Mac's and Wright's prize portions were equal. If Mac's prize money came in higher, so would Wright's. And if Wright wanted this place, who would stop him? The owners had long since awaited a sale. They would not hold out for Mac, not when Wright would be a sure thing.

He swallowed the bile rising in his throat. So *this* was what it felt like to watch a dream slip away.

"Mac?"

He paused on the road and ran a hand through his hair, waiting until he had applied some semblance of order to his emotions before turning to face his friend.

Charles approached on the road. "What is it? You seem distressed."

Mac opened his mouth to tell his friend everything, to confess it all, but he paused, the distress in Charles's eyes enough to curb his tongue. He was troubled, likely as troubled as Mac felt, and he did not need his burdens added to. "I am restless," Mac said, careful to only speak the truth.

He gave a mirthless laugh. "I understand."

"Are you going to offer for Miss Pemberton?" Mac asked.

Charles rested a hand on his hip, the other one pinching the bridge of his nose. "At this point, I wonder if I even have a choice."

"Because you've set her expectations?"

Charles held his gaze. "Precisely. As a gentleman, do I have any other options available to me?"

No, he did not. Charles was far too principled to raise the expectation that he would offer for a woman, only to fail to come up to scratch. Even if he did not love her. He was a better man than Mac. Mac didn't care what any man or woman expected from him. He would never offer for anyone that was not Mabel Sheffield.

"I understand your answer from simply looking at your face," Charles said, a wry smile finding its way to his mouth. "What choice do I have? I could never live with myself otherwise. I invited her here for that sole purpose, and I am nothing if not a man of my word."

"Unless you could convince her to marry Wright. That might solve both of our issues."

"He has no interest in her," Charles said. "He has his eye on Mabel."

Charles didn't say it, but he and Mac both knew that when Mabel wasn't around, Wright clearly had his eye on Miss Sophy. A matched pair, for certain. And that did not help Charles in the least.

"Shall we return?" Mac asked.

Charles hesitated. "I would like you to know that I can be of some assistance, should you need it."

Mac stiffened. He'd already told Captain Sheffield he didn't want a loan. Would he now be forced to deny his friend as well?

"If ever you find yourself with a strong urge to land Wright a facer," Charles said, "you tell me. I might not be as spry in the ring as Jackson, but I can hold my own."

"I would flatten you," Mac said, grinning.

Charles clapped his friend on the arm as they started back toward the group. "You ought to be careful saying such things or I'll be forced to prove you wrong."

Mac chuckled, his mood lightened. Charles's grip was certainly stronger than he'd expected. Apparently building cottages and working the land had added to his strength. It was new for Charles, the concept of manual labor, but it had done well for his physique. Maybe Mac would need to have a round of fives with his friend to test his mettle.

They joined the group and ate their luncheon before deciding that it was time to return home. Charles took Wright's place in their carriage on the way home, claiming the seat opposite Mabel, and forced Mac to sit as far from her as possible in the small cab. Pippa fell asleep against her sister's arm, and the occupants of the carriage remained silent as they traveled home.

Mac watched Mabel for a good portion of the ride, silently wishing she would turn her head and look back at him, but she refrained. He only hoped it was a struggle for her, that she did not feel *nothing* as she pretended to.

They pulled into the Sheffields' drive an hour later and Charles sat up, leaning closer to the window. "Look," he said. "My uncle has returned."

Mabel sat up then, rousing Pippa from her nap. They rolled to a slow stop and the door was opened, the step let down, and the women handed out.

Captain Sheffield stood on the stone steps, waiting patiently with his hands behind his back and a smile under his white beard. "That took you long enough," he said when the group made their way toward him. "MacKenzie."

Mac stilled, the sound taking him back to when he was Captain Sheffield's lieutenant and would obey commands without a moment's hesitation. "Yes, sir?"

The captain held out a thick paper, folded and sealed, the grin widening on his face. "It is done."

Mac's head felt light, as if Pippa could touch him and he would fall to the ground in a heap. It was here, and Captain Sheffield was overjoyed. That *had* to mean that the outcome of their cases in the prize courts had been favorable, did it not? He felt his body move up the steps, his hand reaching for the bundled papers.

"They have accepted our prizes?" he asked, aware of the crowd of guests growing behind him.

Captain Sheffield nodded. "The information is likely outlined in there." He nodded toward the missive in Mac's hand. "Along with the promissory note."

He could have fallen in a heap. The money, as well? He held the key to freeing his father, to retrieving his mother, to...potentially buying a home for himself—whatever home that might be. He needed to accomplish these things quickly, so he could return and convince Mabel to be his bride.

"I must go," he said without thinking. Mabel paused on the steps behind her father and caught Mac's eye, her own growing hard. But he did not have time to consider what that meant. There were too many things that required his attention.

"Yes, son," the captain said, grasping him on the shoulder. "Go."

CHAPTER 27

*S*tanding at a tall, bright window in the upstairs gallery, Mabel traced the impressions of Mac's footprints in the gravel as he carried his saddlebag out of the house and mounted his powerful horse. She followed the steady canter of Orion as it carried Mac away from her, waiting for him to glance back. The back of his head, concealed by a hat, brought a fresh wave of regret and longing.

The moment her father told Mac to go, to see to the things he needed to see to, Mabel's heart constricted, and it had yet to return to a steady, regular rhythm.

A moment's thought had forced her to consider approaching Mac before he left, to wait upon the stairs for him to come down and send him away with her good wishes. But she swallowed the impulse. It had not served her well that time in the vale, and she would prefer not to compound the loss and betrayal she felt from the first time he had left Devon—the first time he had left *her*.

Giulia found her in the gallery and came to stand beside her, giving her the space Mabel needed and the support she longed for. Silently, Giulia sustained Mabel as she processed the events of the day.

"I need to find Gram," she said at last. She'd promised her grandmother she would spend the evening with her, and while it was still later afternoon, Mabel was certain she could not stomach the rest of their party at present. With Gram, she would not need to put on a false face.

"She is in her parlor."

Mabel turned from the window, the empty road a stark reminder of the man who had just ridden away through it. "She never sits in there."

Giulia's eyebrows raised. "I made the same observation. Perhaps she has grown weary of your cousin's guests."

"We might only hope that is not the case. It is very likely that some of those guests will soon become permanent fixtures here."

"And you?" Giulia asked, reaching for Mabel's hand. "What do you plan to do?"

The heavy, unasked question hung in the air between them, so clear and thick that Mabel wished to strike it away, to shout that she did not wish to make any decision about her future at present like Pippa might do in these circumstances.

But she was not a child. She had no excuse for such behavior. A problem faced her, and it would solve nothing to pretend it did not exist.

"I must tell my father how I feel."

Giulia squeezed her fingers. Mabel felt so large and uncouth when her small friend wrapped her hand around hers—so directly opposite from how Mac had made her feel earlier that day on the beach. Slipping her hand free, Mabel brushed her thumb over the tender area the crab had pinched, no sign or marking to show of the creature's misuse.

But the mark of Mac's affection would forever remain in her heart.

"Will he take it well, do you think?"

Mabel shrugged, fixated on her hand. "I am unsure. But he loves me, and I owe him my honesty. I have done nothing I am ashamed of, and I do not begrudge the choice I am making."

"If he does not take it well, you will always have a home at Halstead," Giulia said with a small grin. "I should love to have you, Pippa, and Gram as my permanent guests after the wedding."

Mabel chuckled and wrapped her arms around her slender waist. It was a sign of Giulia's observational abilities that she recognized Mabel, her sister, and her grandmother as a group deal. There was no taking Mabel without accepting the others.

Mabel did not begrudge that. She believed she would be unhappy without them.

"When will you speak to your father?"

"Now," Mabel said, determined. "Or I might lose my nerve. He appeared to be in an affable mood when we arrived home from the seaside. Do you know where Pippa went?"

Giulia nodded. "She's with Hope in the schoolroom."

Good. The last thing Mabel needed was Pippa's excitable interruptions during this important conversation. She made her way downstairs and drew in fortifying breaths her entire way to the study door. Mac was gone. He had not looked back, and he did not seek her out to bid a farewell. Regardless of what he'd said at the seaside, he would have, had he truly cared.

Mabel needed to put him behind her, to focus on herself and her future.

Knocking on the solid oak door, Mabel waited until Papa bid her enter and obeyed. She pushed against the heavy door and paused, her breath catching to find Mr. Wright seated in the chair opposite Papa.

"Forgive me. I can return later." She began to back out of the room when her father lifted a staying hand.

"No. Please, come in."

She could not have this conversation with Mr. Wright present. This felt all too familiar, and it raised the tide of anxiety in her chest.

"Mabel, be seated," Papa said, his white eyebrows lifting.

How could she argue with him? It would be impossible to be honest when in such close proximity to the man she had come here to refuse. But what choice did she have? Closing the door behind her, Mabel crossed over the Aubusson carpet and lowered herself primly into the stiff, leather seat.

"Continue, Wright."

Mr. Wright cleared his throat. "I can only promise another week, Captain. A fortnight, if I must."

"I will take every day I can get, lieutenant."

Mr. Wright chuckled. "Very well, sir." He rose, bowing to her father before turning to bow to Mabel. He regarded her with a thoughtful expression before quitting the room. The door snapped shut behind his retreat and the study became stifling in its silence.

"He is a good man," Papa said, claiming her attention.

Mabel glanced up, swallowing her sudden retort. Mac didn't agree with her father's assessment. Had Mac shared that with his captain? She thought it unlikely.

Gathering courage from the love shining in Papa's eyes, Mabel squared her shoulders. "Papa, I cannot marry him."

He held her gaze, his own failing to give any insight into his feelings. "You are certain? He's given much of his time and effort to be here."

"And for that, I must wed the man?"

"Not for that, no." Papa sat back in his seat, gripping the armrests of his chair. "Is there another man?"

How should she answer that question? Mac's image came unbidden to her mind, his lips spreading into a wide smile as the sea breeze whipped his hair around his forehead, his hazel eyes sparkling from the midday sun. If there had been any inkling of hope within Mabel's breast that Mac would have said something to her father before his departure—an *inkling* that he had intentions toward Mabel—it was dashed at once.

For all she knew, he was not planning to return.

"I cannot marry a man who I do not hold in esteem. Mama has been gone for almost eight years now, but the memory of her regard for you and the love you shared is not forgotten. If I cannot have the love match I witnessed and longed for as a girl, then I do not wish to make any match at all."

Papa stilled, but his throat worked as he swallowed audibly. He seemed to look at Mabel as though through a new light, and she longed to inquire if this was a good or bad development. She'd been bold to mention Mama, she knew, but it was the truth.

He stood and stepped around the desk, then reached for her. She put her hand in his and allowed him to pull her to a stand. Clasping her hand tightly, Papa gave her a sad smile. "I will not press you into a marriage that does not appeal to you, Mabel. It would be my greatest wish for you to find the love match I shared with your mother." He looked her in the eye as if willing her to understand him. "But I do not wish a lonely life for you, and I fear that is what you might face if you refuse Wright."

It was on the tip of her tongue to argue that Mama's life could have been considered lonely to some, her husband so often away at sea. But Mabel liked to think her mother had found contentment in the life she chose, in Mabel and Charles and Gram. Much as Mabel would have for herself.

She was following her mother's path far closer than she had realized.

She took comfort in that startling revelation and allowed her father to pull her in for a hug. It stood to reason that he only wanted what was best for her, as misguided as he currently seemed.

"I have reason to believe that Charles intends to take a wife soon," Papa said, leaning back. "This comfortable life you have might become disrupted if that were to take place."

Mabel nodded. It was a sacrifice she was willing to make, to step back and allow Miss Pemberton the role of mistress. After all, it was Charles who would inherit the estate one day, when Gram was no longer here to be mistress, and not Mabel.

"We found the most picturesque estate on our trip to the sea today, and Mr. Wright mentioned that it was vacant, and he had considered purchasing it." Mabel chuckled, hoping to lighten the feeling in the room. "I had wondered if it would be worth marrying him only to become mistress of that house, but that, I fear, is not a good enough reason to sacrifice the possibility of a love match, nor my freedom."

Papa's eyes twinkled as he shook his head. "Sometimes when you speak, I am fooled into thinking your mother has returned, even for just a moment. You look and sound so much like her."

Mabel's heart burst. "I love you, Papa."

CHAPTER 28

Mac leaned away from the iron-barred door, shaking his head to clear the confusion. "What do you mean, he is gone?"

The man blinked. "He isn't here, gov. Been gone a week hence."

Mac's shoulders dropped. It had taken two days to reach the bustling metropolis and he'd ridden hard with little rest until he saw the hazy coal-fire smog that indicated London on the horizon. Once Captain Sheffield had delivered the promissory note to his hands, Mac had had no other recourse but to free his father and move forward accordingly. But now this gatekeeper claimed his father to be gone.

"Gone where?" Mac asked. "How?"

"Don't know where," the man said, adjusting his cap over a balding head. He indicated the prison behind him with a nod. "Had his debts paid by another prisoner and left."

Mac rolled the words around in his head, trying to make sense of them. How was a man inside the Marshalsea able to afford paying the debts of another prisoner? Particularly one so encumbered as Alexander MacKenzie?

"Who might know where he's gone to?" Mac asked. "Can I speak to the other prisoner?"

"He's gone, too. Tried and punished, I'm afraid," the gate-keeper said gruffly. "Don't know how to find MacKenzie. I didn't bother asking where he meant to go."

Mac blew a frustrated breath through his teeth and turned around, leading Orion down the street. The city was both stifling and busy, and to a man used to the open sea air, it was oppressive. He turned, rubbing Orion's neck and looking his tired horse in the eye. "One night of rest, eh? And then we'll go to Mother."

His horse yanked against his hand, appearing to nod, and Mac rubbed his neck harder. Now to find a reputable inn for the night.

His aunt's townhouse loomed over him, and Mac brushed the dirt from his sleeves, certain he was not about to receive a warm welcome. He'd stopped in a few months ago, before going to Devon, and his mother had seemed content in her situation, but Mac hadn't known how she could be. Her sister was a whiny, wheezy old woman with nothing kind to say about anyone and was prone to far too much prattle.

But Mac was not forced to endure her company day in and out, so he had gritted his teeth and born it for his mother's sake.

And now he would be able to free her from the situation. He would stop in, inform her of Father's sudden disappearance—good riddance—and then he would be off to purchase Camden Court and beg Mabel to become the mistress there. To become his wife.

His chest warmed and he mounted the steps, unable to tamp

down his smile. The butler opened the door, sweeping his gaze over Mac's dirty clothing. "Is my mother in?"

"Indeed, sir," he said, stepping back to allow space. "If you will follow me."

The butler led the way toward the drawing room and opened the door, motioning for Mac to precede him.

Mac stepped into the room and passed over his aunt's face to land on his mother, and then the man beside her. Alexander MacKenzie.

Mac froze, holding his father's gaze, the air fleeing his lungs in the semblance of a scoff. He was tired from his incessant travels and weary.

"It would appear I am the last one to learn the news, Father," he said, taking a step into the room and bowing.

"What a pleasant surprise." His mother rose as though she meant to come toward him.

Mac lifted a hand. "I am covered in dirt. I traveled too much these last few days and would like to change before I soil my aunt's drawing room."

"Of course, dear," Mother said, her eyes round and warm. She gave him a welcoming smile before looking to her sister.

Aunt Marion nodded regally. "You may use the bedchamber you had on your last visit. My man will see to your needs."

"Thank you, Aunt," Mac said, before turning back toward his father. A man who had caused Mac years of grief and hard work, had put his wife through the shame of losing her home and reputation, sat there comfortably as though he'd done no wrong, no thread of repentance on his countenance. "And you, sir. I learned from the gatekeeper at Marshalsea Prison that your debts were paid from a fellow prisoner."

Mother's face flushed, and Mac felt a moment's shame before he shoved it away. There were no servants present and each person in this room was entirely aware of the situation. Mac would learn the truth of it, and he would do so right now.

"Jimmy Poole," Father said, rising from his seat and looking Mac in the eye. He had aged in the years since Mac had been forced from his home and left to join the Royal Navy. Wrinkles lined his father's face and his eyes were deeper-set, sunken. His stringy, gray hair was long and hung past his shoulders. Mac pitied him.

"Who is Jimmy Poole?"

"A smuggler," his father said. "A prisoner of the Admiralty. He was in there for avoiding excises. I told him about—about my boy, my Liam in the navy. A seaman, like Jimmy was."

Was? The gatekeeper had mentioned the other prisoner had been tried and punished.

Mac swallowed. "So you expect me to believe this man became your friend and paid your debts?"

His father lifted his hands as if to say, *I am here, aren't I?* "He did not just pay my debts, Liam. He left me his fortune."

"If he had a fortune, why was he…" Mac could not wrap his mind around his father's explanation. "You mean to say that this Jimmy Poole left you enough money to pay your debts and…and you still have money?"

"Not very much, but enough to be independent," his father said. "Your mother and I plan to find a small house nearby. We don't wish to leave your aunt."

"What…" He turned to his mother. "You do not wish to return with me? To come and live in Devon again?"

Mother crossed the floor and Mac noticed something about her bearing that was different. She no longer appeared content in her situation—she appeared *happy* with it. A weight lifted from Mac's shoulders. He stood straighter, taller, and nodded to his mother.

Resting her hand on his wrist, she looked up into his face. "I cannot return to Devon, Liam. It holds too many difficult memories. Surely you understand that. But your father and I will be happy here. Truly."

"Will you promise me one thing, Mother?" he asked, though he was unsure whether or not he had the right. "You will send for me if you need to? If you find yourself in trouble, I wish to be the person you turn to."

"Of course, Liam."

He swallowed, accepting her promise. He hoped six years in the Marshalsea was enough to cure his father of any compulsions to gamble, but there was no guarantee.

"You will stay, Son, won't you?" Father asked, hopeful, and the look in his eyes pierced Mac's heart.

Mac had spent so long being angry at this imperfect man. But Mac was imperfect too—his history with Mabel proved that —and he'd begged forgiveness from her. Could he not grant his father the same thing?

He tried to smile but paused. He was free. He could go to Camden Court this very moment and purchase the estate, take his prospects and lay them at Mabel's feet, try to convince her he was worth marrying.

But his mother's gaze was pleading, hopeful, and he could not let her down, not when his father had done that so much in their life. No, he could wait a few days.

He gave his father a nod. "I can stay for a few days."

CHAPTER 29

$\mathcal{T}$he fortnight following the trip to the seaside was miserably, dreadfully slow. Despite her rejection of Wright's suit, the man had remained at the house to help finish the cottages. They'd brought on more men from Graton to complete the project quickly, and the houses had been finished two days past.

Giulia and Nick's wedding, the Sunday before, had been a lovely affair. Giulia wore a gown of pale ivory with ornate navy stitching, white and blue flowers tucked in her crown braid. She hadn't ceased grinning from the beginning of the church service to the end of the wedding ceremony, and they had sent her and her new husband away on a wedding trip to visit his home estate directly following the service. Giulia's uncle, Lord Hart, had appeared suspiciously teary-eyed, and Mabel had nudged Hattie to point out the crotchety old earl's sentimentality.

Mabel's heart had been full watching the wedding of her dear friend, but it had hurt all the same. She suppressed the bitterness of wishing for the same thing for herself until she'd been alone later that night, and she missed having Giulia's presence in her house to lean on. The pattern of her life was going to change, and she would do well to conform to it.

Mabel stood in the kitchen doorway now with Mrs. Henderson, going over the list of foods to be prepared for the celebration on the morrow to welcome the new families. Pippa intended to put on her play at the celebration—Mrs. Traynor had agreed to attend and bring her daughters—but refused to do so without Mac. According to the young girl, Mac's role was vital, which only served to anger Mabel more.

Pippa insisted he would return before the celebration, and Mabel didn't have the heart to argue further.

The last time he had left, he hadn't returned for six years. Mabel had foolishly allowed history to repeat itself. She'd fallen for the man again, and then he'd left with no goodbye and no sign of returning. She had done her best to write him off and had begged Pippa to do the same. It was too bad the Sheffield women had such a weakness for Mac.

"It will all be set up in the vale," Mabel finally said. "And we'd like the food and tables there before four." She had not returned to the area since that day she'd accidentally seen Mac there, when they had begun digging up the field of her mother's precious flowers.

Mrs. Henderson nodded. "Cook will be ready, ma'am. It should go off without a hitch."

Mabel trudged back up the servants' stairs. Her leg hadn't so much as twinged in pain since the day at the sea. Her slower pace since returning—mainly due to many evenings spent with Gram, Giulia and Pippa in Gram's private parlor—had given her leg the rest it needed.

Though she hated to admit it, a slower pace was precisely what she required, and it suited her just fine.

Mabel's hand paused just before making contact with the door handle that led to the corridor, and she stilled at the sound of a deep voice just on the other side of it.

"I leave in the morning." Was that Mr. Wright? She quietly stepped back into the shadows of the stairwell, leaning against the wall. He had been cordial since her father had explained that Mabel was not interested in pursuing a connection with him, but still, he remained in Devon for reasons unbeknownst to her.

"And then you will travel to Warwickshire?" a feminine voice asked, little more than a whisper.

Mabel leaned closer. She could not tell who spoke but imagined it to be Sophy Pemberton, her voice sickly sweet and low, as though she feared being overheard.

"Come with me," Mr. Wright said.

"You know I cannot. Not yet. You go and then send word to me here. I refuse an elopement."

A low growl preceded a feminine giggle and Mabel's cheeks heated when she realized they must have been kissing. Turning silently on the stair, she decided to escape down through the kitchen when Mr. Wright made a sudden sound.

"I have a plan. If all goes well, we'll be able to leave together."

"What is it?" she asked him.

"Go, darling. Someone is coming."

Quiet footsteps rang down the corridor and Mabel held her breath, hoping they weren't planning to come down these stairs. If they did, she would be caught. Mr. Wright cleared his throat and she imagined him straightening his cravat and running his fingers over smoothed hair.

"Wright," a familiar voice called, utterly guileless. Charles.

"I was just coming to find you," Mr. Wright lied. "Well met, Charles. Is everything ready for tomorrow?"

"I believe so. Though I heard you are leaving us in the morning. I wanted to thank you for your help with the cottages. Building those was entirely out of my realm of comprehension and I'm grateful for your assistance."

"Of course. We could have finished earlier, perhaps, had not MacKenzie shirked his duty like a lazy—"

"Mac was taking care of an important family matter," Charles said at once, his tone brooking no argument.

A beat of silence passed, marred only by Mabel's ragged breathing.

"Of course," Wright said, his voice tight. "I must go speak to the captain. I will see you at dinner."

Mabel shut her eyes, leaning her head back against the wall. Mr. Wright's indiscretions forgotten, she wondered what exactly had occurred in Mac's family to tear him away so suddenly. And if his family troubles were ever resolved...would he then return to Devon?

Mac stood on the edge of the field, his horse tied to a tree just behind him. Mabel walked ahead of the row of cottages, leading Pippa by the hand, and the smile on her face healed the sorrow in Mac's heart.

He'd been too late. After spending a few days with his family, his heart healed from the anger and bitterness he'd stored within it, he had set off to obtain ownership of Camden Court. But he had missed it by mere days, and the solicitor refused to tell him who had purchased the estate, claiming the buyer wished to remain anonymous. Not that Mac truly wondered. It had to be Wright. Who else would have bought a dilapidated manor house on the northern Devon coastline but the man who'd professed a desire to do just that?

But dreams could change. Just because Mac did not obtain the house he desired, that did not mean he could not settle somewhere else nearby. Now that he knew he had the funds to purchase an estate, he was going to go directly to Mabel and beg her to agree to be his wife. He would never be wealthy—his

THE LADY OF LARKSPUR VALE

portion of the prizes were not so grand as that—but he believed they could be comfortable together.

Starting across the field, he cringed at the trampled, dried petals adorning the ground. The larkspur had been utterly ruined, and the lady of Larkspur Vale, as he'd thought of Mabel, stood in the midst of her ruined vale now, looked peaceably content surrounded by the chaos of the celebration.

"See!" Pippa yelled at once, tugging at Mabel's arm. "I told you, Mae! I told you he would come!"

Mac smiled at the little sprite before hazarding a glance at her older sister. He paused ten feet before her, the majority of the celebration taking place behind her.

"You've come back," she said, her eyes widened.

He could tell he'd surprised her, and he did not know if that was good or not. Had she imagined that he had left for good? And with no goodbye?

Taking a step closer, he dipped his head. "Did you think I would not?"

Pippa ran up to him. "Will you do it? Will you still be my villain?"

Mac could not help but grin down at her hopeful eyes, and he chucked her lightly under the chin. "Of course."

"Good. I will tell my friends to prepare themselves. We must perform within the hour, or the sun will be gone."

"Of course," Mac agreed, nodding seriously. The sun was nowhere near disappearing, but Pippa had no notion of the time, it seemed, and her urgency was darling. She ran off in a flurry of skirts and flying plaits, and Mabel's chuckle lifted on the breeze, wrapping around his heart.

"Mabel," he said, crossing the distance. He paused just before her, using every bit of self-control he had to refrain from reaching out and pulling her into his arms.

She looked confused, her eyebrows drawn together, her body stiff. "Did you have a safe journey?"

He nodded. "Everything—well, nearly everything has been sorted."

"And your business?"

"My...what is it that you thought I was doing for these last few weeks, Mabel?" he asked, stepping closer still.

She lifted one shoulder, looking to the gathered group near the table of delicacies. "I haven't any idea."

"I was seeing my father freed from prison and offering my mother a home of her own."

Mabel's face whipped around, her lips parting as a sigh escaped her lips. "Mac, I had no idea—"

"It does not matter now. My parents have blessedly chosen to remain in Bath." He swallowed. "But that does not mean I can fully escape my name being tainted by the association. I will forever battle my father's indiscretions, and censure will sometimes meet me, regardless of my own spotless reputation. It is the nature of my father's failing, I'm afraid."

"What does that matter?" she asked, shaking her head slightly. Her violet-blue eyes were dark in the late afternoon sun, worry and concern drooping her features.

"It does not, not to me. But I fear for my future wife."

She glanced over her shoulder and Mac wanted to ask who the devil she was looking for. "You," he said, taking her by the hand and not caring a whit who saw him. She faced him and he wanted to kiss the surprise off her face. "Mabel, if you can stand the injustice of it, I would beg you to consider saying yes."

"Injustice of what? That you are proposing marriage to me in the very place you once broke my heart? Really, Mac. Could you not have chosen a new locale?"

He smiled. "No. I would rather replace those wretched, embarrassing memories with better ones."

She shook her head. "Mac, you must see that I cannot say yes."

"Why the devil not?" he asked, tightening his hold on her

hands. He grew thunderous, his chest heating in anger. "Do not say you've agreed to marry that pompous idiot."

"The only pompous man who's proposed to me lately, sir, is yourself."

That sent an inordinate amount of relief through him and Mac relaxed. "Where is Wright, anyway?"

"Gone." She tugged at her hands, but he tightened his hold. "I'm telling you, Mac. It will not work. I cannot accept you."

"Give me a valid reason, and I will allow you to walk away."

She smiled sadly at him, tilting her head to the side. "Do you think I can be persuaded to leave my grandmother and sister behind to live in a house with Charles and Miss Pemberton? The woman is hardly fit to run the house as it is. Her trial period proved so while I was laid up with my wretched leg. How can I subject Gram and Pippa to that?"

"They will come with us, of course. I never expected anything else."

She paused, startled, but then shook her head. "Come where, exactly?"

"Wherever you wish. I will buy the closest available estate if that is what you'd prefer."

She seemed bewildered.

Mac released her fingers, sliding his hands up her arms and gripping her shoulders. Lowering his voice, he looked to her perfect, plump lips. "Mabel, I love you. I cannot offer you the world. I *can* offer you a comfortable home, with a husband who will likely have to work his own land. I am not averse to the life-style, but you must know what you are agreeing to. I only hope, with everything I possess, that you will agree."

She watched him through shocked eyes.

"Please, my love," he begged. "Marry me."

CHAPTER 30

*M*abel felt Mac's hands tighten on her arms, eager to return the embrace, but she was frightened. He had left without a word to her. It was important business he'd gone to see to, she'd grant him that, but where was the communication?

She could see now how he had been afraid to speak his mind before. He could not have asked her this question while his family hung in the balance, waiting to be redeemed from their pitiable circumstances.

"It is not the life you wanted, is it?" Mac asked, so defeated in the deflation of his shoulders, his pulled-together eyebrows, that she wanted to raise her finger and wipe the concerned wrinkles from his brow.

"It is not that," she said. "I simply am not sure if Gram will agree to leave this house. She's spent nearly her whole life here."

"Then we will remain." He stepped closer and she could feel his chest rising and falling against her own. His face was so near, Mabel could feel his breath tickle her lips, and it stunned her. "We can accomplish anything if we do it together. Including raising that sister of yours and caring for Gram."

Somehow, when Mac used the family name, it did not bother Mabel in the slightest. It was ridiculous, really, but she could think of no reason to refuse this man. She loved him, and he loved her in return. The gentle way he held her and the look in his eyes spoke it more clearly than any words ever could. But he'd also said the words, and it had filled her with the warmest love.

"Marry me?" he asked again, his whisper brushing against her lips, so close it seemed to steal her breath.

She looked into his honey-brown eyes, the flecks of gold making an appearance just for her. "Yes, Mac. I'll marry you."

A smile spread wide over his lips before they descended on hers. His hand slid up to Mabel's, the other wrapping around her back and pulling her close. His kiss was soft and gentle, brushing over her lips with delicate care and filling her body with unparalleled warmth.

He pulled back. "Yes?" he asked, as if he needed to confirm.

She bit down on her lip, fighting the joyful smile that no doubt mirrored her heart. "Yes."

Wrapping his arms around her, he picked her up and swung her around, making her feel dainty in a way that no other man could. Chuckling, he set her down again and took her lips in his with a fervor she had not expected.

"Mabel!" Pippa said, running toward them. "I need Mac now. It is time!"

They broke apart and Mabel tried to step back, but Mac would not release her from his hold. Her cheeks warmed from the multitude of eyes that were fastened on them.

"Is it time?" he asked, and Mabel could feel his voice rumbling through his chest.

"Time for what?" Mabel asked.

"Mac has agreed to be my villain," Pippa said as though it was a chore.

"Have you?"

"Indeed. I am to be their pirate."

Pippa gasped. "Say no more, Mac! You will give everything away!"

He laughed again and bent down to kiss the tip of Mabel's nose. "I suppose we ought to go share our news. You have been thoroughly compromised, my dear."

Mabel sought her father out in the crowd and her cheeks warmed further at his raised eyebrows.

"Come, Mac," Pippa said, taking his hand and pulling him away.

Mabel followed them toward the crowd, and they skirted the group toward the place set up with chairs for Pippa's play.

Mabel paused beside her father and he cleared his throat. "I hope you have something to tell me," he said.

"I have agreed to marry Mac, Papa."

"Well I should hope so after that display."

She could not hide her embarrassment, so heavily did it flame on her cheeks. "Do you approve?" she asked.

"I could not have chosen better for you myself," Papa said. He grew contemplative. "In fact, I feel foolish for not having thought of it initially."

"You had your sights set on someone else," Mabel said.

"A failing that turned out to be." He turned, holding her gaze. "I was only trying to help, Mabel. I was afraid you would never leave Graton, and there aren't any men left here to choose from. When Lieutenant Wright expressed his desire to sell out, that he might find a wife and settle a family, I thought perhaps he was my answer."

"It is not your fault—"

Papa shook his head. "The fool was only after my money. He came to see me yesterday and..." He shot her a glance and looked away, uncomfortable. "Needless to say, I didn't know him as well as I thought. He won't be bothering us again."

Mabel's mouth hung open and she closed it, turning back to face the crowd of her neighbors and friends. "What did you have to do to ensure that?"

"It matters not," Papa said.

That could only mean one thing: he'd paid Mr. Wright off. Mabel's stomach soured. When she had overheard Mr. Wright speaking to one of the Pemberton sisters, he'd said he had a scheme. She should have jumped from the stairwell then and demanded to learn what it was. Perhaps she could have done something about it.

"Don't fret, Mabel," Papa said. "All is well."

Pippa announced the play and the group gathered near the chairs, taking their seats.

"Are you coming?" Mabel asked, indicating the seats.

"I will be along shortly. You go on," her father said.

Mabel crossed the field, coming upon Charles standing alone at the back of the crowd, his hands resting lightly behind his back.

"Where is your Miss Pemberton?" Mabel asked, sidling up beside him as people filed into their seats. Hattie and Amelia passed them, raising their eyebrows at her—they had probably witnessed the engagement as well. She needed to choose a more private location next time she let Mac kiss her—and she glanced back at her cousin to find his hardened gaze whip away from Amelia's retreating form.

Oh, dear.

"Miss Pemberton is gone," Charles said, his eyebrows drawn. "She informed me just minutes before we left the house to come here that she was leaving. Miss Sophy is to marry Mr. Wright and is taking her family with her. The only member of their party they did not take with them was Mrs. Boucher."

"Miss Pemberton is leaving because her *sister* is to marry Mr. Wright?" Mabel confirmed.

"Yes. She's rejected me." He stared ahead, eyes hard. "She hopes to return to London. Likely to find herself a better suitor."

Mabel strung her hand around his arm. "Oh, Charles. She is such a foolish girl—"

He shook his head, laughing without mirth. "Fear not, Mabel. I only offered for her because I did not think I had another choice. I had given her expectations, and I needed to see them through. I was relieved when she refused me. She would not have made me happy."

Mabel slid her hand around her cousin's. "I'm sorry, Charles."

He shot her a dry smile. "The rejection stung a little if I'm being honest. But it's for the best for everyone involved. The Pembertons should be gone by the time we return. In fact, they are likely gone now."

Stunned, Mabel faced the stage.

"You will be interested to know, however," Charles continued, amusement in his tone, "that Desmond Pemberton was sorry to leave. Apparently, he's been in a spot of trouble for some time and hoped one of his sisters would marry a rich man who could ease his burdens." He chuckled dryly. "He was sorry it couldn't be me. He liked me."

"He spoke those words?" Mabel asked, laughing. "I think we must be glad to be rid of them."

"Indeed. She never would have made a good mistress of Sheffield House anyway."

"Perhaps not," Mabel agreed, "but the right woman *is* out there, Charles."

He made a noncommittal noise and Mabel followed his gaze to where Amelia sat on a chair beside Hattie.

Pippa called for quiet, glaring at a boy sitting in the front row. "Thank you for coming to my play. It is called *Pirate Tucker's Distress.*"

Oh, heavens. Surely Pippa hadn't created an entire play about her nemesis. Mabel shook her head.

"Will she ever become friends with that Tucker boy?" Charles asked, nodding toward Jacob Tucker in the front row. The child sat with his arms crossed, a smug smile on his face as though he was pleased the villain in Pippa's play was named after him.

"Perhaps," Mabel said, finding Mac's gaze through the dimming twilight sun. "Some enemies turn out to be friends in the end."

Mac sat on the other side of Captain Sheffield's desk, Mabel waiting primly in the chair beside his. The captain watched them through narrowed eyes, working his bottom lip with his teeth, his beard quivering.

"You want to get married," Captain Sheffield said. "And where do you plan to live?"

"We have not made that decision yet, sir."

Mabel leaned forward. "I need to speak to Gram and discover her plans first, Papa."

"What has my mother to say to any of this?" he asked, looking between Mac and Mabel. "Surely you do not intend to remain *here.*"

"I plan to purchase an estate nearby," Mac explained. The room was growing stifling and he longed to run a finger between his cravat and throat to loosen it but chose to hide his weakness from his future father-in-law. Inquisitions upon the ship were much less frightening than this.

"And we will bring Pippa and Gram with us, of course," Mabel added. "And Mrs. Boucher. She has become something of

THE LADY OF LARKSPUR VALE

a companion to Gram, and if she'd like to stay on, I think it would be good. But we'd like to allow Gram some say in the scheme. It cannot be easy for her to leave her home now."

Captain Sheffield's eyes warmed as he looked at his daughter. "If I know my mother, Mabel, she will go wherever you go, and she will not complain...so long as you bring her chair."

"Well, naturally. I wouldn't dream of leaving the chair here."

"And how soon are you hoping to wed?" His probing eyes found Mac once again and Mac fought the urge to fan his face. Was the fire built up this morning? Surely the captain wouldn't build a fire in the heat of the summer.

"Mac planned to speak to the vicar tomorrow," Mabel said. "We'd like to begin the reading of the banns this Sunday."

Captain Sheffield's eyebrows rose a fraction, but he nodded, seemingly impressed. "Then it's settled, I suppose. That gives us just under a month to prepare the house, and you will move into Camden Court at the start of August."

Mac leaned forward, certain he'd misheard. "Forgive me, sir. Did you say Camden Court?"

"Indeed."

"And why, Papa," Mabel asked, appearing as confused as Mac felt, "would you mention it? Mac tried to purchase the estate, but it had already sold."

"It had already sold because I had already purchased it."

Stunned silence fell over Mac and Mabel.

Captain Sheffield looked at his daughter. "You mentioned it a few weeks ago, you might recall. Never before have you asked me for anything, Mabel. I knew you wanted this, so I moved ahead and arranged it."

She frowned. "But that was when I refused to marry Mr. Wright."

The captain nodded. "I assumed Charles would marry soon, and this way you could have your own home. I was unconcerned with you marrying, Mabel, as long as you were happy. Though after watching Mac chase you up the stairs after you hurt your leg, I began to have my suspicions that you wouldn't remain unmarried for long."

Mabel's cheeks flushed.

"I only wanted you to be happy, Amabel." Captain Sheffield turned to Mac. "And I am counting on you to make certain she is."

"I will, sir," Mac pledged. He shifted, taking Mabel's hand in his. "I love your daughter, sir, and I intend to take care of her."

Mabel smiled at him, and Mac was entirely certain he was the luckiest man in England.

"Then consider the estate my wedding gift," Captain Sheffield said.

Mac's stomach constricted. "I could not accept such charity—"

"I did this for my daughter, Mac," the captain said, unwavering. "And I will not hear another word about it."

"Yes, sir." Mac held the man's gaze, an unspoken agreement passing between them. It was clear that he sat across the only other man in the world who could possibly rival him in love for Mabel Sheffield.

Turning to Mabel, he allowed a smile to spread over his lips. "Does that sound agreeable to you?"

She nodded, her wide smile matching his. "I think I might be amenable to the scheme."

EPILOGUE

Eleven months later

"Shhh," Mabel admonished, covering Mac's mouth with one hand and resting a hand over her growing belly with the other. "You will wake Pippa."

"Are you suggesting that my singing voice is not soothing?" Mac asked, leaning down to nuzzle his wife's neck.

She smiled, pulling away from him. "That is precisely what I am suggesting. Now hush, please. Pippa has been in a beastly mood and I am quite happy she fell asleep. I need the rest more than she does, you know."

"I do know. Where is Gram?"

Mabel gestured above them. "She has gone above for a quiet repose, and Mrs. Boucher did the same."

"Are you telling me I am the man of a house of sleeping women?"

"You are," Mabel said. "Giulia, Hattie, and Amelia will arrive within the hour and I hoped to catch a bit of rest before then. Was there something you needed?"

"I wanted to show you something, but it can wait until tomorrow." Mac leaned over the back of the settee to kiss Mabel.

She smiled against his lips and pulled her head back. "You've piqued my interest. Come, help me up."

"You are not so large yet," he joked, coming around the couch.

She gave him a stern look but accepted his hand and he guided her to her feet. Intertwining their fingers, Mac led her outside and down the tree-lined path which led from their home to the beach, their hands swinging between them.

"What is it?" she asked.

But Mac just grinned. "Almost there."

They stepped around the bend and into the small, tree-covered space that opened up to the view of the ocean, and Mabel halted mid-step. Dotting the grass between the trees was a spread of long-stalked, violet-blue flowers. She drew in a breath, her hand resting on her heart.

When the house party from the summer before had come to Camden Cove and eaten their picnic in this very place, there hadn't been a single larkspur in the area. Now, it was littered with them.

"How?" Mabel asked, stunned.

Mac came behind her and strung his arms around her waist, resting his hands on the top of her belly. "When you agreed to marry me, I went out to Larkspur Vale and uprooted as many flowers as I could find that hadn't been trampled from the building. I brought them here and tried to spread them out. I hoped a few would take root, but I had no idea so many would grow."

Mabel leaned back against her husband and wrapped her arms over his. "It's our own little Larkspur Vale," Mabel said.

Mac leaned down and kissed the top of her head. "And you, my love, are my lady of the larkspur."

Leaning back, she considered the irony. Just a year before she never would have imagined she could find herself so content in a sea of larkspur. But this man and his love for her had changed everything, taking something that was once bittersweet and making it lovely again. Mabel felt the beat of Mac's heart behind her, and her own pulse quickened.

How had she become so fortunate?

"Darling?" he asked.

She answered him the best way she knew how. She turned in his arms and kissed him soundly.

ABOUT THE AUTHOR

Kasey Stockton is a staunch lover of all things romantic. She doesn't discriminate between genres and enjoys a wide variety of happily ever afters. Drawn to the Regency period at a young age when gifted a copy of *Sense and Sensibility* by her grandmother, Kasey initially began writing Regency romances. She has since written in a variety of genres, but all of her titles fall under sweet romance. A native of northern California, she now resides in Texas with her own prince charming and their three children. When not reading, writing, or binge-watching chick flicks, she enjoys running, cutting hair, and anything chocolate.

Made in the USA
Columbia, SC
27 March 2021